LUCID TRADE

BOOK TWO OF THE DESIGNED SERIES

LUCID TRADE

BOOK TWO OF THE DESIGNED SERIES

KATE TAILOR

FIFE
PRESS

an imprint of

YOUNG DRAGONS PRESS

OGHMA
CREATIVE MEDIA

Bentonville, Arkansas • Los Angeles, California
www.oghmacreative.com

Library of Congress Cataloging-in-Publication Data

Names: Tailor, Kate, author
Title: Lucid Trade/Kate Tailor | Designed #2
Description: First Edition | Bentonville: Fife, 2020
Identifiers: LCCN: 2020935333 | ISBN: 978-1-63373-572-9 (hardcover) |
ISBN: 978-1-63373-573-6 (trade paperback) | ISBN: 978-1-63373-574-3 (eBook)
BISAC: YOUNG ADULT FICTION/Science Fiction |
YOUNG ADULT FICTION/Loners & Outcasts |
YOUNG ADULT FICTION/Action & Adventure
LC record available at: https://lccn.loc.gov/2020935333

Fife Press trade paperback edition June, 2021

Cover & Interior Design by Casey W. Cowan
Editing by Gordon Bonnet, Linda Knight, & Amy Cowan

Published by Fife Press, an imprint of Young Dragons Press, a subsidiary of The Oghma Book Group.

To My Grandma Eleanore.

ACKNOWLEDGEMENTS

THIS BOOK IS POSSIBLE because of a group of speculators, an accountant, a podiatrist, a Belgian, a set of crazy aunts and their husbands, two lovable children, a father, a missed mother, an extra mother, and a great group of Oghmaniacs.

LUCID DESIGN

C H A P T E R
01

RALEIGH APPROACHED THE cab of the truck, her heartbeat echoing in her ears. The driver was dying, and she'd killed him.

The pelting rain slapped her arm as she reached up and opened the front driver's door and found his body slouched uncomfortably over the wheel. Her fingers didn't bother to check his pulse. The Lucid in her system let her sense his body, and his heart wasn't moving.

Because she'd stopped it.

She reached around and unbuckled the seatbelt, the smell of cigarettes and grease strong on his jacket. After unclipping the belt, she tugged him from the car, stepping out of the way as he tumbled onto the asphalt parking lot, splashing in the pooling water.

It had been her intention to stop his heart for a few beats. If his foot hadn't been on the gas, she would've frozen him, like the two other attackers that stood a few feet away. Like statues, they watched as she got on the ground, hunched over the man, and prepared to perform CPR.

Influencing, she willed his heart to contract. He wasn't completely gone. His mind was alive enough that it obeyed her order and squeezed his heart. It was an uneven contraction. The right side was stronger than the left, but it failed to contract fully. Then she could no longer sense him or influence. He was gone.

"Beat!" Raleigh yelled, pressing down with all her might on his chest.

His ribs sank against her weight. After a minute her breathing became strangled—from the fear, the exertion, or likely a combination of both. Standing, she stared down at him before turning her attention to the other two men.

The three attackers had come out of nowhere. She and Gamma had braved the downpour to get milk from the corner store, and they cut through the parking lot of a deserted office building. It being Saturday and soggy, no one was there to witness the scene. One minute they were talking about their favorite bands and the next a dart flew into Gamma's neck.

The tranquilizer had taken effect quickly. His body slumped, half-tumbling onto the asphalt, making a small dam for the water of the gutter. As she reached down to get him, a van screeched up. Two men barreled out its sliding door. Raleigh scrambled back fast enough that the driver's bullet missed her. From there, she acted on instinct and training. From behind the van, she froze the two men and stopped the heart of the driver. The question was what to do now.

The frozen men stood over Gamma, their hearts galloping wildly in their chests. Who were they? They weren't Grant and Able, or they would've tried to kidnap her, too. Synthetic dealers knew about the Designed but not her, or at least they hadn't before now. If she let these two go, they'd report back to their higher ups. They'd come after her again. Maybe it was a good thing that the driver was already dead.

Raleigh's adrenaline played the world in slow motion, but she still took too long to make her decision. They had to die. But could she do it? With the distaste of the first killing fresh on her tongue, she took a deep breath, preparing to end the other two. Unlike the driver, they wouldn't be an accident. With guns in their holsters they were armed, but no one would consider this a fair fight.

A chill ran down her arms. Her hoodie was drenched, but that wasn't the only reason she felt frozen. This was a war. There was a moral difference between killing a man in cold blood and killing one in battle. It was self-defense. They'd come here to kill her. All the reasons why she should ticked through her head in a chorus of affirmation. This wasn't who she was. She was meant to be a healer. The influencing was supposed to be a tool, not a weapon. Silencing her conscience, it was time.

Without warning they stopped breathing—and not because of her. Their lungs tightened so painfully that she found herself clutching her own chest in empathy. Like all the rest of the sensations they endured and shared with her, she felt their suffocation. If she hadn't hijacked their ability to move, they would've grasped at their throats. Someone else had done what she'd hesitated to do. A Designed. But not Gamma, who was still sedated on the ground.

Startled, she saw Tau walking around the van. Once the two men were dead, their minds no longer reacted to her influencing, they fell lifelessly around Gamma. Tau studied the two men on the ground then turned his attention to her. She remembered the time she'd tortured him in the cellar. Would he witness all her greatest evils? She could think of no harsher judge.

He approached her slowly. "Are you okay?"

"I killed the driver."

"I know."

"They came out of nowhere. What are we going to do? There are three bodies."

"We're going to leave them."

"Shouldn't we put them in the van?" A task he'd have to do because she wasn't strong enough to lift them.

"No. It's not worth it." Tau bent down and slung Gamma over his shoulder with a grunt. "This way."

Raleigh followed his long steps through the rain to a car parked in the middle of the lot, its tires crossing more than one space.

"Would you get the door?" he asked.

Raleigh moved quickly, opening the door so Tau could lay Gamma down across the back seat. Once he was stowed safely in the back, Tau dashed around to the driver's side, and Raleigh hopped in the front passenger seat. The inside of the car was muggy from the rain and had the noxious new-car smell of a rental. She inhaled a deep breath.

Tau revved the engine and sped out of the lot. Raleigh rubbed her hands on her soaked jeans. Were there cameras in the parking lot? She doubted it but was happy that her hoodie hid most of her face—on the off chance that there were cameras. A wave of nausea flipped her stomach. Her fingers found the window button, and she cracked it to let in a breeze. It woke her up from her surreal reality and helped her gulp down the sickness that threatened to come up.

"You're going to be all right," he said. "You're in shock, but you're going to be all right."

"Tau, I killed him."

He turned down a side street. "It was necessary. And I'm not Tau. I'm Chi."

Raleigh whipped her head toward him. This was the reclusive brother who no one had seen since the Designed escaped the island, one of the two living members of the Tau triplet. Being Designed meant that he was likely an ally, but that didn't keep the goosebumps from racing across her arms.

"Chi?"

"Yeah. I've been following the synthetic for the past few years. That's who that was back there, the operation that's based out of Normandy. There were rumors that some of you were in Chicago. I found them, and they found you."

Raleigh tried to ignore the fear. Rumors? "How did they find us?"

Dale, Gamma, Upsilon, and she had gone into hiding a month ago, after she broke free of Grant and Able. In hiding, they'd been careful. No credit cards, no falling into patterns, no hanging out in the same neighborhoods, no smart phones, just prepaid ones they could trash if needed, and no calls home.

"I don't know how. Only that they did. Where am I going?"

Raleigh glanced over her shoulder to the backseat.

"Raleigh, whoever you're hiding with is in danger. Where am I going?"

"One street over. It's one of the beige townhouses on the end."

"Who's there? Is Dale with you?"

Another ripple of fear crossed her shoulders. He knew about Dale. The rest of the Designed only recently learned about the Modified. Grant and Able had created the Designed from scratch with the sole intent of creating and using Lucid. The Modified were a cautionary step years later—people who were altered to produce the drug but not use it. They looked normal, and they were, in all regards, except for producing Lucid. For Chi to know Dale by name was unsettling.

"How do you know about Dale?"

"We have a mole at Grant and Able."

"Who is we?"

"The company I work for."

"You work for a company?" Were there other amoral scientists like Grant and Able exploiting Chi for his Lucid? She couldn't picture any of the Designed working with a formal operation. Small teams were the trend amongst the others.

"Yes, and we have an eye on the synthetic and a mole at Grant and Able." A row of townhouses came into view. Each had a narrow driveway and path to the front door. "Which one's yours?"

"That one." She pointed to the one second from the end.

"We'll leave him in here." Chi pulled into the driveway.

"What? We need to bring him in."

"I don't want your neighbors to see me hauling him. We're lucky enough that no one saw us in that parking lot. That, and your attackers must have eyes on you if they picked you up a handful of blocks away. We won't be staying long." He covered Gamma as best he could with a blanket. Hopefully the rain would help obscure the view inside the vehicle if anyone walked by.

Raleigh's skin prickled. The adrenaline that had racked her system was ebbing, and the chill continued to seep in from the damp hoodie. Her mind reached into the house. Only Dale and Upsilon, from what she could tell. A tight laugh echoed in Dale's throat. He was happy, and they were about to destroy that.

After locking the car, Chi and Raleigh strode quickly up to the front door, and she unlocked and opened it. Once inside, her shoes squeaked as they stepped onto the wood floor.

"That took you long enough," Dale hollered from the kitchen.

Upsilon, able to sense, must've recognized the difference in Gamma and Chi, or that Raleigh was shaken. He was quick to the door, and nearly dropped the measuring cup in his hands. "Chi?"

"We need to go. Grab Dale and your things," Chi said.

"They came at us in a van," said Raleigh. "They shot Gamma with a dart and then jumped out and tried to shoot me."

"Who?" asked Upsilon, crossing the room to her.

"The Normandy synthetic. We need to go," Chi insisted.

Upsilon looked toward the door. "Where's Gamma?"

"In my car, which is where we need you to be. They could be coming here any moment."

Upsilon didn't obey. "What are you doing here?"

Dale entered the room and stared at them. Raleigh had accepted Chi's help, mostly because what he said made sense, and he'd helped her in the parking lot. Images of the man she killed sat on the other side of her eyelids as a wave of nausea roiled her stomach.

She ran forward and wrapped her arms around Dale. "We need to go!"

"What are you doing here, Chi?" Upsilon asked again.

"Helping you."

Raleigh pictured Gamma in the car. "What does it matter? Let's get going."

Upsilon said, "Chi, the last time we saw you was when you ripped out your port and started ranting about the curse of Lucid. Now you show up conveniently when we run into trouble. How do we know this isn't a trick?"

"I'm a Designed! I'm not here to capture you!"

"So, it's a huge coincidence that you just happened to be there to thwart the attack on Raleigh and Gamma?"

"It's not," Chi said. "I work for a company that's trying to take down the synthetic, and I was tailing them. Our intelligence said that you were in Chicago, and when we found the Normandy synthetic sniffing around here, we figured that they caught wind. Now we need to leave. I can explain all of this to you later. But we need to go *now.*"

"Upsilon, please." Raleigh grabbed the pack near the door— the one with the things they'd need in the event they had to get away quickly.

Upsilon stood for a second longer. "Turn off the burners, Dale. I'll grab our stuff."

"We're leaving?" Dale's eyes widened. "But to where?"

"Doesn't matter. Any place but here. Toss your phones, they're no good now." Upsilon's words echoed down the stairwell as he ran up to grab their things.

Raleigh fetched the extraction machine. Then the four of them went to the car.

Thankfully, Gamma was still sleeping in the back seat. Whatever they'd shot him with showed no sign of wearing off. Chi opened the back door and propped him up. Dale slid in on one side of him while Upsilon dumped their bags in the trunk and slid into the other side. Raleigh took shotgun, her adrenaline coming back in a steady wave. The Lucid jolted against her nerves. Stress increased its production, and she prayed the extraction last night would be enough to ward off a blackout.

Chi started the car, and they were off. Raleigh wasn't sure where they were going, but any place seemed like a better option than here.

CHAPTER
02

CHI PARKED IN the basement of a parking garage. A diesel smell irritated Raleigh's nose as she got out of the car. When Dale got out of the car, he grimaced, clearly unhappy about leaving so abruptly.

She placed her hand on his shoulder. "It will be fine." She didn't believe her own words.

"This way," Chi said.

Upsilon shouldered Gamma as they went up a service elevator to the sixth floor. There Chi held up a hand and went into the hall for a moment before beckoning for them to follow. Down the hall they shuffled into an indiscreet apartment. Chi bolted the door, and Upsilon set Gamma down on the sofa.

"Gamma's going to be okay, isn't he?" Dale asked Raleigh.

"Yeah, he's going to be fine."

"You're all going to be all right. I need to call my boss." Chi stepped into the lone bedroom.

Besides the bedroom, the apartment had a simple kitchen with a small table, a sitting area, and a bathroom. It was a cramped place for the five of them to stay, but she didn't dare complain.

"It's not good that he has a boss to call," Upsilon said to Raleigh.

Raleigh thought about how Chi had helped her. Boss or no boss, it was a good thing he'd been there. If nothing else, he provided this apartment.

"All of us are safe," she said, "that's something."

The corner of Upsilon's mouth dipped. "I guess. Speaking of bosses, I'm calling Rho."

Dale sat on the sofa looking at Gamma, fear and apprehension wrinkling his brow. Raleigh could guess what he was thinking—the Designed were so powerful it was rattling to see one helpless. Chi said the attackers were the Normandy synthetic. It wasn't hard to piece together that they were very likely the ones that captured Rho. He was found on a Normandy shore about six months ago. It was the event that kick-started her involvement with the Designed... and the world they lived in.

Raleigh listened as Upsilon filled Rho in, running down the limited amount of information he knew. Then motioned to Raleigh. "He wants to talk to you."

Raleigh took the phone, her hands still shaky. The confession of killing a man knotted in her throat, begging to come up. "Hello."

"Raleigh, are you all right?"

Rho's deep voice slid through the phone and down her spine, calming her fears. "Good. I'm good."

"I'm coming with Kappa. From what Upsilon told me, it sounds like that apartment you're in is the safest place for you right now. With Gamma out it will be too hard to run. Stay put. I've got a few hours' drive."

"You're close to Chicago?"

"Yeah. I was looking into something for Trevor. Shit, I'm sorry

that this happened. Thank goodness you're all right. If Chi didn't show up. . . ."

Raleigh straightened her spine. "I would've been fine. I had it handled." It was true. She'd hesitated when it came to killing them, but she would've done it if Chi didn't arrive or at least she hoped she would've.

"I'll be there. Stay safe. Watch out for Dale."

"I will." She handed the phone to a grimacing Upsilon.

Chi was in the bedroom for a long time talking on his cell, far longer than was needed to explain what'd gone down. Raleigh could hear the muffled sound of his voice through the door. When he came out, he turned on the oven and pulled a frozen pizza from the freezer.

"You mentioned a mole at Grant and Able. Who is it?" Raleigh's mind skipped through the catalogue of researchers, intelligence, and even Receps. None of them had given her any hint that they were working for anyone other than G and A.

"It doesn't matter. I can't tell you."

It made a difference to her. Everyone at Grant and Able knew who she and Dale were by the time they left. She regretted that they hadn't been kept a better secret.

"What are we going to do now?" Dale asked, breaking into their conversation.

Chi crossed his arms and leaned against the counter. "Nothing until Gamma wakes up. I assume that Rho will play a large part in that decision."

"Yeah," said Upsilon. "Who else would?"

Chi's eyes crept slowly over to Raleigh. "I guess that depends on what we decide. How long is it going to take for him to get here?"

"A few hours."

"Then it won't be a long wait."

The wait was agony. The rain continued as the four of them munched on pizza. Two slices were left to the side for when Gamma woke up. As the minutes ticked by, they went from hot to warm to cold. Chi took another phone call in the bedroom, and that was the only conversation that was had. Dale kept darting his eyes to Raleigh, but she didn't know what to say. Upsilon's attention remained on the clock and the front door.

Raleigh curiously observed the patchwork of scars on Chi's arm where his port had been. With the sleeves of his button-down shirt rolled up, they were easy enough to see. He was the one who'd bought all his brothers tickets to the island. The first time he influenced, he'd nearly killed a kid by stopping his heart—a story that Rho told with sorrow and Grant and Able told with an agenda.

The more she thought about the kid, the more she thought about the man she'd killed earlier. It left a niggling in the back of her mind, but she couldn't face it yet. When she tried to think about it, her body went numb and pushed the memories out. It left her in a funk.

The danger was more intense than she'd thought. After leaving Grant and Able, she'd called home once. It was to say goodbye. Her mother demanded she come home, but she didn't wish to bring her problems to her family. Everything was different now after the attack. Her mind looped back around to the man she killed, and she tried to distract herself again.

Rho was coming. The notion both excited and troubled her. Since their failed kiss, her failed kiss, she wasn't quite sure how to approach him. When he arrived, what sort of greeting would she give him? A head bob? Or worse, a handshake? How could she be thinking about her crush with all that had happened?

Raleigh ached to go on a run, to let the rain freeze her skin so that she could no longer feel. There was no way she could, not with the events of the day. If the safe house had felt restrictive, this apartment was downright suffocating.

Finally, there was a knock on the door, and all of them jumped. Chi took measured steps to the handle and lowered his eye to the peephole before turning the lock. If it was the synthetic, Raleigh doubted they'd be so polite as to knock. Kicking the door in was more their speed.

Chi opened the door. Rho and Kappa were outside, their hair and shoulders wet. Raleigh wiped the pizza grease from her hand on the bottom of her hoodie and decided that a head nod was too casual. Before she could raise her hand to shaking position, Rho was across the room.

It took him four long steps to sweep her up into a hug. Inhaling, she smelled the wonderful smell of him mixed with the rain. It transferred to her hair as she let him hold her. A flood of emotion threatened to burble up. She wanted to say it had been the worst day ever. But Gamma was still out cold on the sofa, and there was no need. When Rho released her, his eyes stayed focused on hers.

"Hi, Raleigh." Kappa gave a quick wave of his hand.

She stepped back from Rho, knowing that she'd pay for the long embrace later when Dale and the others made their assumptions. Rho didn't like her like that, and she cursed herself for being giddy in his presence.

"What happened?" Rho asked.

Raleigh recounted the story in more detail than before. She told him that she and Gamma had stepped out to run and get some milk. She explained how Gamma had been sedated, and that they'd tried to kidnap him. Chi arrived and picked up the story, leaving out the brutal way the men in the van died. He said he found Raleigh after she'd disarmed the gunman. Rho and the others seemed to know that meant "killed."

Dale was a little more naïve, asking, "Are we worried about them following you?"

"No, Dale. They died." Raleigh watched his face twist from disbelief to horror to sympathy.

"So, who do we think they were?" Rho asked Chi.

"I know who they were. The Normandy synthetic. The same ones who captured you."

Rho knitted his eyebrows. "You knew who had me and didn't get me out?"

"We didn't know where you were," Chi said. "We have a mole with them, but they were never filled in on your location. Sorry. I would've done everything in my power."

Raleigh wondered just how many people were in Chi's organization if they were able to have so many moles.

"Would you have saved me?" Rho asked.

Chi raised an eyebrow. "I helped Raleigh just now, didn't I?"

"Yeah, but we haven't seen you since you deserted us and went off the grid. We all thought you were living in the mountains. Now you show up and are working for a company that knows far too much," Rho said.

"I didn't come to you sooner because I've been upset about how you sell your Lucid into the black market." Chi leaned back and crossed his arms. "You can't hope to end a trade that you yourself are adding to."

"That was my first impression too." Raleigh remembered when Rho told her. He explained the importance of having money for hiding and justified it that way. But it never sat well with her.

Rho's eyes travel to Gamma on the sofa. "We'll stay until he wakes up. Then we'll be on our way."

"Chicago isn't safe for you," Chi said.

"I assumed as much."

Raleigh didn't like that they had to pick up and move again. They were just starting to fall into a rhythm here. Hiding was tedious. Running would be worse. Thoughts of Paris last summer trickled into her mind, the feeling of looking over her shoulder had crept back while they were in hiding. Now the sensation of being watched prickled the hairs on the back of her neck and left a tumultuous feeling in her stomach that worsened with the butterflies Rho caused.

"I don't want to run," Raleigh said.

Upsilon shook his head. "We can't stay here. We're compromised. There isn't any other option."

"That isn't what she meant," Chi said, his eyes reading hers. "What she meant to say is that she's done running. She wants to face the synthetic head-on. It's not that she wants to stay in Chicago. It's that she doesn't want to worry about some guy holding a gun up to her head when she goes out for milk."

Dale sighed. "It's still better than being trapped at Grant and Able."

Except Raleigh wasn't trapped there. She was well on the path to becoming a doctor. Now, here, that dream was out of her grasp. If she couldn't keep hidden in a big city for a month, how was she supposed to go to school undetected for eight years? It was a frustrating rhetorical question. She, the Designed, and Dale were going to live hastily, without purpose. Not what she wanted.

"You could fight," Chi said to her.

Rho squinted at his long-lost brother. "No. She's already done that. She's got a scar that proves it."

Chi pointed at her shoulder. "That scar on her arm shows that she's her own woman. If she would've just gotten Mu and Tau out, and not stabbed Sigma, she would've been unmarred."

"And how do you plan on fighting the synthetic?" Raleigh asked Chi.

"We have a plan. One that involves you. We've been trying to find you since you left Grant and Able."

"I thought you were in Chicago tracing down the synthetic," Rho shot back.

Chi held up his hands. "That is true. We knew the Normandy synthetic was coming here to get Gamma and Upsilon. We figured that if we followed their lead we would get to you, too."

"What's the plan?" Raleigh asked.

"What's going on?" Gamma's voice broke their concentration. He grasped his head between his fingers, his barricade up as he pressed the sleep from his eyes. "Raleigh? Did they get Raleigh?"

"She's fine." Upsilon ran over to his brother. "They were part of the synthetic. Raleigh and Chi fought them off."

Raleigh was relieved that Gamma was up but frustrated that they'd be spending the next half hour running down the story for a third time. What she wanted was to hear the plan Chi had.

Chi nodded slightly while holding her gaze. He felt the same. As the others doted over Gamma, he said, "There's a cafe nearby which is secure. I'd rather not have everyone here know about my employers. Let's get a cup of coffee and have a talk."

"What? No. We're leaving." Rho started to pick up the extraction machine and bags by the door. "Gamma is up, and we need to leave."

"I want to hear Chi out. We've already been here for hours. What's a few minutes more?" Raleigh asked Rho.

"Gamma, I'll help you stand," offered Upsilon.

Kappa patted Raleigh's shoulder. "Come on. I'll carry your stuff."

"I'm not going until I hear Chi out. If the five of you want to push off, that's fine."

Rho cursed under his breath. "Fine. We'll talk. The three of us. But you better make it quick, Chi."

"Not here," Chi said.

Raleigh guessed he didn't want to answer to the six of them.

"You're leaving us?" Dale said frantically.

"You've got Gamma, Upsilon, and Kappa," Rho said to Dale. "They'll keep you safe while we're gone."

Chi considered Rho. "I don't want you sharing information about my organization with everyone."

"I can keep a secret. Let's go."

CHAPTER
03

IT WAS TEN at night, and the coffee shop Chi took them to doubled as a bar. A band in the corner played acoustic music that drowned out their conversation. Their round table sat to the side of the bar, and there were enough people to give them anonymity but not so many as to infringe on their space. Rho and Chi had beers while Raleigh wrapped her fingers around a hot cocoa, warming them.

"What company do you work for?" Rho asked Chi.

Raleigh regretted that he would be steering the conversation, but she also wanted to know the answer.

"The Vindex Authority. Think of it as a global police force. We work on things ranging from terrorism, to sex trafficking, the drug trade, and everything in-between."

"You work on all that?" Raleigh was impressed. The most she'd done over the last month was master gin rummy.

Chi shook his head. "My company does that. I just work on the Lucid trade."

"It's like the CIA?" Rho asked.

"No. The CIA is an American institution. We keep the world's interests at heart, not any one nation. Our funding comes from wealthy investors and some governments. Not that you need to know about all that. We're only going to focus on ending the synthetic."

"Ending the synthetic is a fantasy," Rho told him.

Drinking a long sip of his beer, Chi turned to Raleigh. "It's a precarious time in the Lucid black market. There were three sellers, not counting the Designed's stuff. The first and strongest is the Normandy group. They're the ones that have the original synthetic made by Grant and Able. They're also the ones who killed Pi and Beta and tried to kidnap Gamma today."

"Who are the other two?" Raleigh asked.

"Other *one*. There was a merger," Chi said. "There used to be two others. One was a synthetic based off the Normandy groups. A former scientist got out with enough of the formula to produce his own synthetic. It wasn't as good, being more addictive and less effective. The other is made by a separate group, and it has more of jolt and wears off quick. During that jolt a lot of people have too much power over themselves, making it more deadly."

"Sounds great." Rho rubbed his hands over his face. "It's a mess."

"These second two combined their operations and their Lucid. Now it has a jolt and lasts longer."

Rho croaked. "Even better."

"It is, because now there are only two groups, and the merged one is still finding its footing. We have a mole at the Normandy one. We know enough about their warehouses and production to take them down."

"Then do it!" Rho looked around to make sure his outburst wasn't heard. "If you can take them down, why haven't you?"

"Two reasons. One, we want to pass Grant and Able the

information so they can handle it. No point in us losing men when it's their fault that the synthetic exists. And two, we want the Normandy synthetic to take down this second group."

Raleigh understood his logic. "You want to get information on the merged group and give it to the Normandy so they can take them down. Then Grant and Able takes out the Normandy group."

"And the synthetic dies," Chi said.

"It's not that simple," said Rho. "Don't make it sound like it's that easy."

"But it is. Lucid isn't like heroin. It's complex to make. The leaders of these two groups have been stingy with who knows the formula. Once we take out the few people who know how to make it, the supply should dry up. We'll have to keep our eye on it, but it will be better."

"Take out the Normandy synthetic and go after the other later," Rho said.

Chi shook his head. "This second synthetic is inferior, but without the Normandy synthetic it will flood the market. People will die, and the second group will be more paranoid than they already are."

Rho's attitude wasn't helping anything. He wasn't along to entertain the idea of ending the synthetic. It irked Raleigh, who was interested.

"What's your plan for taking out the second synthetic?"

"We need to infiltrate them, and we think your Lucid will help. Their product isn't great. We bring them yours and say it's another brand. They know of the Designed's, of mine, but they assume it's just a brand since they don't know about us. That's why it can't be ours and has to be yours. Yours is different enough that we can claim to just have created it. We tell them that we want to go into business with them, learn their secrets, and then pass it to the Normandy."

"You just need Raleigh's Lucid then, not her." Rho let out the breath he was holding. "It's a far-fetched plan, but if she wants to give hers to you, fine. I've kept it off the market because I didn't want to put her in danger."

"I'd like her help going undercover to gain the information. Will you help us, Raleigh?" Chi asked.

"You don't need her," said Rho.

"I don't need you to answer for me," Raleigh said. She didn't know what was more upsetting, that he was interrupting or that she had to point it out.

"No, she doesn't need to come," Chi answered. "But none of our people take Lucid. Raleigh was trained for this at Grant and Able, trained to fight and go into the field. I could use someone to watch my back."

Rho pounded his fist on the table. "You're not risking her. She already got Mu and Tau out. These problems aren't hers. Leave her out."

Raleigh spoke up. "Rho, the problem is mine. Don't tell me that it's not when someone shot at me this morning. Chi, I saw intelligence on the synthetic at Grant and Able. It will be tough."

"I've seen that same information," Chi said.

Raleigh thought of how Gamma was nearly taken that morning. They could run all they wanted, but they would be caught. Raleigh would rather fight and have a chance to control her own fate. She wanted to become a doctor one day, and she wanted Lucid to be regulated. These were lofty goals that could only be achieved with the end of the synthetic.

"I'm in," she said.

"No! We aren't doing this again!" Rho said. "Chi, I need a moment with Raleigh. We'll meet you back at the apartment."

"She can speak for herself," Chi told him.

Rho shot his brother an icy look. "We need a moment."

Chi stood up. "Don't take too long. We all want to get out of Chicago sooner rather than later." He gave them a curt nod before heading out.

Raleigh jumped in before he could try to sway her. "Rho, this is what we've been waiting for. Since I got Dale out, we've been totally stagnant."

"I'm trying to find out more about the Modified."

"Yes, but I've been sitting here in Chicago."

"You've been watching out for Dale. He doesn't trust us the same way."

"He didn't, but he trusts you now. Listen to me. We have to take down the synthetic. If they found us after a month of hiding, then they will get to us a second time."

"They're after me and my brothers. Not you."

"Who knows after today? We have to be more proactive. Chi's organization already has a plan."

"An organization we just learned about a half hour ago. This is too quick, too far-fetched, and too dangerous."

"I'll admit that it's fast. But that doesn't mean that it's too far-fetched." Raleigh could see the apprehension on Rho's face. This wasn't the first time she'd found him to be similar to his Lucidin—steady and calm. She was more like hers, a little wild at times.

"You can't go alone," said Rho.

"Who else would I bring?"

"Brent has lost a few lower level dealers."

"What?" Brent was Rho's man in the Lucid trade and a friend to both of them. It was something she should've known. "Why didn't you tell me this sooner?"

"Because you're not involved in the sale of Lucid. You're focusing on keeping Dale safe. The dealers were being foolish, not being as discreet as they should've been. We've pulled back and are only selling to certain people. The point is these men won't hesitate to kill you."

"I'm well aware." She could picture the gun from this afternoon. The music had taken on a lovelorn tone, and the lights darkened or maybe that was just her imagination because when they entered, she was so worked up she didn't notice how dark it was.

Rho leaned forward, turning her hand over in his. The bottom of her mug held a final sip of cocoa. His beer was almost finished. They should be leaving to find the others. The feeling of his hand on hers kept her sitting.

"If I'd kissed you back, would you be staying?" Rho asked as his fingers traced lines on her palm.

At first, she was offended. Tonight he was rude to try to speak for her. The answer no sat on her tongue, but she wasn't sure. She didn't want to think of herself as the type of girl who made decisions based on a crush. But she couldn't deny that she might've done it. If they were dating, she might be so swept up in it that leaving with Chi would've been devastating.

"You didn't kiss me back, so I guess we'll never know."

She became aware of how close he was. His eyes trained on hers before lowering to her mouth. Unconsciously, she licked her lips, remembering how his lips felt. They'd been nice until the rejection settled in.

"I didn't kiss you back because I didn't want our dating to undermine your position in the group, but most of my brothers assume we are dating, and they don't care. It isn't a valid reason anymore."

He leaned in. She felt her chest tighten with giddiness.

"Stop." She slid away from him, she wouldn't let her foolish heart think about this when there were important issues at hand. "If you really wanted to kiss me, you wouldn't have cared what your brothers thought. If you kiss me now and I stay, I'll have to wonder if that's the reason you did it."

"That isn't the reason I'm doing it."

"Good, because even if you kiss me, I'm going. The synthetic is too big a threat. Dale and the others will be worried." She slid her chair back from the table, swigged down the last of the hot chocolate, and motioned for him to stand. "Let's go back to the others."

They wound their way through the crowd that had formed at the bar. Raleigh tried to keep her eyes from his as they stepped out onto the street and headed in the direction of the apartment.

"I don't want it to be like last time you left. I want you to leave on good terms," Rho said.

"Then don't guilt me or try to talk me out of it. Yes, it's hasty. But we've been pressured into this situation. If I wasn't there, Gamma would've been captured."

"You take too many risks."

"And you don't take enough." Raleigh pushed the door open, and they entered the apartment building.

Inside, the other five were waiting to leave.

Rho walked over to Chi. "She's set on going which means I'm going, too."

"No," Kappa said. "You can't Rho. We can't have both you and Raleigh gone."

"I don't want her to go alone with Chi," Rho said.

Raleigh knew that Chi wasn't considered one of them. Rho didn't trust that he'd have her back, and he might be right.

"I'll go," Gamma said.

Upsilon and Dale's faces dropped at the offer. Raleigh had to wonder if he felt he owed her and Chi for preventing the kidnapping.

"No, Gamma. Thanks, but we look too eerily similar, and, with the race difference, it will be confusing to explain our relation. If I took any of you, I'd say Tau would be best. We could go as twins," Chi said.

Raleigh didn't think Tau would work with her, given their past.

"Yes, Tau," said Rho. "He'll go. And Brent."

"Brent can't influence," Chi said.

"He'll want in," Rho assured him. "The synthetic has threatened and killed some of his guys. Any chance to stop them, and he'll jump at it. It will help to have someone who knows the trade."

"If those are your terms," Chi said, typing into his phone, "have them go to this address in two days."

"Brent's in New York," Rho said, reading it. "I'll buy Tau a ticket."

Things were decided. Finally having a plan was exhilarating, but guilt crept in as she looked to Dale. They hung back as the others walked out of the apartment.

"You've been trained for this," Dale said. "But be careful. Don't be a martyr."

"I won't. Stay with the guys. If we take down the synthetic, we're one step closer to being able to live free."

"Live being the main word. If you die, it isn't worth it," Dale said as the door locked behind them.

She squeezed his arm. She knew she was going to miss him and hoped it wasn't the last time they spoke.

CHAPTER
04

THE NEXT DAY Raleigh and Chi caught a taxi in New York and headed over to Brent's apartment. The noon sun shined down happily, reminding Raleigh of her early morning spent at the airport.

They exited the cab, and Raleigh craned her neck to see the large apartment building. The sun reflected off the windows, stinging her eyes.

"The Lucid trade has done Brent well," Chi said.

"He was rich to start," said Raleigh.

"Worse. He does it for fun."

"He does it for Rho." Although Raleigh couldn't say that Brent didn't enjoy his work.

Once they were in the lobby, they had to be cleared by a doorman before they made their way up to Brent's apartment. The last time she'd seen him was in Paris, before she went to California to meet Sigma and the other Designed. In the brief amount of time they'd spent together, he'd made an impression. Of all Rho's team, he was by far her favorite. A smile was itching at her lips at the thought of his antics. Rapping on his door, she could feel him on the other side, groggily walking toward it.

Chi thumped his fist on the door impatiently.

The locks were undone, and a sleepy-looking Brent pushed open the door. "No need to break it. You could tell I was up and coming. I just had to put on some clothes." The clothes were a pair of drawstring pants.

It was good he'd taken the time—she figured that anything less would be indecent. Raleigh allowed him to draw her into a tight hug. Sensing him, she could taste the morning on his tongue.

"You've gotten into trouble since I saw you last," said Brent. "And you must be Chi. Come in."

The modern apartment had the smell of cologne and soap. Industrial steel reflected the sunshine that came in the large windows. The leather couches reminded Raleigh of how tired her legs were. Besides a cactus on the windowsill, there were very few personal touches.

Brent watched her. "The cactus is named Esmeralda. She's pretty but will stick you. So be careful. Do you guys want coffee?" He began turning knobs and levers on a machine that noisily came to life, as unprepared for the morning as him.

"We'd like to get going. We're expected at the Vindex Authority offices in fifteen minutes. You can get coffee on the way or skip it," Chi said, not moving from the entry.

Brent raised an eyebrow, looking Chi up and down. "Rho warned me that you were friendly. I'll get dressed."

As Brent closed the door to his room, Raleigh said to Chi, "He's a nice guy if you get to know him."

"You do realize that Rho is only having him come along to keep tabs on you, right?"

"Yeah, and if it were anyone else, I'd be mad, but Brent's cool."

"Only if you overlook his profession."

"Let's get going," Brent said, stepping out of his room. The untucked button-down and slacks he wore were the same style as Chi's, but Brent managed to make them look casual instead of stiff.

Raleigh considered her own jeans and T-shirt. She didn't own anything formal enough for a business meeting, but hopefully no one would care.

They got in the back of a cab, Raleigh sandwiched between Brent and Chi. A large plastic divider separated them from the driver who was listening to loud exotic music with a beat that vibrated her bones. Chi was quick to settle into silence, but Brent would have none of it.

"So who's this company you're working for?" asked Brent.

"The Vindex Authority," Chi said as the cab pulled away from the curb.

"Yeah, Rho said it's a secret society. Do you have a handshake?"

"No."

"Any secret passwords?"

Chi adjusted in his seat. "Of course not."

"Rho made it sound like it was a lot more fun."

"It's not fun. It's vital. The purpose of our mission isn't to have a good time."

Brent cracked his knuckles. "But there's nothing to say that we can't have a good time while we accomplish this vital work."

Raleigh elbowed Brent who elbowed her right back. If he wanted Chi to like him, he couldn't goad him.

Raleigh had a question of her own. "How do they make their money if they aren't government sponsored?"

"They provide other services," Chi said. "Some countries pay them for their help. A lot of wealthy people pay to have a stable and safe world."

Vague, not telling her anything that he hadn't told her before. There was too little information to allow her make up her mind about the Vindex Authority. Raleigh half-expected the cab to take them to a back alley and a secret door. Instead, they arrived at a large skyscraper with an impressive metal directory on the front. Lawyers, accountants, and programmers also worked there.

"This looks boring," Brent whispered into Raleigh's ear as they entered the lobby.

"We'll need passes to get you onto the floor," Chi said. "I'll get them. Stay here."

Raleigh and Brent studied the other people loafing around the lobby. The high ceilings collected the voices, and the tall glass windows let the sun douse the room in light. Handshakes were being exchanged, and papers were shoved in briefcases. Her eyes drifted over the crowd and settled on a familiar face.

Tau.

His eyes bore into hers as his barricade pushed her mind out. Further proof that, like her, he wasn't going to forget what transpired between them.

He walked over and held out his hand to Brent. "I'm Tau. You're Rho's guy, Brent. Right?"

"Good to meet you, and this is Raleigh."

"I know her."

"Hi, Tau." She extended her hand.

Tau didn't take it. He looked to the reception desk, instead "Is Chi here?"

"Yes." Chi walked up with three passes printed with the word Visitor in bright blue on blue lanyards. "Glad you made it, Tau. Are we ready to go?"

Into the elevator they went, Brent's eyes hopping between the identical brothers.

"One of them looks strange enough," he said to Raleigh.

She had to agree. Her eyes quickly compared and contrasted the two, noticing that Chi wore their stern expression better. From the curve of his mouth, Tau was quicker to smile—or at least he had been at one point.

The elevator stopped on the fourteenth floor. They waited patiently for a receptionist to approve them to enter. The heavy metal doors swung open slowly. Raleigh rose on her tiptoes to peek around Chi to see what the mysterious Vindex Authority offices looked like. Boring. Cream cubicles obscured their view along the wall. The air smelled of coffee and toner from a printer.

"We're back this way," announced Chi as he led past the other employees toward the meeting rooms.

The people they passed looked blasé and plain. Some of them must be spies, but none wore trench coats like spies did in the film noirs that her father watched. Raleigh supposed they wouldn't want to stand out. Spies need to blend in, which made her wonder how well Chi and Tau would fare.

The meeting room that Chi led them to had a long oval table. A woman hovered near a set of pictures taped up to a board. She was short, round, and had a dizzying amount of caffeine pummeling her system.

"This is Bridget," Chi said.

Bridget nodded toward them, and it occurred to Raleigh that the woman already knew who they were.

"We're glad you decided to come," Bridget said in a heavy German accent. "Please have a seat."

Raleigh plunked into one of the chairs surrounding the table. They were well padded, which meant they might be expected to sit for a long time. Brent sat next to her while Tau selected the chair farthest from them. Chi opted for the chair nearest the whiteboard and Bridget.

"Chi should have filled you in on the basics of the plan," Bridget began. "It's simple enough. We're hoping to infiltrate the newly merged Lucid synthetic."

"Remember not to call it a synthetic. They don't know there's a real kind, so they simply call it Lucid," said Chi.

"Right. And the first thing we're going to do is have you try it." Bridget put a case on the table, undid the clasps, and removed three vials.

Brent picked up one and without hesitation plunged it into his port. Tau followed suit. Raleigh stared at the third vial.

"How is it going to make me feel?" she asked. Raleigh had never taken Lucid. She'd never had the need. She knew hers all too well, and from her kiss with Rho, she had an inkling about the Designeds'.

Brent cleared his throat. "It's crap. But you should know what it's like."

Raleigh fumbled slightly as she injected it into her port, disliking the sensation of pressure that came with pushing in Lucid. As the synthetic hit her system, her body trembled. It was akin to the racecar video games—one small movement sent her careening. Her heart began to flutter. Instinctually she slowed it down, plummeting the rate. Now it was too low, and she kicked it up only to have it too quick again.

Then it was out of her hands. Chi influenced her to a normal rhythm. "Now you can see why someone could hurt themselves."

She tried not to think about her lungs for fear that she'd squeeze out all her breath. "When will it wear off?"

"In a half hour," Bridget assured her. "Keep in mind that people pay lots of money for this. A vial goes for twenty to fifty dollars."

"Considerably less than what I sell Rho's for," Brent said.

Bridget didn't tense the way Chi did at Brent's words. "That's why we think they'll jump on Raleigh's. They're all about profits, which is why they are willing to sell a synthetic as unruly as this."

"So are we just going to waltz in and tell them we have something they want?" Brent asked. "Because that isn't going to work. These people are hidden for a reason."

Raleigh didn't know if he had his own skepticism or if Rho had rubbed off on him.

Bridget turned on her computer and a schematic filled up the white board. "You're right. We have most of the distribution tree developed. When the merger happened, they went with the labs of one and the sales chain of the other."

Pictures flashed across the white board. Ones Raleigh had seen before. "I saw these at Grant and Able."

"Yeah," Chi said. "Some of our information came from them, and we've got a bit more."

"Is your mole in intelligence?" Raleigh hadn't had the opportunity to meet many of those employees, and Gabe rarely gave her time to converse with them one-on-one.

Bridget gave her a pointed look. "If we reveal their identity, it could compromise their safety. Only people who need to know, do."

Raleigh didn't need to ask. She wasn't one of the people who needed to know.

Brent sat up straighter. "You never answered my question. How do we get our product into the hands of the people that matter?"

"We have a low-level seller here in Manhattan that we plan on going through." Bridget pulled up a photo of a guy with studded ruby earrings and a juvenile smirk.

Only a low-level seller? Raleigh darted her eyes toward the large network on the board.

"That's a crap plan," Brent said. "Your maps show what everyone knows. The real trade is in Europe. That kid you just showed us probably doesn't even have his boss's phone number. They call him when they have product to push. We'll be waiting for him to get the call and then hope that his boss finds our Lucid compelling enough to tell his boss about, which means we'll have to wait for that call. This is all going to add up. We could be looking at months before we get it in the hands of anyone that matters."

"But you know who the higher-ups are. Let's just go to them," Tau said.

"We have no reason to know who they are," Chi explained before Bridget could. "Our story is that we're going to them because we don't have the resources in place to make and sell our new brand. If we approach the people at the top, then it comes off as suspicious."

"But months?" Raleigh said. Rho might be correct in thinking it was a long shot.

"There is another option," Brent said. "We can ask for an introduction by someone with influence. I'm thinking of Marcel. I've used him to help sell the Designed's stuff. He's not on your little chart because he only sells the real stuff, but he's been approached by these synthetics to sell theirs."

Bridget tapped the France portion of the map. "We're aware of Marcel. You think that he'd believe that you created this synthetic?"

Brent snorted. "No way he'd buy it. He's had Raleigh's. We had to give it to him for the paperwork we needed to get her back to the States. No. If we decide to get his help, we let him in on the plan."

"And he'd help?" Tau asked.

Brent drummed his fingers. "He'll want something in return. But yes, I think he would. These inferior synthetics give Lucid a bad name and kill off clients. All of us want to see them gone. They've taken out friends of mine and his."

"Rho shouldn't have told Marcel about Raleigh." Chi's jaw was set.

Brent held out his hands. "We needed the papers. Don't worry. Marcel won't tell anyone."

"Then let's go that way," Tau said.

"Marcel is dangerous," Chi interjected before Brent could speak again. "I think we should go with the lower level dealer."

Bridget's eyes focused on the synthetic operations. The guy in Manhattan was far down a complex tree. With her face emotionless, it was impossible for Raleigh to tell if Bridget would side with Brent or Chi.

Bridget's lips formed a thin line as glanced around the table. "Chi and I will discuss this with my superior. We'll have you take a break, and we'll see you in an hour or so."

A warm frustration built in Raleigh's chest. The Vindex Authority had no problems requesting her help, but they didn't seem to value her opinion. They were the ones calling the shots.

Brent stood, shoving his chair. "If you don't go with the Marcel plan, I'm out. The whole reason I'm along is to end the violence toward my sellers and to keep an eye on Raleigh. Your plan has a lot of sitting around, and the only thing she'll be at risk of is boredom."

Raleigh got up and so did Tau. Chi opened the door. Walking past the cubicles, a protest sat in her mouth. It was her Lucid and her help. If anyone had a say, it should be her.

"Chi," said Raleigh, "I think we should approach Marcel."

Chi put up his hand. "We really shouldn't discuss it outside of the conference room. We'll let you know our decision." With that, he deposited them in the elevator and pressed the down button.

"These guys seem great," Brent said sarcastically as the door shut. "We're giving them your Lucid and offering my connections. Yet, they keep the control."

"I don't like it either." Raleigh looked to Tau.

Tau didn't return her gaze. "If they decide to take the route of the lower dealer I'm out, with Brent."

"Yeah. I won't need you to cover my back if I'm just sitting around," Raleigh said.

Tau shook his head as the elevator let them out on the bottom floor. "I'm not here to watch your back. I'm here to watch Rho's. He's convinced that you're no longer with Grant and Able."

"I'm *not* with them!" Raleigh turned to Brent so he could back her up.

Brent was looking down at his phone, not paying attention. As Tau started to walk toward the door, Brent stayed at the elevator.

Raleigh followed Tau. "I can't believe you think that."

"Really?" Tau said, brushing past people in the lobby. "I saw how you interacted with Gabe, and then you stab Sigma for even thinking about hurting them."

"I could've turned you all in then and there."

Tau shook his head. "You might've, but you didn't know about the aerosolized inhibitor. No. You could easily be a mole for them. I bet the only reason you haven't handed over everyone is because Sigma has cut ties, and you're waiting until Rho learns where he is."

Raleigh winced at his words as they stepped out onto the street. "I got you out." If anything, he should owe her. The torture was bad, but it was for a reason that he wasn't acknowledging.

"Doesn't matter if you plan on turning us all in," Tau said. "Rho might be fooled by this naïve helpless girl act you've perfected, but I'm not. Of course, you're interested in the Vindex mole. You don't like anyone spying on your boss."

"You're crazy." Anger rattled her voice. Betraying Agatha was one of the hardest things she'd ever done. In doing so she gave up a lot of her own safety and her family who she couldn't risk involving. "Everything I did was to get you out!"

"Save it for Rho." Tau flicked his hand up to hail a cab. "Just know that I'm watching you."

Tau got in and left Raleigh on the sidewalk, fuming. Grinding her back teeth, she stifled the urge to scream. How dare he say that about her. Brent was walking over.

"Tau thinks I'm still with Grant and Able," she said. "Can you believe that?"

"Yeah, I can. The guy hates you," Brent said bluntly. "But he's loyal to Rho, so we don't have to worry about him giving you trouble. He'll realize eventually that you aren't the enemy."

"I just don't see the point in having him along."

"Play nice or Rho will put his foot down on the whole thing."

"Rho's not in charge of me," she said.

Brent rubbed the bridge of his nose, a headache forming in the back of his head. "Play nice, Raleigh. If we're out, that leaves you with the Vindex Authority, and I don't think they give a shit about you."

Raleigh forced down her anger. "Fine."

"I got a call back there. One of my sellers had an emergency."

"What kind of emergency?"

"He wouldn't say over the phone. Just told me he needed to see me quick."

"Does this happen often?"

"Never. I've got to meet him."

"I'll go with you."

"This is my problem."

Raleigh lifted up her hand to hail a cab. "If you're going to be watching my back, then you can't argue when I watch yours."

"Fair enough. But *I'll* do the talking."

C H A P T E R
05

THE BITING ODOR of the sterilized hospital brought on a wave of nostalgia so strong that Raleigh paused upon entering. Of all the places Brent's client could've chosen, this one never entered her mind. The sound of rolling hospital beds beckoned her mind back to the days spent with Uncle Patrick and Dr. Moore, times when she diagnosed patients, when she didn't know she had her Lucid to thank. It also drudged up the lingering sadness of her blackouts and time spent as a patient. The uncertainty she'd experienced back then was written on the current patients in the waiting area. She'd walked halls like these, with their checkered floors. Taking in a breath, she felt that if she succeeded in taking down the synthetic, she'd be back in a place like this again, but as a healer, a currently unattainable promise.

Brent's breathing had deepened. She knew that, for him, the hospital didn't cast a magical spell of memories and dreams. No. It was a scary unfamiliar place to a healthy man his age. He'd been checking his phone obsessively since the text. With his shoulders drooping, he walked to the elevator door and pressed the up arrow.

"Your guy is on the second floor?" said Raleigh. She wanted to tell him that everything would be all right, a knee-jerk reaction. Neither of them knew what waited for them one story up. Raleigh couldn't help but notice the map to the side of the elevator doors. The ICU was on the second floor. She had a sinking feeling that's where they were headed.

"I'm not familiar with hospitals." His signature charm was snuffed out by worry. "Can we just go in?"

"Usually there are visiting hours in the middle of the day," Raleigh said, stepping into the elevator. Each hospital had its own set of rules, and she wasn't going to claim to be an expert here.

A pair of doctors rushed past them as they stepped out to the second floor. A large nurses' station sat in the middle, an unlucky horseshoe of rooms circling it. Their translucent walls gave the patients little privacy, but curtains offered some cover. The main goal was to have the patients closely observed, which the clear-glass walls allowed.

"Hello. I'm here to see Tristan Williams," Brent told one of the nurses. "I'm Brent, a friend of his."

"Room three," she said. "His brother is expecting you. He's been here all night."

They were expecting Brent but not Raleigh. She planned to keep close to the wall and stay quiet.

They went to room three and opened the door. Behind the blue, sea-green, and cream curtains lay a young man. One leg was immobilized in a sling, and his body was wrapped in bandages—most notably his arm and head. She almost didn't notice the oxygen mask.

A second man sat between the bed and the window with the

tightly-drawn blinds. He stood up and exhaled deeply. It broke the sound of the machines that beeped every so often to let the nurses know everything was stable.

"Ari, is Tristan all right?" Brent asked.

Raleigh knew the answer was no. His problems encompassed a lot of things. His head was banged up pretty bad, a concussion with nausea and pain only calmed by a cocktail of pain relievers. His left leg, wrist, and two ribs were broken. His organs were bruised. Of all the injuries, it was the one to his brain that worried her most. There'd been some bleeding, and the inflammation wasn't doing him any favors. She was so focused on the guy in the bed that she was startled when his brother finally spoke.

"He's in a coma." Ari seemed barely able to get the last word past his lips.

"How long has he been like this?" Brent asked. "What happened?"

"Since last night." Ari walked to the foot of his brother's bed. "He was out on a deal. There's been a lot of overlap between our brand and the others."

"I know." Brent turned to Raleigh. "Our supply isn't enough to keep up with demand. We can't make it fast enough." Brent's eyes made it clear, neither of these men knew the true origins of their Lucid. "When the clients can't get ours, they go to the other brands."

"They'd take ours first every time," Ari said. "There's a group of weightlifters who've been buying a lot. Tristan went to make the delivery."

Raleigh felt Ari's chest tighten as he spoke. Guilt, regret, and sadness ached in him.

"He knew something was wrong," Ari said. "He called me and told me that he thought someone was following him. Still, he made the sale, but on the way out, a car ran over him. The police are calling it a hit–and–run. He's been in surgery for the leg and arm all morning, but he hasn't been conscious since the accident. They think that the trauma to his brain... he might never wake up."

"Have you called your parents?"

"Yeah. They'll be down in a few hours. My mom is freaking out. I've tried to get a hold of his girlfriend. This is my fault. When I started working for you, it was nothing like this. The whole point was that it wasn't illegal or dangerous."

Brent placed a hand on Ari's shoulder. "I know. I'm sorry this happened. You can't blame yourself for him getting hurt. Tristan was always way more into making sales than you."

"Not anymore. We're out. I mean obviously he is, and I can't do it anymore." Ari choked back tears. "I don't blame you, but we're out. You should get out, too."

Hospitals and suffering families were nothing new to Raleigh. For years she'd felt not only the ailments of the sick, but the physical pain it evoked in their loved ones. What was different now was that she wasn't helpless to stop the pain. Now she could influence. True, Grant and Able only dangled the promise of healer in front of her. She was a far better weapon. That didn't matter. She could help Tristan, and she knew it.

Centering herself, she focused her attention on Tristan's brain. She felt the blood surging to the engorged, angry brain tissue. Slowly, she pulled it back without cutting it off completely. The trick was to alleviate some of the pressure that was building up. It took her some time to focus on the delicate process of giving the brain just enough blood while calming the traumatized tissue.

Brent continued to talk with Ari about what would happen next, and Raleigh half listened to their conversation as she pressed around Tristan's brain. If nothing else, she'd alleviated some of the damage, aided in part by the meds they'd given him.

"Is she okay?" Ari asked.

Raleigh knew she looked dopey concentrating so hard on Tristan.

"Yeah, she's fine. She's a bit scared of hospitals. One of my new dealers, although I'm thinking that after this it might be good to pull back on the whole thing. Raleigh, it's time to go." Brent touched her elbow.

Raleigh wanted to stay. She needed a bit longer. The blood in the brain was clotting and leaking into the wrong areas. She could fix it. Tugging her arm from Brent's grasp, she ignored him. Tristan might die without her help. Her interventions would work far better than any the doctors could perform.

"Raleigh, this is starting to get weird," Brent whispered.

Maybe it was. From the way Ari moved, it was clear he expected both of them to leave. She couldn't tell him what she was doing but remained rudely planted near the foot of Tristan's bed.

Then it happened. Tristan took charge of himself. His conscious mind took control as the pressure eased off his brain. Slowly his eyes opened, the small movement capturing Ari's attention. The monitors picked up Tristan's improved heart rate and vitals.

"He's awake!" Ari exclaimed loudly.

Nurses and a doctor rushed in, shock on their faces.

"He's up?" the doctor asked as she walked over to Tristan. "How is that possible?"

"He opened his eyes," Ari told her. "We were talking, and he opened them."

As the nurses and doctor tried to make sense of the sudden shift in Tristan's health, Brent pushed Raleigh toward the door and into the hallway.

"Are you insane?" He pulled her into the empty elevator and jamming the button to close the door. "You can't influence in such a public place! Tristan is known to the synthetic. What if people figure out it was you?"

"No one's going to figure it out."

"The synthetic can't know what you're capable of. No influencing. That's a rule that I should not have to tell you."

"Tristan's the only one who would know, and he was unconscious. He's never going to figure it out. The doctors will say it's a miracle or luck."

The elevator opened to the bottom floor, and Brent stepped out. Raleigh remained in place, her eyes looking up at the top of the lift as she imagined all the people in the ICU that could use her help.

"Raleigh, we need to get out of here."

"Tristan wasn't the only sick one."

Brent kept the doors from closing. "Now isn't the time to mess with this."

"This is what I'm *meant* to do Brent. This is why I make Lucid. It's not so I can save the Designed or fight Grant and Able. I make it because I'm supposed to save these people."

"Not today. If after all this is over you want to be a doctor, that's great. But today you agreed to be a spy. Let's go. Chi texted me back there. They've made their decision. Do you want to explain to them why you were in the hospital influencing? You miraculously saving people is going to put everyone at risk. Not just yourself."

Brent was right. There would be time for this, but not today. Someday people would know what Lucid was, and she would use it openly. Saving Tristan intoxicated her with the potential for what she could do. The roadblock of the synthetic needed to be removed before this could become her calling.

"What if they don't go through Marcel?" she asked as they headed towards the line of cabs.

"We find another way to take the synthetic down, with or without Chi's organization."

RALEIGH SLID INTO her seat in the conference room, the events at the hospital swirling in her head. Chi and Bridget didn't ask where they'd been, and Brent didn't offer up the information. It was better if Chi didn't know. This was Raleigh and Brent's secret.

Tristan was lucky he didn't die in the hit-and-run. The thrill of saving him tingled her nerves, drawing her from the haze that had settled over her since she killed the man. She tried to focus on the synthetic. They needed to be stopped now more than ever.

She was so wrapped up in thinking about the hospital that she almost missed what Bridget said. "It's time to get down to it. We're going to go with your idea, Brent, and ask Marcel for an introduction."

Chi fell into one of the seats, clearly perturbed that he hadn't been able to talk Bridget out of it. That was if it was even Bridget's decision and not someone's higher up. Raleigh hated how much they didn't know about the Vindex Authority.

"Good," Brent said. "I'll call him right now. Usually he can meet with us in a day or two. How fast can we get to Paris? I'm betting you have fake passports, probably more than one. Let Tau take one of yours Chi."

Raleigh expected him to lord the win over everyone.

She was surprised.

"Hold up!" Chi said. "We need to first work on our backstories and identities for this undercover mission."

Raleigh had been a spy, but she'd only ever done it as herself. Grant and Able met with her parents, she simply omitted knowing the Designed. Being herself wasn't an option in this scenario. She'd have to be someone else.

"Do you have any ideas?" she asked.

"Chi and Tau are twins, that much is obvious," Bridget said.

"We'll say that they were users who wanted a better product. They look like users."

"I agree," Brent said. "If anyone thinks they look off, hopefully they'll simply attribute it to that. I'm a dealer. Marcel will say that I got tired of dealing the old stuff and, when two of my clients developed a new synthetic, I got on-board trying to sell it."

"We're too young," Tau said. "Yeah, we're smart, but they aren't going to be giving us an IQ test. Anyone who developed this new synthetic would have to be in the field of biochemistry much longer."

Chi cleared his throat. "We found the scientists and commissioned their work. Scientists aren't businessmen. We don't have to bring any along. If we have the product, that's all that will matter. They'll assume we did the science."

"Then where do I fit in?" Raleigh asked. "One of the scientists?"

Bridget shook he head. "You're far too young. I know you worked in the labs at Grant and Able, and I have no doubt you could talk a fine line about it, but it isn't plausible."

"A sister, then?" Chi asked.

Brent snorted. "Why bring your younger sister? A girlfriend?"

"To whom?" asked Tau. "That's as unbelievable as her being a brilliant scientist. Try again."

Raleigh's mouth flapped open. She fought the urge to kick him under the table.

"Neither of us would bring a girlfriend," Chi said. "Not unless it was really serious. It's hard to fake that kind of intimacy. No. Tau's right. It wouldn't be believable."

That wasn't what Tau implied, but Raleigh held her tongue.

"She's the financier," Bridget said. "We'll say that she also bought from Brent and is friends with you guys. The Lucid helps with her fainting which is why she's so invested in it. She comes from money and she needs to see the production up and running. Her well-being depends on it."

Raleigh shouldn't have been surprised Bridget knew about her fainting, the Vindex Authority had clearly vetted them. But to use her illness as their cover? "My fainting? I'm not going to tell them about my fainting."

"The financier thing sounds good," said Brent. "And it could be any long-term disease. As long as it's treated, how are they to know?"

Bridget raised her eyebrows. "If she doesn't extract, she is likely to faint while there. I was under the impression that it only took a few days for the Lucid to build up. Isn't that right, Raleigh?"

"Yeah, without extractions. But I'm going to extract."

Chi and Bridget were silent, a look passed between them.

"No, you're not," said Chi. "We can't risk bringing an extraction machine. Who knows how closely we'll be watched? They can't know the true origins of Lucid or we're screwed. You and Tau will have your ports removed, and you'll look just like everyone else."

Raleigh rubbed the port lines embedded under her skin. The ridges they caused drew some attention, that was true. "I'll wear long sleeves. We can say it's for medicine. Brent has a port."

"Not as large as yours. There's no reason to have it," Bridget said as her eyes softened.

It was the kindest the woman had appeared since Raleigh arrived, and it wasn't even that empathetic.

"They'll be no extractions," Chi said. "Period."

"I'll faint after a day or two." The Lucid made her powerful. The fainting undercut that advantage. "When I black out, I can lose five minutes at a time."

"Which will serve to strengthen your cover as a sick young woman looking for a treatment," said Bridget. "It fits nicely. By making your cover center around your illness, it lends credibility to it, rather than scrutiny. Tau, Chi, over the next few days I want you to strengthen your backstory. Brent, Chi tells me that you come from money."

"That's one way to put it," Brent said. "I can help Raleigh seem like a socialite. I'm not sure how far we'll get in a few days."

"Maybe it should be weeks," Chi said. "Better to have it right."

Brent looked at Raleigh. A few weeks? How many more of Brent's dealers would be mowed down in that time?

"No," Brent said, "if the merger's new, it's more vulnerable. We need to strike while the iron is hot. I'll see if Marcel can meet us within seven days, and we'll get as far as we can and do our best."

"Tau and Chi, will a week be enough?" Bridget asked.

Tau snorted. "If Raleigh can become a debutante in a week, then I can memorize some fake childhood memories. Don't worry about us."

"Then I won't," Bridget concluded. "Tau and Raleigh, Chi is going to take you to a residence you can stay at while you're here. It's a secure location owned by us."

"Raleigh can crash with me," Brent offered.

Chi shook his head. "This is more secure, and it's nice. You guys will like it. It's getting late. Tomorrow we can start nailing down our identities."

Chi was right, she still had to manage to stay out of the sight of Grant and Able. Any joy of healing Tristan dampened. What was going to be harder, keeping up this cover or enduring the blackouts? Grant and Able had trained her but not for this.

C H A P T E R
06

THE "SAFE HOUSE" was similar to a bed and breakfast, except none of the people seemed happy. Upon entering, they were greeted by a gruff man at the front desk, his jowls and face etched into a perpetual scowl. Raleigh sensed a heavy weight sitting under his shirt, cold against his skin. That was what Chi meant by protection.

Chi walked Raleigh and Tau up to their rooms. "Breakfast and dinner are offered."

Tau still did his best to avoid eye contact, conversation, and being physically close to Raleigh. If Chi noticed, which any reasonable person would, he didn't care to say anything.

"All right," said Chi, "this room is yours, Raleigh." He slid a keycard over the handle and it opened. "Tau is right next door if you need him." With that, Chi left her alone.

There was barely enough room to fit a twin bed and dresser. It felt more like a hallway to the bathroom in the back. Raleigh tossed her bag inside the room and stood wondering what to do. There was a bookcase in the dining room, but after the last two days she couldn't sit still. She needed to run.

As she stretched her legs in the hall Tau was also leaving his room. With his sneakers on and light sweater, it wasn't hard to guess that he had the same thought as her.

"You run?" Raleigh asked.

"Yeah." He tightened the laces on his shoes.

"I was going to go myself. We could run together."

Tau sighed. Raleigh didn't want to run with him much either. However, they were going to have to be cordial and work together. Running was a fine activity to start with because they need not talk. At Grant and Able she'd forged relationships with Receps with runs like this. Tau wasn't the first person she had to work to win over.

He headed towards the stairwell turning just before he headed down to say, "You won't keep up."

"I'm faster than you think." Raleigh refrained from mentioning her training, wisely keeping Grant and Able out of the conversation.

"Fine, but I'm not going to slow down for you."

With that he was down the steps and Raleigh was right behind him. Once they were on the street, the cool October weather fluttered by her, along with the afternoon commuters. It wasn't the busiest street, but she knew that Tau would find one with less foot traffic to dodge.

With each long stride, she left behind the apprehensions of the day. The grim knowledge of Tristan's assault, and her frustration that she couldn't yet be a healer, lessened with each step. Unfortunately, even though each stride brought her further out of her worries, they did little to keep her up with Tau.

He barricaded, and so did she. Thus, she couldn't sense his legs, but she could see them. All the Designed were graceful, built to exceed the physical limitations of humanity. He agilely dodged pedestrians, and she admired that. It was also easy to curse because she couldn't keep up.

It wasn't the first time she'd fallen behind. Even with Lucid making her muscles work more efficiently, it wasn't an absolute cheat. As it was with training, she could only push so hard. She had to rely on endurance to make up for her physical shortcomings. She focused on keeping Tau in sight, hoping that when he slowed she could make up the ground.

Tau didn't slow. He went from being a block ahead to a couple ahead, to a small dot on a vacant street. Avoiding a curb, she glanced down. When she looked up, he was gone. She was alone now—in a part of town that wasn't crowded probably because it wasn't the nicest area.

The stink of trash and urine lingered in the air, and broken glass provided obstacles for her feet. The street had the occasional person sleeping in a doorway or near an alley, but she could perceive others in the apartments and buildings around. Far beneath her feet, the humanity of dozens of passengers flashed past on the subway. To an outsider she would've appeared alone, but Raleigh could tease out the humanity of everyone around her. Not that it helped much.

In her attempt to keep up with Tau, and later just to find him, she'd become hopelessly turned around. She didn't know the exact address of the safe house. She only had a vague idea of the cross streets. The shadows of the buildings crossed the street and crept up the buildings on the other side. The air grew colder making her sweat icy on her skin. If she had a smart phone, she could've looked at a map. But with her toss-away version, phone calls and simple texts were all she could do.

Flipping her cursed phone open, she considered calling a cab, then stopped. Chi wouldn't want her fumbling around looking for the safe house. A Vindex Authority driver had taken them the first time. She punched in Brent's number. He didn't live too far away. She tried not to feel embarrassed for needing his help.

"Can't live without me for a few hours?"

His joke was flat. He hadn't yet recovered from seeing Tristan at the hospital.

"I'm lost."

"Without me?"

"No, Brent. Like I'm lost, lost. I went for a run and can't find my way back to the safe house. I didn't want to call a cab. It's getting late."

"I'll get you. Where are you?"

Raleigh rattled off the street numbers. "Do you know where that is?"

"Yeah. You picked a really safe neighborhood... *not.*"

"I'm fine." Raleigh kept her head down.

"I'll grab my car from the garage and be right there. Stay put."

Raleigh closed her phone and waited. She watched as evening started to settle in. Men lingered in the doorways and crannies of the buildings. Most of them were tired, some high, and others edgy in unsettling ways. With influencing, she was not defenseless. Images of the men she killed in the parking lot came to mind, the pallor of the driver's face the last time she saw him. He was older. He had a past, and people would've been in his life. People who'd wonder why they could no longer reach him and wonder how he died. She pushed out the thoughts.

Five minutes passed. Then ten. At seventeen she wondered if she should've just tried to run back. Then a red car pulled up, and a window rolled down.

"Get in," Brent said. He wasn't smiling.

She dashed around and sat down in the front seat, shut the door, and buckled her seatbelt. "I'm sorry about this."

"Why were you running here?" He scrunched his nose up as the smell of the street wafted into the car.

"I was running with Tau and got lost."

"Where is he?"

"We got separated."

Brent raised his eyebrows. "He shouldn't have left you here! This isn't a great place for you to be alone. Who knows what could happen to you?"

"I'm fine." She tried to ignore the look on his face. "I'm not as helpless as people think."

"True, but Tau is supposed to have your back. I don't think he does. I'm going to call Rho."

"And who's going to replace him? The cover works better if they're twins. No. We've been over this. I won't make the mistake of running with him again."

"If you can't trust him to stay with you running, how are you going to rely on him when we're undercover?"

"That's my problem, not yours."

The car jerked to a stop in front of the safe house. A woman hurried by on the sidewalk as Raleigh collected herself.

"I hurt Tau, back at Grant and Able," she said. "He has reason to hate me."

"You saved his ass, and he needs to get over it. Don't take his shit. You're a good person."

Brent was wrong. Yes, she had the capacity to be good and a hero as she'd been today. There was also something sinister in her, something inside that let her torture Tau and kill the driver. Which one was stronger? She didn't know. She gave him a forced smile before going into the safe house.

Habits die hard, and her mind was trained to sense her surroundings before she entered. Now, as she approached her door, she could feel a woman inside her room. Bridget, she recognized the woman by the amount of caffeine in her system. Stepping closer she put her ear near the door and heard Bridget and Chi. Hopefully nothing was wrong. As a courtesy she knocked on the frame as she entered.

"Raleigh, you're back," Chi said. "Did you go running?"

Wiping her brow she felt the salt crystals that were left from her sweat. "What are you doing here? Did something happen?" A first-aid kit sat on the bed.

Bridget occupied the small chair near the window, and Chi stood. Their calmness made her second think an emergency, but they were both pretty good at keeping their cool.

"No. We're here for your port removal," Bridget said. "Don't worry. It won't hurt. We just took out Tau's, and he said he barely felt it."

Tau had made it back then. Lucky him. Of course Tau wasn't upset about taking out his port. He wasn't going to have to cope with blackouts. She doubted the port held any significance for him.

"Look," said Raleigh, "like I told you before, it's a bad idea."

Bridget reached for the medical box. "The blackouts are part of your cover. We've already decided this."

"No. You decided. You've asked for my help, and I'm willing to do it. But listen to me now when I tell you this is a bad idea."

"You'll still be able to influence, and you'll still be a strong person, just with the blackouts," Chi said. "I know it's frightening."

"No, you don't know."

Chi paused then said, "I thought I was a sick kid. They told me I had kidney disease when I was young, as an excuse to take my Lucid."

"Yes, but I actually was a sick kid, and I'll be ill again if you do this."

Bridget very nicely stood up and started to put her arms into the sleeves of her jacket. "I'm not going to make you do this."

"Great." Raleigh felt a weight lift off her shoulders.

"But if you don't, you can't join the others on the mission."

The weight fell right back down. Ultimatums reflexively made her want to say no. Not this time. It was true that the group might do fine with her Lucid and the plan, but she was strong and ready to fight. Rho's plan to tuck her away wasn't the future she envisioned. With a heavy sigh, she pulled off her sweater and flipped her arm so that the crux faced up.

Bridget took off her jacket and motioned for Raleigh to sit on the bed. With Raleigh positioned in front of her, Bridget sterilized the area with a pungent disinfectant. The tubes of Raleigh's port went in much like an IV, only they were slightly bigger, and solidly in place under the skin.

"On the count of four, I'm going to pull the tubes out." Bridget counted down while Raleigh winced, and the port was withdrawn.

Bridget lied about it not hurting. It burned coming out. Blood dripped down the side of Raleigh's arm as Bridget prepared to stitch her up. All those months ago in Belgium, Raleigh had such anticipation and hope when the port was installed. Now dread clouded her mind like a thick fog. She wasn't the sick girl she was all those months ago. Too much had happened. Yet here she was reverting back to that helplessness.

Chi sat down beside her on the bed, his hand lightly on her back. It was the first time—besides a handshake—that they'd touched, and it seemed contrived.

"You won't be that girl you were the last time you were sick." His deep voice was caring, not stern or serious like usual. "This time around you know how to use your Lucid, and the blackouts can't rob you of your courage."

Raleigh looked into his blue eyes. Was that the term to be granted to the side of her that she didn't like to acknowledge? Was she courageous when she screwed over Grant and Able? Was it courage or something else that made her capable of murder?

Bridget bandaged up Raleigh's arm and gave her hand a small squeeze. "We'll leave you to get some rest."

Chi got up and helped Bridget put her medical supplies away. Raleigh failed to manage even a half-hearted farewell. They were gone, and she felt alone.

C H A P T E R
07

THE NEXT MORNING Raleigh tried not to fidget as she sat in a barber's chair. One seat over a girl sipped a cappuccino as the hairdresser highlighted her hair. No one talked or smiled. It was a stark contrast to the chain store Raleigh usually went to for cuts. She heard the snipping of scissors near her ear. With each snap a brown tendril fell to the floor. She'd never been the type of girl who spent hours getting ready, and she hoped her hair wouldn't be too short to pull into a ponytail.

"Your boyfriend is cute," the man cutting her hair said. "He's so involved. Most of them don't care."

Cute wasn't how she'd describe Brent. This was as serious as he got, and perhaps only because Marcel had agreed to the meeting in a few days. The incident with Tristan seemed to have lit a fire under Brent, and he wanted the synthetic gone.

It wasn't Raleigh's idea to cut her hair. It was Brent's. She knew she had split ends and that they needed to be trimmed, but who knew how well she'd be able to pull off this cut? Styling was an art she'd never learned. Her eyes drifted over to the display wall of gels, mousses, and other products.

The stylist took his work seriously, like all good professionals. He stood back more than once, head cocked to the side as if he was evaluating a work of art. He turned Raleigh away from the mirror—to not ruin the surprise—but his expression made her worry.

"It's finished." He turned toward Brent.

"She looks great. You're very good."

The man nodded his head as he swiveled Raleigh's chair around so she could see. Her hair was beautiful. It was layered. The shortest one framed her face and the others tiered down to her shoulders. It was softer and lighter. Raleigh's fingers tentatively touched the ends, worried by how easily she might ruin the effect. Her appearance was lovely and should have given her confidence, but it didn't. Inside she wasn't soft and girly, she was hard and dangerous.

"Thanks. I love it."

Really. She ought to love it.

Brent got her out of the seat and paid at the front. Then they headed to the clothing stores. Raleigh kept catching glimpses of herself in the store's windows. Was that really her?

Shopping was one of her least favorite activities. Brent was indifferent, neither excited nor bored by the task. It may've all been in her head, but she had the impression that everyone knew she was out of her depth.

In the past, Raleigh's mother helped her pick out practical pants and shirts, mostly from sporting goods stores. Every now and then her older sister Lana would go the mall, but Raleigh rarely did. Thalia, her younger sister, picked up a lot of her Goth clothes from second-hand stores. Raleigh assumed this experience would be on par with shopping at the mall. She couldn't have been more wrong.

The store Brent took her to was a boutique, not a department store, which meant it was quaint rather than large. Outfits were spaced out on hangers so that customers could see them, and there weren't a lot of choices. Raleigh ran her fingers down the smooth cotton of a dress while trying to avoid drawing the attention of the sales people who'd already offered up help twice.

"That isn't really your color," Brent said nicely.

"At these prices, that's probably a good thing."

"Don't talk like that. From now on, you don't even look at prices."

"How am I going to afford this?" Raleigh had a handful of dollars in her pocket, all the money she had to her name. Rho hadn't been selling her Lucid, so she had no income, and Brent wouldn't be selling much for a while, so frugality was a must.

"The Vindex Authority is paying. If you feel guilty, know that the Lucid they took goes for way more. Fashion is part of your cover, so it's important."

The door chimed, and a slender woman entered. Raleigh gave her little notice until she walked over to them and honed in on Brent.

"What was so important that I had to drop everything?" The woman's casual tone warred with her poise.

Raleigh felt the woman's animosity toward Brent—underneath the composure. Her first guess was an ex-girlfriend, but Brent struck Raleigh as a guy who had one-night stands, not relationships.

"Lilia, hi," he said, hugging her.

The woman's arms half-embraced him. As she pulled back, the line of her mouth dipped into a frown. "We haven't heard from you in months and then you call me and say you need my help... at a clothing store?"

"My friend here needs a bit of polish for a job interview, and I thought you'd be the best to help with that. Meet Raleigh." He guided Lilia's attention to her. "And Raleigh, meet my sister Lilia."

Raleigh remembered Brent saying that he had smattering of half-sisters, stepsisters, and any other type you could imagine. It surprised her to meet one of them. None of the Designed kept up with their families because it was too risky, but Brent wasn't Designed. Raleigh wasn't the only one who seemed shocked. Lilia, too, seemed baffled.

"It's nice to meet you." Raleigh stuck out her hand. "Brent's told me about you. It's nice that you're willing to come help me shop."

"Nice to meet you." Lilia shook her hand. It was a delicate yet firm shake, her skin soft and smooth. She turned to her brother. "Where have you been, Brent? None of us have been able to get a hold of you. Dad's been worried."

"That's because Dad gets upset when I don't do what he wants. So Raleigh needs clothes. Ones that will make her seem older. It's for a job overseas. Raleigh's more than qualified, but she doesn't come from the right social circles. You know how it is."

Lilia tucked her bottom lip between her teeth, no doubt deciding if she should help. From the look on her face, she wanted to interrogate her brother, but Brent was going to evade her questions, and Raleigh knew he had to. Lilia clearly got the message.

She put on a smile and walked over to a rack of dressed. "Not too formal, right?"

"Maybe one party dress," said Brent, "and anything you could teach her about designer labels would be helpful."

With that, Lilia started to pull things off hangers. When she held something up, Raleigh would either nod or take it and put it back on the hanger. Eventually, they had a small collection, and they headed into the dressing room while Brent sat outside.

Raleigh slipped behind a thick cloth curtain and tried on the first outfit. Lilia's heeled shoes peeked through the bottom of the drape. Raleigh perceived Lilia's calm demeanor and even heart rate as she walked out in the dress. Lilia's eyes scrutinized her, settling on the bandage on her arm where the port had been.

"That dress really suits you," Lilia said. "Will you have any time for alterations?"

How could clothes this expensive need alterations? Raleigh repressed her outrage and tried to act like a socialite. She guessed alterations would take some time.

"Probably not. My interview's at the end of the week."

"Then try a size smaller."

"All right. Do you think this makes me look stuffy?"

"No. I think it makes you look elegant." Then Lilia opened her mouth as if to speak, then shut it.

"What?"

"Nothing. It's just we haven't seen Brent in nine months and now he brings me to meet a girlfriend, which he's never done before. He's brought home girls who've hung all over him and danced with people at our family's charity functions. But none of them have been serious, like he cared about them."

"I'm not his girlfriend," Raleigh said. "We're just friends. Nothing romantic."

"That's even odder, then. You're a cute girl, not his normal flashy type, and he clearly thinks you're pretty. Like I said, he obviously cares about you. So, why aren't you dating? Is it because he's into something bad?"

"No. He's not into anything bad." Raleigh stepped behind the curtain to hide the lie on her face. She put on the next outfit slowly. "It might be because one of his friends...." How did she explain Rho? "Brent thinks one of his friends likes me, but he doesn't. And, well, Brent...."

"It's complicated?" Lilia jumped in. "That explains it. Brent doesn't do complicated, at least not with girls. I can't claim to know if his life is or isn't chaotic because I'm not really a part of it these days."

Despite Lilia being here, Brent wasn't an active member of his family. The thought of Raleigh's mother and father left a sour taste in her mouth as she stepped out in the new outfit. "And this one?"

"I'll find the skirt in a slightly smaller size, too." Lilia left the dressing room.

Raleigh tried on another dress. When she stepped out to take a look, Lilia was already back.

"I think that one's a bit too long on you," Lilia said. "You're in good shape. Might as well get something that shows that off. Here, try this one."

The longer they shopped, the more relaxed things became. They talked about clothes, and Lilia choked down questions about her bother. Brent was smart to invite his sister. She did a great job. By the end of the day, Raleigh had enough clothes to fill her new suitcase.

"Lilia, she looks great," Brent said as they left. "Any chance you can help again tomorrow?"

The shopping bag straps cut into Raleigh's arms. "I think I have enough clothes."

Brent shook his head and looked to Lilia. "Not clothes. The people she's interviewing with will expect her to be from certain social circles. She needs some hints at how to act the part."

"I'd love to, but tomorrow night is the Breast Cancer fundraiser."

"Jeff's yearly one?"

"Yes, that one."

"Great. Do you think you can snag two more tickets? Jeff never can say no to you. It will be a good place for Raleigh to practice her small talk."

"I can manage the tickets," Lilia said. "Raleigh, you can come over early, and we can get ready together."

Brent nodded. "Excellent. Can I drop her off at your place in the morning?"

"Sure. Nine would be fine. We'll have the day to get her ready."

Brent hugged Lilia and walked away with Raleigh. Shopping had been one thing, but this sounded like etiquette lessons.

Raleigh grabbed Brent's arm. "I'm not sure it's fair to your sister. I'm not going to be very easy to teach."

"Lilia's good. You'll see. You look the part. Now you just have to get a bit more confidence."

Raleigh had confidence, what she needed was poise. She was going to have to possess the same commanding authority Lilia had, a candor that would not be achieved in a week. Heading back, she tried to ignore the fact that anything but a socialite would be a better cover.

———

BACK AT THE safe house, Raleigh bumped the shopping bags against the wall as she held the door to her room open with her foot. Most of the garments had to be hung up and handled with care, so she was careful when she put them down on the bed.

Getting new clothes meant she'd have to part with the old. She opened up her suitcase and reached her hands in, the clothes were soft from use, but they weren't how she left them. Someone had been through her things. It was undeniable, a month on the run, and she was hyper-aware of her environment and where she left things. There were few enough clothes that she quickly determined nothing was taken, but someone had rifled through them. Someone careless, because there were cameras staring down each hallway.

She rang the front desk.

"Good evening," answered a gruff baritone voice.

"Good evening. I'm Raleigh Groves, and I'm staying on the second floor."

"Yes. I know who you are."

Right, they were probably watching her make this call right now. The eerie thought prompted her to scan the room. She pressed a hand to her chest. "I think someone has been in my room."

"No one but your partner has been in your room."

"My partner?"

"A young man by the name of Tau. Your keys work in both locks." He sounded almost bored. "This is a secure location. We have excellent surveillance. No one has been in your hallway with the exception of you and him."

"Do you have cameras in the room?" Raleigh wanted the evidence that Tau had rifled through her things—almost enough that she was willing to not be upset about her privacy being violated.

"Not yours—is that all you need?"

"Yeah...." The line went dead before she got all the words out of her mouth. "Thanks."

Tau had been in her room and gone through her stuff. It was invasive and wrong. How dare he! They didn't have the best past, but none of it justified this kind of behavior. Whirling toward the door, she left her room and marched over to his.

She took her frustration out on the door, pounding it as hard as she could and liking the heavy boom that happened with each hit. She didn't sense anyone inside, but that meant little as Tau barricaded.

"Calm down," Tau said as he opened the door.

With her fist raised for yet another knock she had to rein herself in to not hit him in the face. Lowering her hand she stormed in, not wanting to have this fight on camera. The room was the same as hers.

"I didn't invite you in," he said.

"Really? You go into my room uninvited and go through my stuff, and then *you* lecture *me* on being invited?"

Tau stood there, with absolutely no sign of remorse or guilt. "You're observant."

"Don't go into my room. Don't touch my things."

"Why would you mind, if you have nothing to hide?"

Raleigh had spent too much time around the Receps. Her initial response was to shove him and make threats. Neither of which she did.

"Don't go through my things again."

"It'll come out, you know. You're going to slip up one of these days. Grant and Able will want intelligence."

"Get off this! I saved your ass. Is this a pride thing? Your ego's hurt because you're not as strong as me?"

"You're not stronger than me. I was starved and weak. I'm not anymore. If you mess with my brothers or me, I promise you'll find out just how capable I am."

"And now you're threatening me?"

"No. Just telling you how it is. If you're so innocent, why are you feeling so guilty all the time? Yesterday when we had the second meeting at the Vindex Authority you were distracted. Why? Did you talk with Gabe?"

She missed a beat. Tristan was none of his business. Brent wanted to keep it a secret. Tau was observant, and she was going to have to mask her face much better around him—a skill that would no doubt be helpful as a spy.

"Stay out of my stuff." She opened his door and slammed it shut behind her. As she went to her room, her head was too full of things to worry about without adding Tau.

CHAPTER
08

THE NEXT DAY her attention wasn't on Tau's invasion but on her inadequate manners. Quickly she learned that *please* and *thank you* were not going to be enough to prove that she had a privileged upbringing.

Brent had dropped her off at Lilia's at the designated time. All morning Lilia had taught her how to walk, sit, and stand. Initially, Raleigh thought these things would be easy, but now she knew better. Forcing her body to sit steadily in a position it didn't like became near painful.

"You look so rigid," Lilia chastised her as they walked from the cab to the restaurant for lunch. "If you stomp like that, you'll break your heels."

The two-inch heels on Raleigh's feet seemed like weapons in their own right—maybe she wouldn't need her Lucid after all— and she wasn't worried about harming them. Even so, Lilia's point wasn't lost on her. Marching wasn't dainty. Neither was crossing her legs at the knees, letting out blustery breaths, or exaggerated gesturing. Raleigh knew because Lilia pointed out all these missteps.

Now, with the prospect of eating, she hoped she'd get a break from training. But as they entered the small café, it became apparent this was another lesson. Lilia sat on the edge of her chair and crossed her ankles. Picking up the napkin, she left it folded in half as she neatly placed it her on her lap.

Raleigh followed suit, making sure that her motions were small and light. The menu had a lot of complex salads and soups, and she ended up ordering the same as Lilia because none of it really appealed to her. When the salad arrived, she dug in.

"No big bites," Lilia said. "Small."

Raleigh put her loaded fork into her mouth. As she chewed her greens, she looked at the other women in the restaurant. They were all perched on their seats like Lilia, barely filling their forks. They drank small sips that left behind whispers of lipstick. With her second bite, Raleigh skewered a few spinach leaves and half a walnut.

This meal was going to take a long time to finish.

"Is my brother dealing drugs?" Lilia asked.

It was good that Raleigh's bite was small because she nearly choked. All day they'd stuck to the plan—teaching Raleigh etiquette. Lilia had been patient and kind, but now she was straying from the script.

"Why would you think that?" Raleigh didn't have the heart to lie and say he wasn't.

"I don't know." Lilia's eyes drifted down to her food. "We used to talk all the time. He went through a rough patch in high school where he was experimenting with a lot of things."

Brent told Raleigh about his rebellious period, and that he ultimately decided that recreational drugs weren't for him. When he found Lucid, he could understand the difference between it and the illicit substances.

Raleigh said, "I've never seen him take any."

"No, and he looks healthier than I've ever seen him, but you don't have to use to sell. My father thought he'd be working with him by now. We all did. Brent didn't want to join the firm, but with all the pressure my father's been putting on him, we all figured he'd cave. Not that Brent caves easily. It's just that it's been the plan for a long time."

"Brent doesn't do things he doesn't want to do." Raleigh knew what it was like to not follow the wishes of one's parents.

"No. Still, he isn't working at any of the firms. No one knows what he's up to. He's got a bit of an ego. If it was something good, he'd brag. So, it must be bad."

Raleigh felt the tears welling up in Lilia who was working hard to hold them back. Raleigh wasn't sure how to comfort her, opting to give her a sympathetic smile. Would Raleigh's own sisters be tainted with the same regret? They knew less than Lilia, would they assume the worst? At first Thalia would enjoy being the center of attention. How long would it take for her to worry? Raleigh's family had stood by her all those years, and now she'd cut off ties and destroyed the relationship. Her guilt would have to wait for another time, because this conversation wasn't about her.

Raleigh couldn't tell Lilia about Lucid. So she talked about other things. "Brent's doing well from what I can tell. He has friends, and he's a hard worker."

"But you can't tell me what he does?"

"I think he has to do that."

Lilia rolled back her shoulders and took a bite of salad. "If he wanted me to know, he would've told me. As long as it isn't illegal."

"It isn't." At least it wasn't yet.

"You're much more down to Earth than I expected a friend of his to be. Just make sure he knows that I'm here for him. I don't want him to think that the only things I can help with are shopping and etiquette lessons."

"I'll let him know, and I do appreciate your insight. Hopefully I'll land that job."

"You look the part. Now all we have to do is smooth you out. Tonight we'll get a chance. Have you ever been to a charity event?"

Raleigh shook her head. She didn't think the few hospital functions she'd attended would compare with what was planned for tonight. This was confirmed when Lilia started to go into what was expected. If Raleigh was out of place at lunch at a café, she imagined that tonight she'd be a complete outsider. Thankfully, she'd have both Brent and Lilia to walk her through it.

Lilia's phone buzzed and she apologized profusely. "Do you mind if I take this? It might be Kent, my boyfriend. He's supposed to drive us tonight."

"Sure," Raleigh said, planning on wolfing down a few bites while Lilia's attention was elsewhere.

Lilia answered the phone, her voice happy and light before being slightly disappointed. The conversation was short, and Raleigh couldn't really hear. It was soon over.

"Is he not going to make it?" Raleigh asked.

"It was Brent. He can't go."

"Can I go without a date?"

"No. You'll need a date, and he's found someone. A friend of his."

"Who?"

"He didn't say. Either way, you'll do fine. Smaller bites."

Raleigh's appetite left her. Brent's friends in New York were probably as intimidating as Lilia. The growing apprehension gnawed at her as she reluctantly ate.

FOUR HOURS LATER Raleigh appeared ready to go. Lilia helped her pin up her brown hair and covered her freckles with a liberal amount of makeup. Raleigh's emerald-green dress gave her a nice balance between modest and flirty. It was tempting to twirl, and, if she wasn't such a bad dancer, this would be the perfect dress to show off some moves.

"What's your boyfriend like?" Raleigh asked. Every time Lilia brought him up, Raleigh could feel a few lovesick butterflies in her stomach.

"He's great. We've been dating for three months. He's spontaneous. My mom says that I should be settling down, but I like the guys who can't be tied down easily. Maybe I pick them out because I don't want things to be too serious."

Raleigh shrugged. She didn't know Lilia well enough to analyze her perspective on relationships and didn't have any experience of her own to speak from.

"I've never dated anyone, so I really don't know."

"No one?"

Raleigh shook her head. She absentmindedly rubbed the place where her port had been. Back, before getting treatment, her days were filled with appointments to see doctors. Raleigh had been on the odd date, and she had been invited to school dances, but nothing ever as serious as a boyfriend.

"You're young, and I dated too much in high school, which really took the fun out of dating in college. I've dated so many jerks. You've had crushes, right?"

A recent one came to mind. "Yeah. My last one didn't end so well. He wasn't interested."

"Putting yourself out there is hard."

"And now I wonder if we would've ever worked. He can be too protective." The conversation Rho had with Chi—when he spoke for her—still bothered her.

Lilia gave Raleigh a curious look. "My brother would make an interesting first boyfriend, and you'd be good for him."

"Thanks. But it isn't an option." Raleigh couldn't date Brent even if they magically started to have some chemistry. She couldn't date anyone with enough receptors to get addicted. Brent wasn't as at-risk as the Receps or Collin, but he was still off the table.

"I know he's flirtatious and unreliable, but like I said, it should be all about fun when you start out."

Lilia reminded Raleigh of Lana and Thalia. These were the types of conversations a person had with their girlfriends and sisters. It made her think that she'd been around Receps and Designed too long. Maybe if she could've talked through her feelings about Rho with someone like Lilia she wouldn't have rushed into stupidly kissing him. Raleigh longed for a friend to talk to and not only about boys. There were times when she wondered if she was in over her head, and others when she wanted to talk to someone about her family.

There was a knock on the door. Lilia looked at the clock in the kitchen. "That must be Kent."

Raleigh stopped cold, her stilettos sinking into the white carpet. Kent wasn't on the other side of the door, not unless he was adept at barricading, which Raleigh doubted. That left Chi, Tau, or a Recep. Did Grant and Able monitor Brent's family? It seemed like a long shot. Regardless, she secured her own barricade and readied herself for a fight.

Lilia opened the door and gasped.

Raleigh took three crooked steps in her direction. She wasn't used to fistfights in heels, but if that's what it was going to take....

"Hello. I'm Tau. I'm here to take Raleigh to the event."

"Come in. I'm Lilia, Brent's sister."

Tau stepped into the apartment, his eyes landing on Raleigh. She broke her fists, hoping he hadn't guessed she was about to fight him. "Brent sent you?"

"Yes. He said he had something he needed to do. So I'm here."

"Why not Chi?"

"Yeah. That's the obvious choice. But no. It's me."

Lilia looked back and forth at them. Then she glanced down at her stockings. "I've got to swap these out. They've gotten a run. I'll be right back. Answer the door if Kent comes, will you?" She disappeared to her room.

"Sure." Raleigh turned back to Tau. "You got a suit."

"It's Chi's. The others want us to pretend to get along better."

"I think they want us to actually get along."

Tau rubbed the back of his neck. "The cover is that we're friends. So I'm going to work on seeming like that."

It was a step in the right direction, but Raleigh would've preferred it if they tried to build a real friendship rather than pretend. She wondered if Brent really had something pressing to do or if this was the plan all along.

There was another knock on the door. Lilia ran out of her bedroom, new nylons on but shoes off.

This time, Raleigh wasn't worried. On the other side of the door stood a perfectly normal guy—at least in her eyes. Kent stepped into the apartment and said his hellos.

Lilia grabbed her shoes, and Raleigh applied her lipstick again. The lessons from earlier in the day sat like a checklist in her head. It reminded her of cramming for a test. Leaving the apartment, Raleigh cursed Brent for not being by her side. If this didn't go smoothly, it would be on his head.

CHAPTER
09

AT THE FUNDRAISER, grand chandeliers hung overhead, and a polished wood floor was underfoot. Tall tables lined the perimeter of the room, and a bar sat along the far wall. Glasses hung over the bartenders' heads, and backlit liquor bottles decorated the counter. People in groups of three and four socialized, their voices drifting up and getting lost in the vaulted ceilings. Some of the guests spoke in quiet voices as they brokered deals, others with big booming laughs encouraged by the alcohol in their veins.

The four of them fit in just fine, although Raleigh was on the younger end of the spectrum. With her makeup and hair done, she managed not to stand out, but she was aware of the age difference.

"I'll get some wine," Kent offered.

"I'll help." Tau followed him, leaving Lilia and Raleigh standing together by the tables.

Lilia watched as they left. "He's the most handsome man I've ever seen."

"That's good," Raleigh had never been great at talking about guys. "Did you help him pick out the suit? It matches your dress."

"Not Kent," Lilia said. *"Tau.* He's your and Brent's friend?"

"Yeah."

"No wonder you're not interested in Brent."

Raleigh wasn't sure how to respond. There was no contest in her mind. Brent was much better company than Tau. "Your brother's a lot kinder."

"My brother is more of flirt, and Tau is way hotter."

"A bad personality will make even the most beautiful person ugly." Sigma came to Raleigh's mind. He was identical to Rho, but Raleigh wasn't attracted to him.

Lilia's eyes were wide. Her mouth opening slightly, yet to be supplied with the correct question.

Raleigh spoke before she could ask. "I'm not talking about Tau. I'm thinking of someone else. I don't know Tau well. But I do know your brother, and his is the type of personality that makes someone more attractive."

"Watch it, Raleigh. You're dangerously close to getting a crush on him. Too many girls fall for his charms. Not that I'm going to talk you out of it. Hell knows, Brent could use a girl like you to settle him down."

Tau and Kent arrived with drinks in hand. Kent's held two thin glasses with sparkling wine, and Tau had a mixed drink loosely held in one hand and a soda in the other.

Tau handed Raleigh the soda. "Here."

"What were you ladies talking about?" Kent asked.

Lilia gave Raleigh a secretive smile. "Brent."

"He's up to no good?" Annoyance hung in Kent's voice.

Raleigh wondered what he and Lilia had speculated about what was going on with her brother.

Lilia shook her head. "No. I think he and Raleigh would make a good match."

"Lilia!" Raleigh gave her a warning glance.

"Please, you think so, too." Lilia winked. "It's too bad he canceled tonight. I was going to let it pass, but now I'm going to insist that the four of us double."

"And I'm not a decent date?" Tau's voice was playful, but his eyes gave Raleigh a somber look. "For what it's worth, I don't think Brent's interested in Raleigh."

"Oh, you don't know that," Lilia said.

Before Tau could go into how much Brent and Raleigh weren't a couple, a woman walked over and hugged Lilia. Introductions were made, and Raleigh learned that she was an entrepreneur named Nicole.

Lilia worked in consulting, Brent told Raleigh in what capacity, but she hadn't fully understood. She was trying her best to keep up with the conversation but kept getting a bit lost.

Kent and Tau moved on, leaving the three ladies. Raleigh was left feeling out of the loop.

"And what do you do, Raleigh?" Nicole eventually asked, drawing her in. "All this finance talk is probably boring you."

"No, it's not. But I don't have much to add. I'm interested in biology. I'm taking a year off before college. Right now I'm pursuing an internship in Europe." It sounded real, perhaps because aspects of it were. If she didn't have the problem with Lucid, this would simply be a year off.

"And you're from here? You don't have the accent."

"Denver."

"Wonderful. And you stopped in New York for a bit of fun?"

Lilia broke in, a little tipsy from her second glass of sparkling wine. "No. Brent hoped I could help her act a bit more refined."

"Oh, yes," Nicole said. "Colorado isn't nearly as stiff as we are here. There you can wear jeans to business meetings. It's enviable. Europe is different in their social codes, too. It's too bad we ended up with such traditional notions. I'd rather strike a deal on the slopes instead of at events like this. But that's probably what I ought to be doing. Good to see you." Nicole gave Lilia one last light hug and left.

Raleigh turned toward Lilia. "Is that true? Are rich people from Denver less refined?"

"Don't take it personally. I'm sure it's a generalization. A lot of people think Denver has an air of casualness about it. Lots of new businesses and start-ups are laying down roots there, and they don't care as much for formality. San Francisco is similar, but California is superficial in ways that even I can't seem to keep up with."

Raleigh didn't take it personally. For the first time she saw a way she might be able to pass as a socialite. From now on she'd play up the Denver angle. Hopefully any missteps would be attributed to that. She looked the part and could probably fake the rest.

"Do you know how to dance?" Lilia asked.

Raleigh shook her head. "No. And I don't need to learn either. I can't see it coming up at the interview."

"Too bad. It's fun."

The music got louder. Kent came over, a seductive smile on his lips, and whisked Lilia away.

Tau was nowhere to be found. Raleigh was alone. She considered mingling with other people. Her talk with Nicole had bolstered her confidence, but she didn't really know how to break into any of the conversations.

As she contemplated how to initiate small talk, a college-aged guy approached. His hair was neatly combed, and his smile was kind. "Would you like to dance?"

Despite his calm demeanor, Raleigh could sense that he was nervous. "I don't dance."

His face dropped, and he shoved his hands into his pockets. "Sure. Yeah. Thanks, anyway."

It wasn't just a line to reject him, but that's how'd he taken it. She reached out her hand. "No, wait. I'm just not very good."

"Not many people out there are."

After watching the dancers, she had to agree. On the whole, the group was made up of ungraceful people.

He stepped closer. "We'll fit right in."

"All right." She stepped closer to him.

Raleigh let him take her hand as they wove through the dancers to an open spot. The band played an unfamiliar fast-paced song. He started to dance, and she tried some of her own moves, remembering to move her top half as well and not just her feet. It was difficult to banish her self-consciousness. He didn't seem to mind.

The song ended. "Another one?"

"Sure." Dancing wasn't that bad. Most of the people were too drunk or self-absorbed to notice her, and he seemed nice enough.

The band struck up another song, and Raleigh prepared to pick up the same moves she used a second ago. But the rhythm was slower and more melodic, not for a lively dance. Seamlessly, the mood on the dance floor became romantic. Couples who'd been standing feet apart were now pressed together. Out of the corner of her eye, she caught Lilia snuggling into Kent. Raleigh turned to the tables when her partner's hand reached around her waist.

"You still want to dance, right?" His eyebrows rose.

The last time she'd danced to a slow song was at a middle school dance. She and the guy swayed back and forth for three painfully slow minutes. It failed to endear her to the practice of slow dancing.

But this was one dance, and she'd already agreed. "Sure."

With the one hand on her waist, his other lifted her hand up to his shoulder. All right. She could do this. If she could train with Receps and go undercover with the Vindex Authority, she could do this.

In some ways it was easier than the fast-paced number. He led, and she didn't have to worry about what to do with her hands because they stayed on him. As he moved closer to her, his breath crossed her exposed shoulder. Since he was only an inch taller, they moved nearly eye to eye, their lips dangerously close on his forward steps. Her illness had made her miss out on this kind of thing. She didn't know his name, but for a second she wanted to lean in.

"Excuse me. That's my date," Tau said, interrupting them.

The guy instantly pulled back. "Sorry. I didn't know."

Tau smiled, but his eyes remained harsh. "That's fine. Do you mind if I finish the dance?"

"Yeah. Sure." The guy shrugged back, staring at Tau before leaving.

Tau put his hand on her hip, and she settled hers on his shoulder. The height difference between them was noticeable.

"I'm surprised you stepped in," she said.

"Are you trying to get caught?"

"What?" Her mind went over all Lilia had taught her. As far as she knew, she wasn't breaking any social rules.

"That guy was way too close. One kiss… and if he has any receptors at all…."

"I wasn't going to kiss him."

"Because you're too busy trying to hook up with Brent?"

"I'm not trying to hook up with Brent." She withdrew from his grasp.

Tau moved his hand to her lower back, locking her in place. "Then why does Lilia think you are?"

"Lilia wants me to. She's been pushing it."

"She'd like it until her brother became addicted. Then, not so much."

"I'd never go out with Brent."

"Right, because then you'd lose your hold over Rho, and then he might look at the situation and see how shifty it is."

"Give it up. I'm so sick of your theories."

"You just have to slip up once."

Raleigh tried to think of a retort when a flood of sensation captured her attention. She could feel the bubbles of wine sliding down the throats of the people at the bar. The woman nearest the band had a headache from the noise. Lilia danced a few feet away, her heart tight in her chest, as Kent held her. All the sensations vied for her attention. Looking up, she locked onto Tau's blue eyes, disrupting his barricade as the Lucid swirled violently through her system.

She sensed a steady pulse racing through his veins, the strength of his arms as he held her slightly at bay, and the warmth of her skin under his fingers. His pupils dilated. She saw and felt it. Then everything went black.

———

"IS SHE GOING to be all right?" Lilia's voice edged on hysterical.

Raleigh remained in that groggy state between consciousness and unconsciousness.

"She does this," Tau replied. "Brent didn't tell you?"

"No, Brent didn't tell me. Are you sure it wasn't a heart attack?"

"Her heart is fine."

"How do you know?"

"I just do. She's breathing. If her heart was bad, her pulse wouldn't be so steady."

Lilia's nimble fingers checked along Raleigh's neck.

"I'm fine. I just had an episode," croaked Raleigh.

Lilia's face relaxed at the sound of Raleigh's voice.

"I should get her home," Tau said.

Raleigh was behind some tables on the far side of the room, cradled in Tau's arms. The fabric of his suit rubbed against the bare skin of her shoulder. A pain shot through her ankle as he helped her stand.

"You twisted that," Tau said.

"That's why I hate heels." Raleigh winced as she put weight on it, but she knew it wasn't sprained.

Tentatively Lilia put a hand on Raleigh's shoulder. "Everyone was worried. Tau insisted that it was normal for you and that you don't need an ambulance. That's why we're over here."

None of the partiers had come over. Sometimes her blackouts created quite the disturbance, but whatever Tau had said had cleared the crowd.

Kent watched from a few feet back and asked Tau, "Do you want me to call a cab?"

"That would be great." Tau placed a firm hand on Raleigh's back, steadying her. Raleigh didn't need it, but Lilia and Kent seemed calmed by him taking charge.

"I'll get her coat." Lilia dashed over to get her jacket from the coat check.

Soon Raleigh and Tau were outside waiting for the cab. Tau remained close enough to catch her if she fell.

"Are you going to be all right?" Now that the others were gone, he didn't pretend to know what her blackouts entailed. "Are all of them like that?"

"Not all of them are that long. Most of them are around three minutes. I'm assuming I was out for a while."

"Ten minutes. And that wasn't what I was asking. With all of them, do you sense so much?"

She gave a quick nod. "Yeah. That's my cue that it's going to happen. Usually I'm so overwhelmed, I can't really think about much else, like talking."

"I've never felt so many people so deeply, all at once. You broke my barricade and funneled them all in."

"Sorry about that. I didn't mean to break it."

Tau paused. "It was the most amazing thing I've ever sensed."

"I guess that's one silver lining."

"We need to meet with the others."

"It's late. We'll catch up with them tomorrow."

"No. I've already texted Brent and Chi to meet at the safe house."

His conviction was unwavering. Raleigh didn't have time to protest before the cab pulled up to the curb.

Fifteen minutes later they neared Tau's room. Brent and Chi were talking inside. Raleigh's ankle prevented her from walking as quickly as Tau, who'd burst in ahead of her and interrupted their conversation.

"Lilia's been freaking out." Brent held up his phone. "Raleigh just fainted. Didn't you tell Lilia that it's normal for her?"

Raleigh entered in time to see Tau toss his hands up and say, "There was nothing normal about that. One minute she was dancing, and the next she sensed the entire room. Then she collapsed like a pile of bricks. People tried to call ambulances. It was awful. We're not going to be able to manage these blackouts."

Chi held up his hands. "Look, we've already taken them into account. They're part of her cover. It will work out fine. We're sticking to the story."

"You weren't *there!*" Tau boomed at his brother. "I know you and Bridget have decided to make all the decisions, but I'm letting you know right now that I'm not going if she is."

Brent snorted. "You've been trying to get rid of her since she signed on. Rho says you can't get over thinking that she's working for Grant and Able."

"I can't get over it because she is, but the blackouts are a far bigger problem. It's bad for her, too. She twisted her ankle. I was standing right there, and she managed to hurt herself."

Chi's eyes scanned down Raleigh's leg to her swollen ankle. "We don't need Raleigh to come along. Tau and I can have each other's backs. Brent, we'll need you, of course. But we don't need Raleigh."

Raleigh didn't want to be out. "Just put in my port!"

"We're not bringing an extraction machine, and we're not having this argument again," Chi said.

Brent scrunched his nose. "Marcel won't meet with us if she's not there."

Chi's eyebrows shot up. "I thought you said he was loyal to us."

"No. I said he wasn't dangerous," Brent said. "There's a difference between keeping your secrets and doing you a favor. Raleigh intrigues him. Ever since they met he's been asking about her. We have to bring her if this is going to work."

Chi rubbed his chin and looked at Tau and Raleigh. "Then she comes. We'll handle the blackouts as planned. Tau, if you think they'll inconvenience you too much, you don't have to come."

"But Rho wants him along," Brent said.

Tau squinted, his muscles taut in frustration. "I'll stay. Someone needs to make sure she doesn't turn you all in. I'm going to get out of this suit. This mission is feeling more and more like a long shot."

Brent turned to Raleigh. "Besides the fainting, how did it go?"

Raleigh stared at him wondering if it was an honest question or a joke. "Fine." She wanted out of the impractical heels and evening gown. It might be a long shot, but if she didn't let the fainting hold her back before, she certainly wasn't going to let it hold her back now.

CHAPTER
10

PARIS WAS COZIER in the autumn than in summer. The last time Raleigh stood on its old streets, she was innocent to the life that sat before her. Now she knew the obstacles—and was stronger. They were at a hotel this time, and they'd each gotten a few hours of sleep. Now, jet-lagged, Raleigh's internal clock was off. It didn't seem like five in the afternoon, despite what her watch said.

Brent met her in the hotel hallway freshly showered and rolling down the sleeves of his shirt. "Ready?"

"Yeah, but Chi said you thought he should stay here."

Brent styled his hair by twisting damp strands through his fingers. "Yeah, I didn't want Chi to dominate the conversation. This is *my* connection, and I told him it was best to let me navigate the introduction."

"And he's letting you?"

"It surprised me, too."

"So it's just you and me."

"And Tau," Brent said. "We have to prove to Marcel that the Designed are involved."

Raleigh wondered if Marcel would need Rho's approval. During their last encounter, Marcel offered her his future help—with strings attached. That help wasn't dependent on the Designed, something she was about to remind Brent of when Tau joined them in the hall. Like them, he had only a few hours of sleep. Unlike them, it didn't show. The Designed weren't prone to jet lag, yet another advantage.

"Ready to go?" Brent asked rhetorically as he headed out.

A cab dropped them off at *Orange,* Marcel's club. Raleigh put up her barricade.

That prompted Tau to ask, "What kind of guy is Marcel? He's friendly, right?"

"Friendly isn't the right word," Brent said. "He's slippery. Don't agree to anything. You're there to show that we're with the Designed. Let me make the deal."

Tau stood up straight, his face emotionless and stern. The Designed were capable of being intimidating. "What are we giving him?"

Brent grimaced. "As little as possible." He walked to the door and rapped on it.

A bouncer answered. The burly man didn't take long to assess them before letting them in. Once inside, the bright white walls welcomed them. Marcel stood at the bar discussing a drink menu with a bartender in French. He put down the menu when he saw them.

"Brent." Marcel walked over and extended his hand. "Good to see you again, Raleigh." He kissed her cheeks.

Raleigh smiled. The greeting was a cultural norm, but she wasn't comfortable with it.

Marcel gazed at Tau for a moment. "And you must be one of the brothers."

"I'm Tau."

"No Rho this time? Pity. Please, come in. Have a seat," Marcel said, motioning to Tau and Brent. He stopped Raleigh before she sat down. "Raleigh, I was hoping we could talk upstairs. Alone."

Brent leaned forward. "I'm the one in charge of the deals."

"No." Marcel motioned for Brent to continue sitting. "You're in charge of Rho's deals, and as far as I can tell he's not here. I appreciate that you brought his brother, a clear sign that he's in on whatever you're asking, but this is Raleigh's deal, not yours."

Brent opened his mouth to protest, but Raleigh jumped in. "It's all right, Brent. I can handle it."

Marcel directed Raleigh up the steps to the darker room upstairs. Unlike last time, there were no bodyguards.

"No security?" Her voice came off cooler than she expected.

"No. We both know you're strong enough to overpower any men I'd have."

In contrast to the white-walled and decorated floor beneath, this one was drenched in black. Even in the daytime the shadows were swallowed up by all the black with only the occasional pop of orange. Leather armchairs sat around low tables. The table nearest the bar had two closely positioned chairs and two drinks sitting atop it. One was caramel-colored and took up the bottom of the tumbler—straight liquor. The other was pink and in a tall, narrow glass. Raleigh sat down and inspected the pink one.

"It's a new cocktail." Marcel sat down. "American girls enjoy cocktails, don't they?"

"Yes, they do." But in America you had to be twenty-one, so Raleigh didn't know if she was one of those girls.

"Try it."

It could be drugged. Tau was one floor down. If she dropped her barricade he'd be able to tell if she was in trouble—not that she liked depending on him for backup. She took a sip. The sugar hid the bitter taste of the alcohol.

"It's good."

Marcel swirled the hard liquor in his glass. "What have you come here for?"

"I'm hoping to end the synthetic trade."

A thin grin lined the bottom of his face. "No. Really? Why are you back in my city?"

"That's it."

"I'm not involved in the synthetic trade."

"I know." Raleigh moved to the edge of her seat and employed the professionalism Lilia taught her. "Because you don't like it."

"It has no place in my clubs. The addicts it produces are volatile. It kills. And once you've had the real stuff... I needn't explain it to you. How are you planning on doing this?"

"There are two sellers of the synthetic. The first group is the one that captured Rho, and they know about Lucid's true origins. The second is recently formed by a merger of two smaller factions. This second group doesn't know where true Lucid comes from. We're hoping to partner with them, learn their secrets, and then give the information to the first group who will want to bring them down."

"Then, only one synthetic will have the trade. You will make them stronger." Marcel shifted back in his seat.

"We have someone who will handle them when the time comes."

"And there will be no blood on your hands. Not that you should feel guilty about them, they're terrible people. I'm surprised Rho is letting you."

Raleigh leveled him with her gaze. "Rho isn't my boss."

Marcel laughed his deep laugh. "Oh, but how he wishes he could be. That's what I like about you. You're a strong woman.

Some men prefer meek, obedient girls. I go for the ones that can handle themselves."

Raleigh took another sip of the pink cocktail. She knew Brent would be better at selling the plan. Despite what he'd said, she felt like she amused Marcel more than she intimidated him.

Raleigh said, "I need an introduction to the head of the second group. I need you to tell them that Brent has a new synthetic, but he still needs the means to both produce and sell it."

"You have a new synthetic?" Marcel marveled at this, and then his eyes darkened. "No. You're going to pass off yours."

"Right. They don't know that people make it."

"Even if they did, they wouldn't suspect you." He felt the hem of her skirt with his fingertips. "These are fancier clothes than the last time we met. What role am I to say you are playing?"

"I'm the financier. Brent's our connection, and Tau and Chi, another brother, are the ones who got the formula for the new synthetic. That's the story."

"You wish me to mislead these men? These are people who kill their enemies."

Raleigh gulped. "They wouldn't know you knew. There's no reason you can't claim ignorance and that you thought it was legit."

Marcel lifted his glass off the table and swigged down the bronze liquor. Raleigh took another sip of her drink.

Marcel stood. "I'm going to make us both a drink. Finish up that one."

Raleigh didn't really want to finish the first one, let alone have a second. But she also didn't want the deal to go south. As he went to the bar she drank down the rest of the cocktail and began feeling a little fuzzy. "You know, getting me drunk doesn't affect the Lucid, or my ability to use it."

Marcel glanced up over the bar, his eyes twinkling. "I'm not a fool. I know. Even if it did affect you, you have a Designed with you, but I find that people are more honest when they've had a few drinks."

He pulled out two glasses and filled them with a green liquid. Then he put spoons over the tops and balanced sugar cubes on top.

Raleigh craned her neck to see. "What are you doing?"

"It's called absinthe. It used to be banned here and in America, too. Before that it was a nineteenth-century muse. It's strong, which is why we dilute it."

He placed the two glasses under a large metal contraption with two faucets that he turned on. The water dissolved the sugar, leaving a cloudy green drink beneath. When the glasses were full, he turned off the spigot. He returned to the table and sat down, handing her a glass. It had the pungent smell of licorice.

"Why was it banned?"

"A component of it can cause hallucinations. Don't worry. It's really too small an amount to do anything."

Marcel clinked his glass to hers and waited for her to take a drink.

Raleigh took a small sip. It was strong, and she wasn't sure she liked it. "Interesting."

Marcel grinned his Cheshire Cat smile. "So you want my help. But what do I get out of it?"

"The synthetic trade will no longer bother you."

"I'm not Rho," he said playfully. "It's not much of a bother to me."

"Is that true? Brent said they've gotten more aggressive. If they've threatened our people, then they must've threatened yours, too."

"That may be. But to incite them? How do you know a new synthetic won't jump in when they're gone?"

"It's hard to make, and everyone is really secretive about their individual formulas."

"That I believe. It's why they haven't made anything good."
Marcel took a long sip of his drink and looked at Raleigh.

She did the same.

"Do you want another?" he asked after polishing his off.

"No. I want to walk away from here with a deal, not a headache."

"What do I get for helping you out, Raleigh?" he asked, moving in closer.

In the pit of her stomach, Raleigh knew that what he wanted she wouldn't give. "What do you want?"

"You and I both know that the thing of value you have is running through your blood." He ran his hand down her arm to her wrist, which he then turned over. Her veins made a lattice pattern under her skin. "I want your Lucid."

"I can give you some after it's all over."

"Once the synthetic trade falls, so, too, will the real one. I'm not in it to make money... well, not *only* to make money. I'm in it because I like to feel like a god. Once this ends, Lucid will be hard to come by."

"It will. But we can supply you."

"Not we. *You.* I prefer yours to theirs. In fact, I'd prefer you to come live here with me. That way you won't have to injure your arm again with another port."

Marcel was observant if nothing else.

"I'm not that type of girl."

"And what type of girl is that? I'm simply asking you to be with me. It doesn't even have to be exclusive. If Rho comes into town, you can spend your nights with him. I have no problem with it being a casual, open affair."

The guys liked to tease her about Rho, but Marcel's blunt way of talking about sex made her uneasy. Raleigh tried to gauge just how old he was. She guessed mid-thirties, but he acted even older. Fifteen years easily sat between them—not that he seemed to mind.

Marcel ran his fingers over her veins. "If I had your Lucid, I could tell how fast your heart is beating." His fingers moved from her wrist to her throat, tracing a finger down the *v* of her neck.

Raleigh froze his finger, withdrew his hand, and folded it neatly in his lap. She'd learned a lot since she saw him last. Yes, she needed his help, but she wasn't going to let him cross that line.

"I can sense that pain in your shoulder. How did you hurt it?"

He sat back. "Tennis." Sighing, he took another long sip of his drink before staring at her solidly in the eyes. "Twenty-four vials a year for four years."

"That I can do."

"I'll get in contact with the people you wish to meet. I'll let Brent know the time you should come back."

The deal was made. But, unlike him, she didn't stand.

Marcel cocked an eyebrow. "Thinking you might stay a bit longer? I could come up with ways to entertain you. But tell me, how riled is Brent right now?"

Raleigh shut her eyes and sensed Brent one floor below. The muscles in his hands were taut, and she could feel his feet bouncing on the floor. "He's not happy. But Marcel, there's something I should tell you." She wasn't sure how to word what she wanted to say.

Marcel took her hand and helped her up. She was slightly shorter than him, and, predictably, he had no qualms getting into her space.

"What concerns you?"

"If I die, I won't be able to get you the vials. Rho and the others can't be committed to doing so. If I die, the deal dies with me."

He laughed. "Fine. I won't expect the others to pay your due but don't die, Raleigh."

With that they walked down the steps. Brent leapt up from his chair upon their arrival. Tau was less quick to stand, an icy expression on his face.

"We have a deal," Marcel announced and shook Brent's hand. "I'll call you when I've made the arrangements."

"Thank you," Brent said.

"Tau, it was lovely meeting you," Marcel said. "And Raleigh, as always, it was a pleasure."

He kissed her cheek longer than needed for a customary goodbye, but Raleigh didn't step back. The kiss was intended to upset Brent, not her.

"Goodbye," she said.

Three of them headed out the front door and into the street. Brent slipped his arm through hers, and they all walked to a small café that was closed for the day.

With no one in earshot, Brent asked, "Have you been drinking?"

Raleigh nodded. "I made the deal."

"It was my job to make it," said Brent. "You should've insisted that I go up with you. After you agreed, I couldn't very well barge up there. Marcel's crafty. I was supposed to be the one."

"It went fine. "He was more candid without you there."

"What's the deal?" Brent asked.

Raleigh squinted at him. "I'm not an idiot, you know. You might just thank me. It's not like Marcel's that easy a person to work with."

"Thank you. What's the deal?" Brent asked again.

"Twenty-four vials a year for the next four years."

Brent relaxed. "That's still a little high."

"They're for personal use. Believe me, his first offer was steeper."

"What was it?" Brent's brows drooped.

Raleigh didn't meet his eyes with hers. "I said no, and don't pretend not to know. There's a reason he didn't want you in the room. Now, let's go find Chi and tell him the good news."

Brent looked toward the club. "Marcel shouldn't have."

"I wasn't in danger." Raleigh thought of the man in Chicago she'd killed—and the fear that entered Marcel when she influenced his hand. "You know I'm not helpless."

"What was the steeper deal?" Tau asked.

"Sex. Isn't it obvious?" Brent said.

Raleigh felt cheap the way he said it. "A relationship, which he said could be open."

Tau lost his formality. "Really? He wants to date you?" His eyes traveled, as Brent's had, toward the club. "That's kind of creepy and gross."

"He *is* a lot older," Raleigh agreed.

Tau nodded. "What some people won't do for Lucid. I assume that's why he wants you. The Lucid. Probably why Gabe was so into you, too."

"What does that mean? That the only attractive thing about me is my Lucid?" The alcohol had finally loosened her tongue.

Tau took a step back. "I'm just saying. I imagine that Marcel usually hangs out with girls that are little more, *you know.* Gabe, well, I'm not sure who his type is, but I doubt you're it."

"Gabe wasn't interested in me," Raleigh retorted. "Despite your juvenile assumptions."

"I'm just glad he has standards."

Raleigh's eyebrows shot up.

"I mean I'm glad he wouldn't cross that line with his trainees even with the promise of extra Lucid," said Tau rather quickly.

"Tau, you're an asshole. If I was created to be beautiful like you, people would be fawning all over me, too. I'm plain all right, but maybe it's better than your artificially-created beauty."

Brent stepped between them. "This is what Marcel wants. He enjoys ruffling feathers. Remember last time with Rho? You did a great job with setting up the deal. Twenty-four vials a year isn't that much. Let's tell Chi. I'll hail a cab."

Before Brent could hail a cab, Tau turned to her. "I'm not like Rho or Chi. I don't feel bad about being Designed. It's who I am. I refuse to apologize for it."

A thickness formed in Raleigh's throat. Tau could be such a jerk. "If I knew you were such an ass, I might've left you in that basement."

"It's not like going undercover and pretending to give a damn about you is that much better."

Brent tugged on Raleigh's arm. "You made progress with Marcel. Tau is part of the team. The two of you need to play nice. Tau, get over yourself. Keep in mind that if you give a damn about the mission or Rho, you give one about Raleigh. Let's get that cab and talk with Chi."

With Brent sandwiched between Tau and Raleigh, the car ride was uncomfortable. The hairs on her arms stood on end at the thought of Marcel's offer. Who was he to think he could talk like that? And who was Tau to be so damn annoying all the time? She wanted to go for a run or to hit something. In such a cramped car, she couldn't even kick her foot in frustration.

The phone in Brent's pocket gave two short chirps. This late in the day in Paris would be mid-morning in the States. Was it Rho? He knew they were meeting with Marcel.

"Yeah. Sure. We'll be there," Brent said.

"Was that Rho?" Raleigh asked quietly.

Brent looked at her. "No. Marcel. He's got everything set. The introduction is in two days."

"Two *days!*" Tau turned his attention from the window into the interior of the cab. "That was fast."

Brent studied the phone in his hand. "I know. I was thinking it would take at least a week to set up. Hopefully, it's a good thing. Maybe they know their product is crap. It also means they think highly of Marcel or respect him at least."

"That's why we went through him, right?" Raleigh asked.

"Yeah," Brent said. "You can take credit for this, Raleigh. Marcel clearly called the moment we left and was very persuasive."

Persuasive was a word that aptly described Marcel. Her stomach cramped at the thought of another meeting, although it may've been wooziness from the booze. If Marcel was one of the good guys, and he made her skin crawl, what would this new guy be like?

The taxi parked at their hotel, and they got out. Dirt clung to the older hotel—a far cry from the posh apartment they stayed in on their last Paris trip—but clean. They climbed the spiral stairs to their rooms. Raleigh's was small. Chi had the largest. They knocked on his door and walked in.

Hunched over his computer, Chi stretched and stood. "How was it?"

"Raleigh made a deal," said Brent.

Chi lifted an eyebrow. "So, he's willing to make an introduction?"

Brent said, "He called us on our way over. It's with half the partnership from the merger, in two days."

"Forty-eight hours? Did he say which half?"

"No."

Chi rubbed his neck. "I can't picture Glen knowing Marcel or being so motivated by his call. It's got to be Ilario."

"Who's Ilario?" Raleigh asked.

Chi unfolded one of the diagrams he kept in a folder and smoothed it across one of the beds. The diagram resembled a family tree. Noah, the contact the Vindex Authority had suggested, was circled near the bottom while Ilario's name was at the top. Raleigh's muddled brain quickly put together that it was the hierarchy of the synthetic—or at least the half Ilario led.

"If we have this, why do we even need to meet them?" Tau asked.

Chi's fingers tapped two different spots. "We don't have all the names, nor do we know the locations of the warehouses. If it is Ilario you're meeting, he has this information. Good work, Brent. Going through Marcel was a wise decision."

"Thank Raleigh. She convinced him," Brent said. "How much do you know about Ilario?"

Chi's lips turned down. "He had the synthetic that was more fatal and less addictive. He sticks to clubs and doesn't keep many long-term clients. That's why it's probably him. Marcel has clubs, so they would've crossed paths."

"Marcel hates those guys," Brent said.

Chi flicked Ilario's picture. "He doesn't value human life, but not many of them do. He lives a flashy, dangerous, impulsive lifestyle which helps explain why the meeting's in two days. In person he's not that mean, unlike his counterpart, who's calculating and severe. But both of them are ruthless, which is a trait that serves them well in the Lucid trade."

"Great," Tau said.

Raleigh's stomach tumbled, and a wave of nausea clenched her throat. "I need to go to my room and lie down."

"That's fine." Chi gave her an evaluative stare. "We have a little over a day to prepare for the meeting."

"Tomorrow I'll read up on Ilario," Raleigh said, heading toward the door.

Chi helped her open it. "You know all you need to know about him right now. There will be more chance of you slipping up if you know too much. Easier to keep your cover if you don't have to constantly remember what you're supposed to know."

They had more to discuss, but Raleigh couldn't really think with the absinthe in her system. She'd make better sense of everything tomorrow. For now, she was going to go to sleep—hopefully without getting sick.

11

WITH EVERYONE STILL muddled by the change in time, the two days passed quickly. Too soon Raleigh found herself exiting the cab in front of Marcel's club a second time.

"Don't barricade." The mantra was becoming Chi's new motto.

Raleigh understood why. Barricading was reflexive for her now, like yanking her hand away from a hot fire.

"Ilario doesn't know the extent of Lucid's uses," said Chi. "Let's not fill him in on anything."

"No problem," Raleigh said, letting her barricade drop.

Tau was more reluctant. He waited until they were just outside the club to dismantle his barricade. When Raleigh confronted him in that basement a month and a half ago, he'd been weak. Now he was stronger. His eyes flicked to her, guessing that she sensed him.

Brent leaned close to Raleigh. "Let me do most of the dealing. I understand why it was you last time. But I'm supposed to broker the deals, so let me do it."

Raleigh gave him a nod. There was no danger of her taking on that role. It'd been stressful enough dealing with Marcel. Chi might step in, but he knew Brent was the main negotiator.

Chi put his hand on the door. "Everyone ready?"

He and Tau wore charcoal-colored suits. Individually, they were both stunning. But matching and formally attired, they commanded attention. Raleigh desperately tried not to look at them. Tau seemed to take her staring as a personal affront.

Brent whispered in her ear. "Here I spent all that time helping you pick out clothes only to see no one is going to notice either one of us when we're with them."

The same bouncer that let them in two days ago did so now. He walked them up the steps to the dark second floor. This conversation wouldn't be at the small table near the bar. It would take place in the corner with two sofas and a chair around an oblong table.

Marcel sat on one sofa, wearing a navy suit and an insincere expression. His body language was closed off, his arms against his sides rather than across the back of the couch as she would've expected. A man she assumed was Ilario sat in the chair, a foot resting over a knee as his hand tugged at the bottom of his trouser. From the briefing, she knew he was Italian. She'd been expecting someone with darker coloring. His sandy-blond hair and brown eyes didn't fit her assumption.

As they neared the table, Raleigh sensed both men effortlessly. Marcel was his usual self, despite being sober. Ilario's body had all the hallmarks of an addict—muscles that twitched, a parched feeling in the back of his throat that seemed impossible to quench, and a tension spanning his back like a rubber band wound too tight just under the skin. He didn't simply sell his product. He used it. It was hard to guess his receptor volume, but he definitely had some. Usually, the more receptors the greater the risk of addiction. But being addicted didn't guarantee you had a lot, and it really didn't apply in his case, given his access to large quantities.

Ilario was saying something in Italian when they walked up. His hand used sweeping gestures to prove his point. Marcel's reply in Italian was laced with his French accent.

"Marcel." Brent shook his hand.

"Brent," Marcel said, slipping into English, "I see you've brought Raleigh, Tau, and you must be Chi."

Chi stuck out his hand. "Thanks for arranging this meeting." For all the disdain Chi had for dealers, none of it showed on his face.

"This is Ilario, the man you asked me to introduce you to," Marcel said.

Ilario stood and gave each of them a hearty handshake and a wide grin. Only his eyes belied that he wasn't excited to meet them. The way they roamed over the group hinted that he was skeptical and uncertain. "Americans in this part of the world? I'd think you'd be doing your business in the States." He spoke English well and wouldn't need a translator.

Marcel motioned for them to have a seat. Chi, Tau, and Raleigh filled up one sofa while Brent shared the neighboring one with Marcel. Ilario sank back down into his chair.

"I can tell you would like to get right to the point," Marcel said to Ilario.

Ilario held open his palms. "It is merely for our guests. Americans tend to spend too much time on pleasantries."

Brent leaned forward and did his thing. "We have a new brand of Lucid."

"But what does this have to do with me? If you have a new formula, then you must know that we are in competition." Ilario's thick accent was misleading. He was fluent in English—with good inflection. His eyes darkened.

Brent kept his face and voice light. "We have a few bottles here of our new synthetic formula. What we lack is the space to make it, the workers, and the sellers. We need you for those things. We'd like to partner up. Our synthetic, your production and distribution."

Ilario looked to Marcel and said something in Italian. It reminded Raleigh of when her parents used to spell things out around her when she was young.

"I have a partner, and I have a version of the drug," Ilario said.

It took Raleigh a moment to realize they were once again part of the conversation.

"Ours is better, and your partner can stay." Brent took a vial from his pocket. He rested it on the table. "You can try it now. That is, if Lucid affects you. Otherwise, you can take Marcel's word for it."

Ilario's eyes dilated at the sight of the vial. Rolling up his sleeve he gave Marcel a short glance before injecting it into a small port like Brent's. This guy had the marks of a veteran user. His hunger for Lucid momentarily quieted. His muscles relaxed slightly, his back bowed, and a soft groan escaped his lips. It resembled someone biting into rich chocolate, their ecstasy clear for a moment.

Leaning back in his chair, Ilario splayed his fingers before returning his attention to Marcel and the group, sensing them, no doubt. Raleigh tried to think of pleasant things to keep her body relaxed.

"There is no point denying it," Ilario said. "It's the best I've ever tried. Marcel, it's better than that expensive stuff I've had at your club. This could be worth a fortune."

Brent nodded. "Yes, it could. But the market is shifting, and we're having a hard time finding our footing. We want to get in now, before sanctions and regulations are put in. It's crucial that we find our place in the market before it becomes illegal."

Ilario studied them. "And, who, exactly, are you?"

"Brent used to supply me with that very expensive Lucid," Marcel said. "But his higher-ups have had less and less to sell."

"It's true. Tau and Chi are some of my best clients." Brent motioned to them. "But you could tell that by looking at them, couldn't you?"

Ilario tapped his knee. "Yes. I can tell they are a lot like me in that way."

Raleigh consciously had to keep her eyes from rolling. This guy had the cockiness of a Recep, too.

"You use, too?" Ilario asked, addressing Raleigh for the first time.

She nodded. "I have a condition. Traditional medicine hasn't helped, but Lucid seems to lessen the symptoms. This newer formula works the best. Brent said he needed money to help get it developed. It was my dollars that did that."

"I'm guessing the development was pricy?" offered Ilario.

"Can you put a price on health?" Raleigh replied.

Ilario grinned, "A lot of people have to. A lot of Americans have to."

Raleigh lifted her chin. "Money isn't a concern for me. I'm here to make sure that my investment pays off, that there's enough Lucid to keep me healthy."

"Which is part of the reason we're seeking an established business to work with," said Brent.

Ilario's smile faded. "This seems almost too good to be true."

"Not that good," Brent said. "It's going to be fifty-fifty."

"The overhead on something like this...."

"The profits. The profits are split fifty-fifty."

Ilario rolled his tongue along his teeth. Raleigh could feel the way he chewed on the offer. Finally he spoke. "I already have a partner, and he cuts into my profits."

"But you'll be making more," Marcel said. "The product you

have right now isn't enough to compete. Yes, you have a lot of Italy and a lot of the clubs, but this would expand you to the rest of Europe. This would give you a presence in the States and Asia. Think of the potential."

Ilario grinned at Marcel. "And you want to be a part of this, too? What fee are you taking?"

"Two percent finder's fee," said Marcel.

Ilario shifted in his seat and gave a small snort, "I suppose that comes out of my fifty percent?"

"Consider it part of the overhead," Brent said.

Ilario rubbed his hands together before addressing Marcel. "And you'll sell it in Paris? With our enemies based in France, we've yet to gain a stronghold here. In the past you haven't sold our Lucid because the product didn't meet your standards. And now?"

"I'll stay out of it. My focus is on my clubs. Yes, I'll sell the odd vial here and there, but I don't want it to be my primary line of work."

"You're a smart man," Ilario said. "Keeping your fingers in everything but never getting dirty. Too bad that this money has to be made in the trenches. You could be a richer man than you are."

"I'm comfortable," Marcel said. "Besides, you'll pay me for this introduction."

"If I decide to take the deal." Ilario looked to his bodyguards standing silently along the back wall. "I'm going to have to think about it. Right now I'm doing well."

Brent held open his hands. "Not as well as you could be. That's why we came to you. Yes, there is a market. And yes, you have the means to produce Lucid. But you lack a decent product, and we have it."

"Mine isn't that bad," Ilario said.

Marcel cleared his throat. "It's deadlier."

"Death is a risk of drug use," Ilario shrugged. "Part of the reason people like it is the gamble."

The hairs on the nape of Raleigh's neck rose. She felt Tau's shoulders tighten. Chi's body didn't change at all. His expectations of Ilario had clearly been appropriately set.

"How long till you decide?" Brent asked.

Ilario opened his mouth and then stopped. "A few days. I need a few more vials. I need to consider this. How many do you have?"

"Around sixty," Brent said, handing over another two.

Ilario snorted. "That's very little."

"If we had more, we wouldn't really need you," Brent said.

"I'll bring these to my partner. I'll consider your offer. If it's a yes, Marcel will contact you. If it's a no, then I expect you to get out of Europe. Sell your product in your own country. The market here is competitive enough without you." Ilario stood. He slipped the vials into his pocket and flicked his fingers toward the door, his bodyguards fell in line to follow him down the steps.

They sat in silence until Ilario was gone.

"How do you think that went?" Raleigh asked Marcel.

Marcel's pressed his lips together and nodded toward the stairs. "It's hard to tell. Ilario is impulsive. He likes risks, and he likes power. Your drug offers him both. Is he hesitant? Yes. You're outsiders. He doesn't trust you. It could go either way."

Chi rose. "Thank you for the introduction. I assume you'll pass on the message from Ilario when it arrives?"

Marcel clasped Chi's hand as they shook goodbye. "A word of advice. If he rejects your offer, it won't be a phone call to me but a hit put out on you. In his world, if you're not a friend, you're an enemy."

"I don't think a man like that has very many friends," Chi said.

Marcel's mouth hitched up in the corner. "Maybe ally is a better word. Either way, if he decides he doesn't want to deal with you, he'll want you dead. Watch your backs. Then again, you probably already are."

"You're right," Brent said. "It's nothing new. We have stronger enemies than him."

"But he plays dirty and won't have a reason to keep you alive," Marcel said. "But you did want the introduction. Raleigh, as always, if you like, you may stay here, and I will personally see to your safety."

"I'm able to look out for myself," she told him.

Marcel kissed her cheek. "Until we meet again. Don't forget our deal or the two percent."

"We won't," Chi said.

The group made their way down the stairs and left. Once they were out on the street Tau immediately put up his barricade. "Ilario is creepier than Marcel, and I never thought I'd hear myself saying that."

Brent's eyes remained on the club. "What kind of people did you expect in the black market?"

Tau shook his head. "I suppose you're right."

Chi shoved his hands in his pocket and grimaced. "Marcel is right. While we're here, we stay on the offensive. Let's get back. Then we wait."

A cab pulled up to the sidewalk, and Raleigh checked around before she got in. The moment Ilario decided to forgo the deal they'd be in danger. She had no clue when that would be, and it could be now.

12

RALEIGH'S MUSCLES WERE coiled and ready to spring as she arrived back at the hotel. Her body was on edge, like it was a haunted house, and at any given moment she might be grabbed. What if Ilario decides against them tonight?

"Do you think Marcel is right, and that Ilario will attack if he rejects the offer?" Tau asked Chi as they made it to their floor.

"Absolutely." Chi opened his door and welcomed them in.

Raleigh went over to the window and inspected the street through the chipped white frame. The hotel, advantageously, sat at the end of the street, and they could see all the traffic coming their way. The building was against a tall wall, so there was no way to surprise them on that side. It struck her that it wasn't just luck. "You picked this place because it's easy to monitor."

"Yes, I did," Chi said. "There are members of the Vindex Authority that have their eyes on us. We won't have to alternate taking watch."

"Are these agents going to have our backs the whole time?" Brent asked.

Chi shook his hand and lifted his suitcase onto his bed. "No. Which is why I haven't mentioned them sooner. When we go deeper undercover, we'll be on our own. Ilario is based out of Italy and lives in a remote area. If that's where we're headed, they won't be able to cover us without being seen." Unzipping his case, he set some shirts aside and removed a gun.

Raleigh shivered at the sight of it. "Why do you have that?"

"Not all of us can influence." Chi handed it to Brent. "I assume you know how to use this?"

"Yeah. I carried one for a while."

Raleigh gaped at Brent. "What? You carried a gun *for a while?*"

"Don't look at me like that. You know some of my men have been threatened."

His eyes seemed to say *Tristan*. A reminder she didn't need. She'd thought of him rising from his coma every hour since they left New York. Raleigh could understand Brent's need for protection, but she hated to think of him using it.

Chi rested a hand on her shoulder. "Tau and I know how to use one from our time on the island. It wouldn't be a bad idea for you to understand how it works."

"I don't want to use it," Raleigh told him. "I can influence."

"There are times when you can't influence," Tau said.

Raleigh rubbed the scar on her shoulder and thought of the man she'd killed. The couple of times she'd been around a firearm, things had deteriorated fast.

Chi's face softened. He knew she was thinking of the van. "It's not like we're going to be able to shoot it here, or really anywhere nearby. I'm just going to have you hold it and familiarize yourself with the basic parts."

Raleigh put out her palm. It sat heavy in her hands. Influencing was deadlier, she was already more fatal than this gun. "Okay, let's go over the parts."

Chi succinctly went over not only the parts of the weapon but how to safely hold and use it. By the end, Raleigh was more concerned about accidentally shooting herself than the possibility of killing someone else. It was short and sweet, and Raleigh could tell from the delicate tone of Chi's voice that he felt they were ready to go it alone without the Vindex Authority.

"Enough about the gun," Tau said. "What should we know about Ilario's partner?"

Chi went to his notes and unfolded the second part of the diagram. "Glen. His partner's name is Glen. We don't know a lot about him. He's a chemist and worked for the Normandy group at one time, which is why his is a variation of theirs. They don't let the scientists have the full formula, so he had to fudge his way through. As far as personality, probably not the greatest of guys if he partnered with Ilario. Know their names and faces but don't slip. Wait until people are introduced to call them by name."

Raleigh studied the thirty or so people. There was no danger of her slipping. She doubted a few days would be enough to learn them all.

Tau spoke up. "I did it yesterday, when you showed us the first time."

"You what?" Raleigh asked. "We saw it for a moment."

"We're beautiful and smart. With the way you look at Rho, we all know which of those attributes you're more in tune to." Tau pushed the paper toward her.

Raleigh bristled.

Brent stepped in. "I'll take a look at that, too. Chi, you aren't going to bring this with us if we go, are you?"

"No. I'll mail it back to the States if and when we leave."

Raleigh hadn't thought about that. "When do you think Ilario will get back to us?"

Chi shook his head. "Tough to say. Hopefully, not too long."

They were in this now, and she'd chosen her fate. There was no point in expressing or fussing over the feeling of dread that prodded her at the mere thought of Ilario.

13

TONIGHT THEY'D LEAVE the watchful eyes of the Vindex Authority. Chi booked them on the overnight train to Rome minutes after Ilario invited them. Packed and bound for Italy, they walked down the train platform. The terminal bustled with people hurrying to their trains. Her mind flitted from one to the next, always landing on Brent, where she could feel the weight of the gun pressed up against his ribs hidden from view by his jacket. Raleigh tried to take her mind off it, focusing her attention on the trip.

"How does this work? Do we sleep in our seats?" Raleigh didn't like sleeping in the open where anyone could walk by. During sleep, she was at her most vulnerable, and she wondered if they'd take shifts keeping watch.

"No, there are sleeper cars," Chi said.

She stepped up the metal steps of the locomotive and grabbed onto a handle near the door. "Will there be strangers in our room?"

"No. We purchased two whole rooms. Tau and I will take

this one. Raleigh, you and Brent take the second one." His hand directed them down the narrow hallway.

Raleigh toted her bag through the small passageway behind Brent to their room. Once inside she saw that with four beds it was small but manageable.

"We can't fit in one room?" she asked Brent.

"Not all of us."

She, Tau, Chi, and Brent should've fit perfectly. Guilt swarmed in her stomach. Did Tau hate her that much that he insisted on being in a separate car? Did he think that she'd hurt him while he slept? Would he hold back from hurting her? Maybe Chi had made the arrangements to lessen the strain. Before she could ask Brent if that was the case, there was a knock on the door.

"I thought we weren't going to have strangers?" She didn't have the wherewithal to dredge up conversations with anyone new.

"We won't." Brent gave her a grin as he opened it.

On the other side stood Rho, Mu, and Collin.

"Rho!" Her guilt was replaced by an entirely different emotion. "What are you doing here?"

"Finding a place to sleep for the night." He walked in and tossed his bag on the upper bunk near her head. "Do you mind if I take the top cot?"

Raleigh looked at Brent and then back at Rho. "Yeah, that would be great."

"Good to see you, Raleigh," Mu said. "Collin is setting up in here too. I hope you don't mind if I ride with Chi and Tau."

"No, of course not. Hi, Collin."

"Raleigh." Unlike the rest of the guys, he wasn't smiling. Instead, he glared at her.

A whistle pierced the air, and the train jolted to a move, causing Raleigh to sway. The twelve-hour journey had officially begun.

"I want dinner," Brent said. "Who else wants to come with me to the dining car?"

"Me." Mu stepped into the hallway.

Collin shook his head. "I'm not hungry."

Brent rolled his eyes. "You are so dense," he whispered, pulling Collin out. "You're joining us."

Chi and Tau joined the group, poking their head in to say hi to Rho as they went toward dinner.

"We'll pick you up something," Chi said to Raleigh.

They shut the door, and Raleigh found herself alone with Rho.

"Did everyone else know you were going to be here?"

Rho nodded. "Yeah. I called Chi yesterday. The Vindex Authority wanted to know exactly where I'd been held captive in Normandy. Collin and I went back so we could give them the location."

"Did you find the spot?"

"Yeah. No one was there, but it can't hurt to know. If you're on your way to Italy, the meeting with Marcel must've gone well."

Rho sat on the bottom of the bed. Raleigh paused, wondering if she should sit beside or across from him. Did either one send the wrong signal? It depended on what she was trying to imply, and she herself didn't know what she wanted yet. Sitting down next to him, she pulled her legs up, tucking them under her chin.

"We're working with Ilario. He's a pretty unnerving guy," she told him.

"Did you expect anything less?"

"No. But we'll have to be careful."

"There was a reason I didn't want you taking this mission."

Raleigh wasn't going to spend the night rehashing an argument they'd already had. "I met Brent's sister."

"I know. Even I've never done that. What's she like?"

"Nice, not quite as outgoing as Brent."

"No one is."

Raleigh lifted her toes in her shoes and rocked slowly back and forth. "She's worried about him. She doesn't know why he's gone all the time. She even thought he was dealing drugs. I wish we could've told her, but it's better she doesn't know."

"It made you think of your own sisters?"

Raleigh stopped fidgeting and looked at Rho. "Yes."

"You sisters won't assume the worst of you."

"That doesn't mean they'll understand."

"True. I had Trevor check in on them."

"Really?" She put her feet on the floor and listened closely. "How are they?"

"Thalia is getting good grades in school."

"Wow, that's a first." Most of the family conversations revolved around Raleigh's condition or how Thalia had to bring up her grades. Now with her gone and Thalia doing well, Raleigh had no idea what they all discussed at the dinner table.

"Your mom's flower store is doing well."

Raleigh wondered then if her parents weren't better off without her. How simple their lives would've been if they'd not had her as a daughter. All the worry that she'd burdened them with over the years took a toll. With her gone, they appeared to be living the lives they perhaps always should have.

"I'm glad they're doing well." It was true. She wanted them to be fine. "And Dale?"

"Good as well."

"How often do you check in with him?"

"I check in with Gamma every other day. Brent usually calls me every other day, and Tau has been texting me daily. He wants Trevor to look into your phone, to see if you've deleted any texts."

"Can Trevor retrieve deleted texts?"

Rho shook his head. "No better than anyone else. You aren't surprised that Tau has asked?"

"No. I think he's here to keep an eye on me."

"Not the kind of eye I was hoping for."

"Then you admit, he's a babysitter."

"Raleigh." Rho lifted his hand and let it hover a few inches from her own before he pulled it back. "We all need someone to watch our back. I didn't know Chi well enough to assume he had yours, not with his allegiance to the Vindex Authority."

"I still know next to nothing about the Vindex Authority. Chi's fanatical about them. It creeps me out how much they seem to know about you guys."

"Information that they have yet to use against us."

Raleigh hadn't really considered that. It was true. The Vindex Authority could've turned her, Dale, Gamma, and Upsilon over to Grant and Able instead of sending Chi.

"I miss you," Rho said simply.

Did she tell him it was the same for her? She'd been thinking about him too much. Seeing him now only seemed to bolster any infatuation she had. He was more handsome than she remembered, her memory not capturing his perfection, or maybe she recalled his face well enough. Maybe it was his vitality and charisma that was hard to keep fresh in her mind.

They'd intentionally left things on a good note, unlike last time. Rho disapproved of her choice to come, but he still spoke to her. She wondered what was more troubling to him, that she went or that she didn't listen to him. Rho was a leader, which was only attractive to someone wishing to be led.

He scooted back on the bed until his shoulders touched the wall. Then he stared at the undercarriage of the top bunk before looking at her. Did he still see the girl that rescued him? Or did he see the one who'd stabbed his brother and forced his hand at disbanding his family? Raleigh could barely recognize who she was these days. In her skin she felt confident, but she didn't know herself.

"They cut your hair," he said.

"It's part of the cover."

"It looks good on you, makes your eyes stand out."

The compliment dangled between them. It wasn't a simple pleasantry. It couldn't be, not when he knew how she felt about him. She remembered the touch of his lips and the taste of his Lucid. Resting her hand on the mattress, she marveled at how easy it would be to move it a little further and touch his. It wasn't the contact that scared her. It was the rejection. No matter how sweet the kiss, it had lost all appeal when coupled with embarrassment. She could feel his eyes on her, and she looked up. The silence sat as heavy between them as the potential.

"Knock, knock," Brent said from the other side of the door.

"Come in." Rho's voice caught a bit on the first word.

"Sorry, didn't know how long we should be gone. They just had wrapped sandwiches." Brent's eyes studied them both. "We can leave...."

"No. Stay." Rho sat up from his lounging as he moved to the edge of the short mattress.

Collin came in and handed Rho a sandwich before tossing one across the bed to Raleigh. "They're not very good."

Raleigh unwrapped the paper and took a bite of the sandwich. Her teeth crunched on stale bread. Not the best but better than she expected for a train. The nerves riddling her stomach over the impending meeting with Ilario—and from sitting with Rho—took away her appetite. Chewing slowly, she watched as Brent, Collin, and Rho slipped into their well-worn friendships. Had it really only been a handful of months since she first set out with all of them?

"Time for cards," Mu called from the door.

Everyone wanted in on the game, including Mu and Chi. With all seven, the room quickly became cramped.

"Can you scoot over?" Mu took a seat next to Raleigh, who slid closer to Rho.

The two bottom bunks served as seats, with Brent, Mu, Raleigh, and Rho on one cot and Collin, Tau, and Chi on the other. Raleigh's suitcase served as their card table.

Rho bumped her shoulder and whispered, "Gamma said that in Chicago you perfected your game."

Raleigh had never been bad at cards. She nodded as Tau took the deck and began to shuffle.

Brent cut the deck. "No poker. I've got a good poker face, but it's another story when you can all read my body."

"I've got a game." Mu began rattling off a list of rules.

Raleigh listened to him almost as closely as she listed to Rho's breathing. He was close to her now, with his leg pressed up the length of hers. So was Mu's, but only the skin on the side of Rho burned as if on fire. It was hard to pay attention to the cards or anything really. Pretending to be engrossed in the game, she hoped the others wouldn't notice.

The first hand went around. Raleigh watched the cards and knew that Rho too paid more attention to her than the game. Turning, she was fast enough to catch him flick his eyes to the pile. He barricaded, and so did she. It was hard to tell if he felt the same spark that sat on her skin. After playing each card, his hand fell to his leg and a millimeter closer to hers. If she lifted her thigh, his fingers would brush her knee.

With each round, they moved a little closer. She paid less and less attention to winning and more to how much she wanted to kiss him. The thought made her breath catch in her throat.

Not that she'd do it. Even if she mustered up the courage and the reasoning that it was a good idea, all his brothers were in the room with them, his brothers and Collin who also stared at her with the opposite of admiration.

"Your turn," Tau said. It took her a moment to register that he spoke to her. His expression was too similar to Collin's.

Yanking an eight from her hand, she tossed it onto the pile.

"You had an eight!" Collin shouted.

"Yeah. Do you see the eight little hearts on it?" Raleigh spat back. One thing she didn't miss about traveling with Rho was Collin.

"Then why didn't you play it before?" Collin asked. "Back when I would've taken it?"

Raleigh tried to scan back over the hands. Had she misplayed? It seemed more than possible. She hadn't been really paying attention. The rules were silly and complex. "I'm sorry." She backtracked, handing it to him.

"Don't just hand it to him," Tau said. "It's too late now. This changes the whole game."

"Let's remember, it's just a game," Rho said.

Collin threw down his cards into the pile. "Figure you'd take her side, even when she's cheating."

Chi put both his hands out to the side, mediating. "It was an honest mistake. We're all preoccupied with the mission tomorrow."

"Raleigh isn't thinking about the mission. She's spent the whole game sneaking looks at Rho," Collin said. "That preoccupation I would believe."

Rho sat forward in his seat. "Knock it off, Collin. We'll just start another hand."

Tau stood up, swaying with the motion of the train as he did. "I'm done."

"Me, too," Collin said.

Both of them skirted the others as they left. Embarrassment edged up her neck. They'd left on her account because she'd been too interested in Rho to keep up with the game and now they all knew. "I'm sorry, guys."

"It wasn't you," Chi said. "Collin's been using Lucid more. It's making him moody. Rho, you have to stop supplying him."

"It's not that simple." Rho collected the cards off the suitcase, not meeting Chi's eyes.

"It's bad for Collin, and you know it."

"Fine. I'll tell him to go off it for a while. He takes breaks, and he's overdue."

Mu gave a worried expression in the direction of the door. "Why do you think Tau's in a huff? It isn't the Lucid."

The straightforward question left a wave of discomfort in its wake. No one answered. Rho looked at Chi.

Everyone knew but Mu.

Raleigh cleared her throat. "He thinks that I'm a spy for Grant and Able. He thinks I'm waiting to learn of Sigma's location, and then I'm going to turn you all over."

Mu smiled. "No really. Why is he grumpy?"

"That's the reason," Chi said. "You were there. You saw Raleigh break his barricade."

Raleigh recalled Mu starved and tired in that basement. Gabe had chosen Tau for her to torture. She wondered how different things would be if he'd chosen Mu.

Mu remembered, too, his lax body straightening. "Yeah, Tau was freaked out about that. But then she got us out."

"It doesn't matter to him," Rho said. "He thinks it's part of her larger plan."

Raleigh asked, "Do you trust me, Mu?"

"Completely." When Mu spoke he looked her directly in the

eye, unflinching. "I can tell Tau that if you want. But if Rho and Chi haven't talked him out of it...."

Brent jumped in. "Tau's got to drop this, or we've got to drop *him.*"

"Not now," Chi said. "It's too suspicious, and we can't afford to come off as disorganized. No. We need him tomorrow. He'll have to get over it. When Grant and Able don't ambush Rho in Rome that will help support that Raleigh isn't a spy. We're a team, and he knows how important playing along is."

They stopped talking. The quiet drifted in while they mulled everything over. Raleigh's ears burned. Next door Tau and Collin were likely discussing the reasons that she shouldn't have been included in the mission.

Rho broke the silence and their thoughts. "Let's get some sleep. Tomorrow's a big day for you."

Raleigh nodded. Earlier, the small window had displayed breathtaking views of the countryside as they whisked past. Now it was pitch-black with the occasional light popping up in the distance. Grabbing her toiletry bag and nightgown, she went to the bathroom to change.

In the small single-person bathroom, she could only hear the sound of the wheels pounding along the track. Over the last few hours, she'd run the gamut of emotions. Now she was spent and ready to sleep. Walking back to her cabin, she entered and quickly slid into her bunk. Rho was above her, and she could tell when he fell asleep by his light breathing. Like her, he barricaded. Across the way was Collin, his slumbering face less harsh than when he was awake. Soon enough the sound of the clacking rails and rocking of the cabin lulled her to sleep.

"Raleigh?"

Rho's voice woke her up. Tucked into the small cot she squirmed against the hard mattress. The restful sleep left her head heavy and dazed. It was the best night of rest she'd gotten in a while, and it took her a moment to shake the drowsiness.

"Is it morning?"

"Yeah, it's morning," Collin said. "Are you going to sleep all day?"

Rho turned and gave Collin a look that made him shut his mouth. Rho said, "The train stops in a half hour."

Their time together had come to an end, with a few moments remaining for a short goodbye. She rushed to the small bathroom, dressed, and brushed her teeth. Back in the room she packed. Collin was gone, and Brent soon left. Once again she was alone with Rho. The train station came into view, and the intercom announced their arrival.

"Be careful." Rho pulled her into a snug embrace. As he stepped away, he reached one hand up and cupped the back of her head.

Raleigh's breath swirled in her lungs, she almost forgot to breath. Her eyes looked up at him as her heart slammed against the inside of her ribs.

Collin stuck his head into their cabin interrupting the moment. "Come on! It's time to go."

Rho let his hand fall. "If you need me, call. Cover or no cover, I will come."

Raleigh believed him as he lifted her bag and followed her out of the train. On the platform Mu, Collin, and Rho headed one direction, Brent, Chi, and Tau the other. Brent beckoned for her to follow. They had a meeting with Ilario to prepare.

Raleigh looked one last time in Rho's direction and then forward at her crew. They were in Rome, and there was work to be done.

CHAPTER
14

ILARIO LIVED AN hour outside Rome where the city streets gave way to rolling green hills. Chi booked rooms at a local villa that'd been converted into a bed and breakfast. It was a three-story mansion with four rooms on each floor, collectively they took over the second story. The rooms were quaint, with just enough space for a bed and a chair. Its setting resembled home more than a hotel, complete with a homemade quilt. It should've been comforting, but instead it made Raleigh homesick for her own purple quilt that she'd wrapped up in many a night.

After delicately hanging and folding all her clothes, Raleigh stood in front of the small mirror, trying her best to do her makeup. Lilia's pointers came in handy. But Raleigh still wasn't good at recreating the look.

There was a knock on the door, and she glanced at the small clock on the bedside table. It was ten in the morning, and they were due to visit Ilario and his partner in two hours.

"Come in," Raleigh said, trying to remove the mascara that'd gotten on her cheek.

"I need your phone." Tau walked in and held out his hand.

Raleigh took it from her purse, turning it on. "It gets lousy reception here. Is yours not working?" Handing it to him, she went back to mirror.

"Did you call them?"

"Them?"

"Grant and Able."

Raleigh smudged her top eyelid before turning to him. "Are you serious?"

"Rho was so into you, and you're not together. Why? Is it that you can't bring yourself to betray someone you're dating?"

The observation was like a hook to the gut. "It's not that."

"Collin thinks you're with Grant and Able, too. He said that you've been stringing Rho along since the beginning and that's he's blind to you. Chi and I aren't Grant and Able's endgame. They want Rho and Sigma. That's all I ever heard them talking about. Our leaders." He scrolled through the phone. "You haven't called them yet? Or you deleted it?"

"I'm not in contact with them." Raleigh grabbed the phone from his hand. "What do I have to say to you to prove it?"

"Rho making it out of Rome unmarred would be a start. If he's intercepted by them, we'll know why. He shouldn't have been on that train, but you convinced him."

"I didn't even know he was going to be there!"

"You're leading him on, and he's taking risks, like being on that train. He shouldn't be in Europe any longer than needed."

Raleigh twisted her hands together. Maybe if she came clean with Tau he'd stop accusing her. Unlike the other accusations, there was an easy way to put this conspiracy theory to bed.

"I kissed him, and he didn't kiss me back."

"Yesterday? I don't buy that. He couldn't take his eyes off you."

"A month ago. He said he couldn't date me because it would alter the dynamics of the group. Maybe it was because he didn't like me enough. I don't know. He didn't start acting all interested until I came on this mission. It might not even be genuine. I think he's hoping that if I'm so smitten with him, I'll do whatever he says."

Tau's face twisted in mortification. It was the first time that he'd acted like he might've misjudged her. Some of the anger left his voice. "Rho's intentions have been genuine. You might be a good actor, but Rho is painfully honest. With the amount of times he checks in with Brent about your welfare, he cares."

"I can't date Rho. He's right. It would change the dynamics of the group that I have to be an active part of. The Lucid trade isn't some game, it's a serious problem that we have to solve. Rho would rather run and hide, but sometimes you have to step out into the open to actually get stuff done."

Tau stood there staring at her. "You shouldn't lead him on."

"You're worried about him getting hurt? Last I checked, he's the one who rejected me. It's not like I go around making passes at people. It took a lot of courage only to get shot down. Now we have a little more than an hour and a half to get ready for the meeting which is a lot more important than if Rho and I are dating."

Raleigh pointed to the door. Tau turned, glancing over his shoulder one last time before leaving. Irked at Tau, Raleigh returned to the mirror, pulling out her lipstick. It was time to take her own advice. Now was the time to focus on the task at hand.

TWO HOURS LATER, they drove to Ilario's house. The mild autumn weather, along with the white puffy clouds, tried to convince her that today would be nice. If she closed her eyes, she could almost imagine that she was a tourist and that this particularly beautiful day was meant to be enjoyed. That illusion was broken as the large estate came in view through the front windshield.

Rolling down his window, Brent spoke into the small metal box positioned before an ominous metal gate. "I'm Brent, and I'm here to see Ilario."

"*Un momento,*" a voice from the speaker box said.

The gates creaked open, revealing a twisted drive to a large old house in the distance. Raleigh and the others jostled in their seats as Brent drove over the pebbled path up to the front door where he parked.

Silence filled the interior of the car. With no one barricading, Raleigh could feel the apprehension. It sat in the knotted muscles of Tau's back and in the curl of Brent's toes.

Chi cleared his throat. "Everyone ready?"

No one answered. Instead, they opened their doors, Brent scurried to help Raleigh out. "Remember, I'm supposed to open that for you."

"Right." Her first act as a socialite here, and she'd failed. It wasn't hard to remember to hold onto Brent's arm as they walked up to the front door because the small stones were difficult to navigate in her heels.

Chi rang the doorbell, and they listened to its chime echo through the cavernous inside. It took a moment before a burly man opened the door and stepped aside for them to enter. They slipped into the small entrance.

The doorman held his hand out to her. Raleigh shrugged out of her jacket and fought the urge to rub her cool arms. Now was not the time to appear nervous. "Thank you."

The man hung her jacket in the nearby closet and then ushered them through a short hall to the living room.

"You're here!" Ilario boomed rising from his seat. "Sometimes I have a habit of scaring people off."

"Not when there's money to be made." Chi shook Ilario's hand.

Ilario made a show of greeting each of them in turn, ending with small air kisses on Raleigh's cheeks.

"Welcome to my home." Ilario spun in a circle with his arms outstretched. "Please have some wine. I know Americans like beer, or, if you're friends with Marcel, I'd guess hard liquor. But you can't be so close to the vineyards and not try the wine."

"Are the vineyards yours?" Raleigh asked.

"Yes, but I don't run the wine operation. It would require too much of my time." He poured her a glass of red from a decanter.

Raleigh took a hesitant drink. Ilario's lips turned down. She'd forgotten that when tasting wine she was supposed to swirl it around the glass and smell it before taking a sip. Lilia had given her a long speech that the taste was only one of the ways to appreciate the wine. Ilario would know the etiquette of studying a wine. Her quick sip damaged her cover. Hoping it wasn't too late, she performed the swirl and smell.

"It's nice."

"It's nice?" Ilario smiled. Maybe he'd not noticed or chose not to care. "That's a five hundred euro bottle of wine." He proceeded to fill the guys' glasses. "Come. I'll give you a short tour."

Wine in hand, they followed him into an impressive living room with a large television hanging amidst priceless works of art.

Raleigh walked over to one of the pieces and studied it. The cracking in the paint looked old, and she figured it was an original. How old was it? She wasn't about to ask. A girl with her background wouldn't be impressed by originals. She couldn't afford another slip.

"Do you like it?" inquired Ilario.

"I'm more into modern, but this fits the decor of your home better," she said diplomatically. The last thing she needed was to be drawn into a conversation about Renaissance art and prove she was pretending.

He gave a casual shrug. "I know nothing about art. It's an investment. People buy them for me. The house, too. It's a bit older than my taste, but I'm told it will resell well."

They walked through a short corridor to a glass wall that divided them from a pool.

Ilario flicked his fingers in the direction of the turquoise waters. "I had this added. It cost two hundred and fifty thousand euros to install without harming the house. But I wanted it indoors."

Raleigh remembered Lilia saying that people who were new to money were the only ones who bragged about the cost. Ilario was showing just what a novice he was to his new station in life.

"Do you swim?" Ilario asked Raleigh.

Raleigh shook her head. "Not with my condition. Fainting in the water could be fatal."

"But you have so many of these strapping young men to catch you." He eyed Tau and Chi. "Another time."

Ilario put his arm though hers and escorted them back to the first sitting room. Raleigh didn't like being so close to him, but she knew it would be rude to pull it back.

"Where's your partner?" Brent asked.

Ilario's nose scrunched. "Where he always is, the lab. He can't stop tinkering with Lucid. Today he's making sure that yours is truly different from the other kinds out there."

"It is. We figured you could tell." Tau nodded to the small injection port in Ilario's arm.

All of them knew Lucid the way people around here knew wine.

Ilario smiled. "Yes. I can tell it's better. But Glen is methodical. Too much so. It takes the fun out of all of this. He puts all his money in the bank and tells me to live simply. He doesn't want us to gain attention. But what would the cops do? Nothing is illegal. That's what separates Lucid from the others. You can sell without concern of retaliation from the law."

The doorbell rang, and the sound of the door opening could faintly be heard. Shortly after, Glen walked in. He was a petite, trim man with a hawk-like nose and small beady eyes. Dressed in a tweed vest and loafers, his age wasn't only apparent in his face but his style.

Raleigh sensed the vinegar taste in his mouth. She wondered if he'd been eating pickles. Ilario introduced them one by one and then, clapping his hands, alerted his staff that they were headed to the dining room.

China sat on fresh linens. The table could easily accommodate twice the number—each seat had plenty of room. Ilario pulled out her chair, and she sat while the guys took care of themselves. Chi and Tau seated themselves across from Raleigh and Brent while Glen and Ilario took the heads. From her vantage point she could see past the table out the large window that overlooked the rows of grapes. It was breathtaking—and sad that the person who got to enjoy it had made his fortune in such a ruthless trade.

"Salad comes at the end of the meal," Ilario told her. "Americans have it first. Who wants to fill up on salad?"

The servers put out small plates of meats and olives. Raleigh could tell that he must've had at least one cook—and from the taste of the spices used and the balance of flavors—a good one. She remembered to take small bites and pause occasionally, a hard task since she was hungry and the food delicious.

Glen was the only one not eating. Instead, he scrutinized them.

"Why are you trying to partner with us? I tested your Lucid. It's new and better than ours."

Chi put down his fork. "We don't have warehouses, and we don't have sellers lined up to produce and distribute."

Glen's still didn't eat. "You'll make more if you take the time and set it up. Today you've come to the home of your competition. We'd be better off if your product never entered the market, which means we're not only competitors but rivals."

"You'll be better off if we were allies and you help us sell our product," Brent insisted.

Glen shook his head. "We have a place in the market, and once we expand to Asia, we'll easily sell ours. With ours we don't have to pay half the profits. The mere fact that you've come here shows you're fools. I don't do business with fools."

"Our product is better," Tau said. His eyes flicked to Brent's.

Raleigh perceived both Brent and Tau's shoulders tense. Would Ilario invite them to lunch with the intent of ending them so they couldn't enter the market? Taking another bite of food, Raleigh calmed her heart. Sensing, she could tell there were three servers—two in the kitchen—and the bodyguard from the front door. There was a pressure on his left side. A gun. Ilario had dosed before they arrived. But even if he could influence, he wouldn't be strong enough to break their barricades if they put them up.

"It *is* better," Ilario agreed.

"But in a month we'll roll out the sublingual version, and we'll be more competitive without their help," Glen said.

"A sublingual?" Brent asked.

Glen leaned back. "It goes under the tongue."

"I know what it means, thank you. I didn't know anyone had it," Brent replied.

"Not yet," Ilario said. "But soon. We could use it for yours."

"We don't *need* theirs!" Glen pounded his fist on the table causing the delicate plates to clatter. "I'm fine with our version, and I don't wish to share the profits. I told you, Ilario, that I thought bringing them here was a mistake. Only fools would walk into the home of their enemy and hope to make a deal."

Ilario pulled a gun from under the table and leveled it at Brent. Raleigh looked to Chi. They could all stop his finger if they needed to. Chi imperceptibly shook his head. They didn't want to blow their cover or tip Ilario off to influencing. Raleigh focused her attention on his trigger finger. If he moved it at all, she would stop him.

"My partner thinks I should kill you all," Ilario said. "What do you think?"

"I think it would be a mistake." Brent laughed in a way that bubbled up through his dry mouth. "But I'm biased."

Ilario smirked and moved his hand a little to the right, training it now on Glen. Without saying another word, he pulled the trigger. Raleigh and the others were able to stop him but didn't. The bullet shot across the table into Glen's head, propelling him backwards, a spray of blood falling on Brent's and Tau's arms. Raleigh felt her chest tighten and had to gulp down her scream. The gruesome scene was nauseating. Glen was dead.

Or he would be in a moment.

Raleigh shifted in her seat. She had the urge to run over and try to heal him. But there was no amount of influencing that could piece his brain back together.

Ilario pocketed his gun and took another bite of food. "Glen is no longer in our way. Let's hope for your sake that I made the right choice. There are much worse ways to go if you cross me."

Raleigh shakily took a sip of her water. It was no longer hard not to eat. She felt like someone had tied her stomach and intestines into one large knot. Ilario dug back into his food as the servants cleaned up the body and brought in the next course. They were working with a murderer.

Lunch wrapped up, but Raleigh barely remembered what was said. Ilario bragged, and Brent schmoozed. She stayed silent.

Ilario kissed her cheek goodbye. "Glen was right, you *are* innocent. Not a bad trait in a woman."

Raleigh forced a smile and stepped back into Chi who put his hands delicately on her shoulders.

"Where do we go from here?" Chi asked.

"Tonight you will come to my club," Ilario said. "You'll meet my right-hand man Rubio, and he'll tell you about our operation. I'll talk to the warehouses and see how quickly they can make your product."

Brent said, "We'll need to see the warehouses. We aren't going to just give you the formula. We'll give you parts. That way we don't end up like Glen."

Ilario opened the door. "That is fine for now. First though, you understand the sales."

"Thank you for having us." Tau shook Ilario's hand. "We'll see you tonight."

With that, the four of them left. Raleigh waited at the car door for Brent to open it. None of them said a word as the car drove down the path and through the large gate onto the street.

As the estate disappeared from view Tau yelled, "What the *fuck* was that!"

Brent's hands gripped the steering wheel. "We knew he was rash."

"That's not rash! That's maniacal. At the dinner table. Who does that?"

Raleigh added, "And this is what he does to people he's *partners* with?"

Chi leaned forward so he could better speak to Raleigh and

Brent. "That was good for us. Glen opposed our deal. Ilario showed us that his partnership with Glen is over so ours can begin."

"It was awful," Tau said.

Brent sped up, the sports car hugging the road at each turn. "Either we had to die or Glen. Up until Ilario pulled the trigger, I was convinced it was going to be us."

"We can stop him. We would've stopped him," Raleigh assured Brent. "I had a feel for everyone in that house. We're not as helpless as Glen."

"Good to know." Anger seeped into Brent's words. Then his face softened. "Chi is right. Now Ilario needs a partner, and it's us. One hurdle down. Let's make sure that we don't mess things up at the club."

They nodded and headed back to the inn. Raleigh shivered. In her heart she harbored guilt for the man she murdered. Now she knew how different a death in cold blood was. She doubted that Ilario would lose sleep tonight the way she had been. Perhaps he was right, not about being naive to the world of Lucid, but the violence of it.

15

FOUR HOURS DIDN'T give them much time to recover from the murder before they headed off to Rome. After returning from Ilario's, Chi reported to his superiors. The others retreated to their rooms. Raleigh spent some time studying the map of the city while trying not to replay Glen getting shot over and over in her mind. This wasn't a game, and she had no illusions that she was special to Ilario. He would readily kill her if he had a reason.

When they convened outside the inn, the mood was thick, cautious. Brent frowned, and Tau kicked the dirt by their car with his foot.

Chi's expression was stone as he said, "You look nice."

Raleigh was dressed in the copper dress Lilia had recommended for nightclubs or parties. It was tight but conservative in length. Once again she wore heels. Her ankle had recently stopped complaining about the last time she'd fallen while wearing them. Fashion was important, overriding the practicality of flats. This rule seemed particularly true in Italy where some of the shoes bordered on works of art.

"You can have the front seat." Brent opened the front door for Raleigh.

"Thanks."

Everyone buckled up, Brent put the car into drive, and they sped off. For the first few minutes, not much was said.

Tau broke the silence. "I think Ilario will kill us the moment we're no longer useful."

"Yeah," Chi said. "That tends to be how he operates. But I really didn't think he'd off Glen quite like that."

Raleigh pulled at the hemline of her dress. Chi was right. They had to be careful, but they weren't as defenseless as Glen. In a pinch she could drop her cover and influence Ilario and so could Chi and Tau.

She snuck a glance at Brent. "How are you feeling?"

"You're asking because of the four of us I have no defenses?"

Raleigh wasn't surprised he was thinking the same thing. "Yes."

Brent kept a straight face as the car accelerated slightly. "We just won't get caught or become useless. Chi, what do you know about this right-hand man?"

"Not much. One of the reasons we needed to infiltrate them was that we didn't know all the levels of the pyramid. An advantage to climbing the ladder is we have had more time to learn about everyone."

"Too late for that now," Brent said. "We'll play it safe. If we need to leave, we will. Worst-case scenario is that we all run. Then we'll go into hiding."

"Worst-case scenario is that we all die while running." Raleigh regretted saying her thoughts aloud.

Brent raised his eyebrow and looked at her. "Don't tell me

that you're just now realizing this is dangerous. There's a reason Rho begged you not to go."

"I don't need Rho to tell me how dangerous it is. It's worth the risk. Ending the synthetic is vital. It wasn't like I was much safer in hiding."

"Yes, at least we're not fighting without a cause."

Raleigh considered how defenseless Brent was, was this really his cause? "You're in a lot more danger than the rest of us since you can't influence, it's a bigger risk for you."

This prompted a smile from Brent. "Are you going to act like Rho? Are you going to tell me how I can opt out? I know that I can. But it would look odd to Ilario since he accepted our deal."

"Yes, the plan is working," Chi said.

Almost too well. It had cost a man his life. Raleigh reminded herself that Glen was probably not a great guy himself.

Chi went over the rules again as they entered the city. "Remember not to barricade, and remember that some of them will sense how you're feeling. Try not to be nervous."

Brent reached over and grabbed Raleigh's hand to stop her fingers from fidgeting. Right, Chi was talking about her. Time to forget about the ordeal at lunch and get into character.

They parked the car halfway on a sidewalk, like the stream of parked cars before them. The ancient streets had been planned long before cars existed, and now people made do as best they could. Despite being cramped, the streets were beautiful and old in a way that Raleigh wasn't used to seeing. Her mind scrambled to remember her history lessons. The only things Roman that came to mind were gladiators and Julius Caesar. Both were foreboding. Hopefully, the night wouldn't end bloody like that.

"Ready?" Chi asked.

She swallowed her fears. "Yes."

"Then let's do this," Brent said.

The car gave a sharp beep as he locked it. With Chi's arm through Raleigh's, they walked down the block.

Unlike Marcel's club which took over a large space, Ilario's did not. A short stairwell led down to the front door. The two stories above housed other businesses. They were dark this time of night, not bothered by the club in the basement. Two bouncers blocked the heavy door, and a small cluster of partiers hung outside.

Brent walked up to the bouncers. "I'm Brent, and Ilario is expecting us."

One of the men looked to the other who nodded slowly. "All right. Back room."

The first stepped out of the way, and the four of them gained admittance. Raleigh held on to Chi a little tighter as they descended into the club

With the brick walls and lattice of vents overhead, the space resembled more of a cellar than a basement. None of the partiers seemed to be aware of the dank, dark interior. They trained their attention on the loud fast American music, or at least the words sounded that way—synthesizers obscured the lyrics.

The crowd was young. Raleigh and the guys fit in effortlessly. As people passed, Raleigh perceived a myriad of drugs in their systems. A lot of them were drunk, some were on uppers, and as they walked through the throng, Raleigh noted a few that felt like they had Lucid, which wasn't surprising in a club frequented by Ilario and his men. Per the bouncers' instructions, they wound through the people to the back. Once there they found a small passageway that skirted the back wall and led to large private room. It was quieter and out view of the other patrons. Velvet sofas and antique chairs made small meeting areas—not unlike the set-up in Marcel's club.

With the exception of bodyguards along the wall, only two men were in the wide space, Ilario and who she guessed was Rubio, the right-hand man. He fell short of her expectations possessing neither the air nor the appearance she expected the second-in-command of a drug empire to have. His medium build, short brown hair, and round face were unremarkable. When he smiled, he looked sincere.

"This is Rubio," Ilario said.

They shook hands before all sitting in the small area. Raleigh remembered her posture, remaining ridged as the boys lounged into the seats. Moments of silence trickled by. Raleigh didn't know what to expect from Rubio.

Brent cautiously tested the waters. "You're in charge of sales?"

Rubio held up a hand, but Ilario batted away the comment.

"Tonight is not about business," he said. "Tonight is about getting to know you. Come, have a drink and we'll just *hang*. That's what you Americans call it, right?"

Tau's shoulders eased. Raleigh could tell this wasn't as awful as they'd expected, or maybe it was. Maybe this was all part of them giving the team a false sense of security. She had no interest in hanging out in the club. She wanted to get the finer points of the deal hashed out. The less time they spent in the company of these two, the better.

Ilario ordered a round of shots. Raleigh downed hers and tried not to wince at the taste. Tau, Chi, and Brent slipped easily into casual conversation with their hosts. It started with sports, football—the actual kind—not the American version. Then Tau started talking about rock climbing and that turned to jet skiing. The drinks kept coming, and Raleigh politely declined. It felt surreal sitting there. As the conversation progressed, she felt more and more out of the loop. Ilario got up to excuse himself.

Brent leaned over. "Feel free to add anything."

"It's male bonding."

"You're telling me that after the last few months you've had, you don't know how to shoot the breeze with a bunch of guys?"

"I do. But I don't think a socialite would," she whispered back.

Rubio caught them whispering. "If you two need a room, I have an office behind the bar."

Raleigh's eyebrows shot up, and patches of heat bloomed on her face.

Brent answered, "Raleigh and I are just friends, but thanks."

"I was wondering when we'd get to the topic of girls." Ilario strutted into the room.

There were six women with him. Now the females outnumbered the males seven to five, including Raleigh. The way the ladies sat on the sofa and draped around the others, she realized she'd get little help from them or any chance of a normal discussion. Raleigh thought that Brent might ignore them, to help keep her engaged in the group. All it took was one of the brunettes to put her hand on his thigh, and he no longer noticed Raleigh. Either it was an act to stay in character and prove something to Ilario or it was simply his nature. Each of the guys had a girl, and Ilario had two. She no longer belonged in this group. Sitting quietly during their conversation was bad enough, but this was awkward.

The girl lounging between Raleigh and Chi kept flicking her long blond hair onto Raleigh. The long strands swayed into her face. That was it, Raleigh was done. "I'm going to get some air."

When she stood, she felt invisible.

Tau had been muddling through a conversation with one of the girls. Her English was lacking, as was his Italian. He looked up as Raleigh stood. Other than that, none of them cared.

Raleigh tucked her tiny purse under her arm as she left the secluded area and immediately found herself immersed in the melee of dancers. It felt good to get away from them. A rock formed in her stomach. Was she singlehandedly blowing this? She headed towards the bar needing water more than air. It might take the edge off the alcohol, not that sobriety was doing much for her.

Pushing through to the bartender, she recalled the word for water, *acqua*. After hollering it through the line of people, the bartender pulled out a glass for her and then aided the next person who requested a drink. Raleigh took a long sip and fought the urge to press the cool glass to her forehead—a move that was decidedly unladylike. It was important to act her cover. She never knew who was watching.

"Raleigh?" a familiar voice asked.

All the hairs on her arm stood up. Her barricade filled in despite her knowing that it was better left undone. As she turned her head, she saw Adam a few feet away. Adam, the Recep that she'd trained with under Gabe. He was one of the few Receps she counted as a friend, who she'd truly betrayed a month ago. Caught. She hadn't even considered the possibility that Grant and Able would be here.

"Adam." She kept the nerves from her voice.

Adam's forehead wrinkled, his mouth forming a tight line, and going slack. "You need to leave. Gabe and Dustin are here."

Of course, Gabe and Dustin would be. That was the only thing that could make this already awful night worse. This wasn't a coincidence. A chance meeting with this group across the globe was nil. From the surprise on Adam's face, she knew that they weren't after her. They must be sniffing around Ilario.

"Adam, I'm sorry."

"Don't. There isn't time. You need to get out of here now."

Raleigh didn't wait to be told again. Pushing off from the counter, she skirted her way through the dancers toward the front door. Her heart jumped in her throat, finding Gabe feet from the exit. There had to be a back door, right? In case of a fire, there had to be another way out if the front door was blocked. It was reasonable to think that even in a city as ancient as Rome they respected modern fire codes. Ducking back into the crowd, she noticed an exit sign in the same direction as the bathrooms. Pulling out her phone, she texted the guys.

G and A are here. Stay put or get out the back. Quick.

She prayed they would get out, too. Only it didn't send. The reception underground—in a city that already had iffy coverage—was nonexistent.

As she considered running back to grab them, a sharp pain pinched her neck. For the briefest moment she feared a wasp. When the world and all she sensed about it went silent, she knew what it really was—a dart with the inhibitor. Now the only thing she had to defend herself was barricading. Influencing wasn't an option.

Wheeling around, her eyes leveled at Dustin's chest. He moved close to her, his meaty hand clamping onto her bicep. Without a sound, he yanked her toward the back exit. Raleigh opened her mouth to scream, but his free hand smothered her mouth and extinguished her yell. Most of the people were on the dance floor. Those that hung to the sides were either too high or engrossed in their phones to notice her. It was probably better for them. None of the partygoers would be powerful enough to go up against Dustin.

They spilled into the back alley, the high brick walls of the buildings shielding them from view. Raleigh struggled against him, her manicured fingers digging into his arm. She gave one swift kick back, hitting his heels, and he released her. Stumbling forward, she didn't know if she should plead for her life or threaten him. It didn't matter—she had the chance to do neither. His fist found her gut, doubling her over and knocking the air from her. Instinctively, she wanted to curl up into a ball but forced herself to stand only to be met with a second blow. This time she buckled to the ground.

"Not so strong now, are you? You know there's a reason they make the women healers. Because when you strip away the Lucid, you're left with someone small and weak. Someone like you who can't even begin to go up against someone like me." To drive home his words, he kicked her hard in the same place he'd punched.

Pain rallied around her side. Tears blotted out her vision. The dirt from the ground scraped her arm, and her shallow breath took in the smell of trash.

"Dustin," she huffed, unable to say anything else. This beating was something he had been dying to give her, and as she cradled her ribs, she wondered if he was volatile enough to kill.

He bent over and yanked her hair, pulling her to sitting. "Beg me not to hurt you." His face was inches from hers, the spit flying from his lips and landing on her face. "Say how weak you are. How pathetic you are. I always knew you were worthless. I saw through you when no one else did. Take away your Lucid, and you aren't worth shit."

"Gabe will be mad if you kill me."

Dustin's eyes darkened. "You're right. But who's to say how mad he'd be if I beat the shit out of you?"

With her legs curled beneath her she couldn't get enough force behind a decent punch. She clawed at him and tried to kick out her leg, but nothing worked. She could do little to hurt him. He stood over her and kicked her repeatedly in the side.

The metal door they'd come out of clanged open. Dustin paused to see who it was. Raleigh didn't look and focused on escaping. Pressing her palms against the ground she tried to lift herself. Pain wracked her side, and she gritted through it, needing to get away.

"Oh! It's one of them. I can see why you left us Raleigh. He's pretty isn't he?"

Raleigh turned, her hair obscuring her vision. It was Tau, his fists clenched and his blue eye flashing anger.

"Run!" Raleigh wheezed. *"Run!"*

He didn't run, his eyes finding her and softening. A delay that would cost him. Dustin threw the dart at Tau's shoulder, making him as mute as her.

Tau was shocked only for a moment. "Do you really think that I need the Lucid to mess you up?" He darted forward and cut Dustin across the cheek with his right fist.

Dustin stumbled back, and Tau threw a left. Relief flooded through Raleigh. Tau was going to win. Dustin was a solid guy but no match. As that thought crossed her mind, Dustin landed a solid blow across Tau's jaw. It wasn't long before Tau found his footing and placed his own hit. They were going to be fine. Raleigh forced herself to kneel, and then, squaring her right foot on the ground, staggered to a stand.

The door opened again. She hoped to see Chi but instead met the steely stare of Gabe. Two against two if Raleigh counted herself, which was too generous. Tau could still do it. Then Gabe pulled something from his pocket. A gun. No. A Taser. A volt zapped across the small distance hitting Tau in the chest, jolting him to the ground and sending him into convulsions.

"Stop it!" Raleigh shouted. She was unable to fathom his being tortured a second time. This time it would truly be her fault.

Her Lucid swarmed around her system, appalled at the inhibitor that blocked its path. It surged in heaping waves, muscling aside the inhibitor and bringing the world into stark clarity. Raleigh felt everything—the trail of electricity left in Tau's system, the throbbing pain of Dustin's busted cheek, and the tight anger of

Gabe's muscles. She could sense, which meant she could influence. A blackout was hurling her way, and before it enveloped her in dark silence, she unloaded as much pain as she could on Dustin and Gabe. The last thing she heard was a chorus of their screams.

C H A P T E R
16

RALEIGH CHOKED ON the adrenaline when she woke. The rush startled her, and she found herself cramped between someone and metal. It was odd to only have her five senses to go off of. The person behind her was warm, a contrast to her chilled skin. Her stomach plummeted, thinking it might be Dustin. Struggling to turn around, she still couldn't see. No light was to be found.

"Calm down." Tau's voice was inches from her ear.

"Where's Dustin? Where are we? What happened?"

"We're in the trunk of a car."

That explained the jostling and the sound of tires.

"You blacked out. But first you gave Dustin and Gabe one hell of a jab."

"I broke through the inhibitor?"

"You did. Before you pass out, your system floods with Lucid. There's got to be a way we can use that."

"I'm not sure how much longer we have. You should've run."

Tau let out a slow breath. "When you left, I thought it might be to contact Grant and Able. I spotted you texting, and then I saw Gabe by the door."

"And you thought that I alerted them to you?"

"Yeah. I was mad. I couldn't go back to Chi and Brent and tell them, not without blowing our cover. Instead I texted them what had happened. Then went looking for you."

"Well, you found me."

"Dustin was beating the shit out of you."

"Yeah. I was conscious for that part."

Tau took in a deep breath. As his lungs filled his chest pressed up against her. "You didn't call Gabe and Dustin."

"No. They just happened to be there."

Tau snorted. "I'm sure they're sniffing around the synthetic trade just like we are. You're no longer involved with them. I've been wrong this whole time. Shit. It's over now."

Raleigh couldn't console him by telling him otherwise. "How long have we been in here?"

"Maybe five or ten minutes."

Raleigh took a deep breath that came up short, her ribs screaming in protest.

Tau's hand fell on her side. "It's bad, isn't it?"

"Can you sense?"

"No. I can feel the pain in your voice. They gave us both another shot of inhibitor before loading us up. We aren't going to be able to rely on influencing."

Raleigh nodded. "How are you?"

"Really not that bad. I think Dustin is worse off."

"Or at least he *was*," Raleigh said. "We're the ones crammed back here."

"I'm sorry I didn't believe you."

"It doesn't matter now. We have to figure out how to open this trunk." Her fingers scanned the inside of the trunk looking for a handle or a place to pop it open. Even if it did open, they'd be faced with having to jump out of a moving car. No such luck. "I can't find a handle."

"I think that we're trapped. I could try to fight them as they open it. But I think they'll be ready."

"Gabe has a Taser. No. We're going to have to talk our way out of this one."

"Good luck. Those guys are furious."

"Yeah. But you said yourself, I was one of them once. They'll remember that."

There was silence from Tau before he said, "It may be better if they don't."

The car took many turns over the course of the next fifteen minutes. Each time it swayed, Raleigh braced herself in the small spot, trying not to lean into Tau too hard. Occasionally they stopped, only to start back up. The rumble of cars outside reminded her of a rushing river. The illusion was only broken by the occasional beep, screech, and siren. If she had to guess, they were still in the city. Eventually, the stopping became less frequent, and the traffic sounds tapered to the occasional blip.

"We're in the countryside," Tau said. "But not far because we haven't been in here long."

Raleigh didn't like being out of the city. Fewer eyes were there to watch what was happening—not that being in the city had stopped Dustin from attacking her.

The smooth pavement turned to a coarser terrain before they came to a dead stop. Car doors opened and echoed closed.

"Don't say anything about Rho," Tau said. "No matter what they do, don't say anything."

"I won't."

"Raleigh?" Gabe's voice said from the other side. "Are you awake?"

"Yes." She listened to her voice reverberate through the trunk.

"We're going to let you out. Dustin has a gun trained on you both. Any sudden movements and you're both dead."

"Understood," Raleigh shouted. Then she whispered, "Gabe's not bluffing. Don't try anything."

"It might be better to be shot now than go through what they have planned."

Raleigh shuddered at his words. They weren't said with fear or hysteria. Instead, his voice was calm, logical, as if he was weighing the options. Would he really rather die than be captured by Grant and Able a second time?

The trunk opened, and Gabe stood ready on the other side. "No fast movements. Adam, help Raleigh out."

Adam lifted her under the arms and hoisted her from the cramped space, her legs unfurling before he gently set her down on the ground. Raleigh looked at him solidly in the eyes. He didn't return her gaze. He stared at the trunk with Tau inside. It struck her that this was the first time Adam had seen a Designed in the flesh—and the perspiration along the side of his face marked his fear.

To the side of them stood Dustin, his gun trained on Tau and the inside of the trunk. His face had started to swell where Tau hit him. She didn't need Lucid to tell that his finger was heavy against the trigger. Raleigh knew he wouldn't shoot unless Gabe gave the order. As long as Gabe was there, neither Adam or Dustin would be making any decisions.

Drawing her attention from the gun and the car she surveyed the scene. They stood next to an old house. Paint chipped off the sides and rusted farm equipment sat discarded on the lawn. A yellow-tinted bulb sat over the front entrance, more foreboding than welcoming. There were lights in the distance, just close enough for her to know it was another house, but far enough away to squash any notion that her scream would be heard.

"All right, Tau. Now you. If you try anything, you're both dead. Do you understand?" Gabe asked.

Tau didn't receive any help. Gabe's hands were full with his gun. Tau swung one leg out of the car and then the other and was soon standing beside Raleigh. Gabe's face was expressionless as he pushed Raleigh and Tau toward the front door of the small farmhouse.

Adam unlocked the door, and the five of them entered. The plan must've been discussed in the car because Adam and Dustin set about grabbing ropes as Gabe took them to a side room. With only a bare mattress and chair, the bedroom was sparse, a far cry from the luxury Grant and Able had in Phoenix.

Adam entered with a matching chair to the one already in the room and Dustin with a length of rope. It was nylon and thick and would be hard to get out of.

Gabe said, "You two, sit. Dustin, tie them up."

The backs of the chairs were placed together so the rope could loop around them both. Back-to-back, Raleigh and Tau sat as Dustin secured the restraint. The chairs creaked with each tug of the rope and Raleigh's breath hitched from the pressure.

Dustin smiled at Raleigh, his beaten face making him look more sinister. "You can't sense it, but trust me, the pain I give you will be ten times more than what he did to my eye."

"Adam," Gabe said. "The cuffs."

Tau's and Raleigh's arms were secured by the rope, their wrists and hands peeking out the bottom. Adam cuffed their wrists together, further immobilizing them. Tau's pulse beat against her skin. It wasn't as fast as hers. He was still in control, which was good because she was frantic.

Gabe sat down on the bed facing Raleigh. Only a few feet away, she recognized the familiar lines of his face. His eyes were inquisitive, the wrinkles in his brow showing more curiosity and regret than anger.

"You left us," Gabe said simply.

"Betrayed," Dustin corrected.

Gabe looked over at him and then back at Raleigh. "Agatha was crushed."

"She's okay?"

"You don't get to ask that." Gabe cast his eyes down. "I am mad. I admit that I was unable to think of anything but killing you for the first week after you left. But now I'm more interested in knowing why. Why, after all that we did for you, did you leave?"

Raleigh looked at him. "You know why, Gabe. What you did to the Designed wasn't right."

"Obviously you don't understand yet." Gabe glanced up and focused on the top of Tau's head. "They're evil."

"That isn't true. You know it isn't. Some of them are bad but not all. That's why you have that chart. You dehumanized them so you could justify capturing and draining them of their Lucid."

"You took Dale."

"Dale wanted to come. Trust me, you all would've come up with reasons to imprison him in the long run."

"We aren't bad people. You trained with us. Adam!"

Adam stepped forward, his face concerned.

"You and Adam were *friends,"* said Gabe.

"Adam still is my friend, and as my friend I would encourage him to leave. Lucid isn't a good thing. It changes you. Tell me, since we've been gone you've had less. After the initial withdrawal, you've felt better, haven't you?"

Gabe said, "It isn't as addictive as you think...."

"It *is*, "Tau interrupted. "We've seen that addiction in the clubs, in people like Collin."

Raleigh flinched at the name. Gabe and Collin had been best friends on the island. Collin left with the Designed, but Gabe had been under the impression he died.

Gabe got up and walked over to Tau. "Collin? You *killed* Collin. Or don't you remember?"

Raleigh spoke up. "He survived. He's with us."

Gabe went back to Raleigh. "He *survived?*"

"I've met him. He's a lot like you, just more of an asshole," Raleigh said. "He's indebted to Rho. So much so that he hates me."

Stepping back, Gabe ran his fingers hastily through his buzzed hair. Then he squared off at her, no longer troubled. "I want to know where Rho is, where Sigma is, where they all are."

"Yeah, after I stabbed Sigma, the group broke up," Raleigh said.

"I guess you were good for something. Where's Rho?"

"That I won't tell you. You can torture me, go ahead." Raleigh inhaled deeply. With the inhibitor she couldn't use her Lucid to hurt them, but she could use it to numb her own pain and bolster her barricade.

Lifting his arm, Gabe prepared to backhand her. Raleigh squeezed her eyes shut and braced for the impact. No strike came. As much as he hated her, he wasn't the type of guy who hit girls—at least not helpless ones. It was a strange code to have, but for a man like Gabe, morals were what he clung to.

"For fuck's sake!" Dustin said walking over.

Raleigh opened her eyes to find Dustin making a fist. Gabe grabbed it before he could strike.

"I'd rather you hit Tau," Gabe told Dustin.

"We already know that won't work," Adam said.

Raleigh didn't know if he was trying to save Tau or if he was simply stating what they all knew. After all, during Tau's months in captivity, neither he or Mu had ever cracked until they went up against Raleigh. She was the only one in the room strong enough to pull the information from Tau and, luckily, this time they were on the same side.

"Raleigh will crack," Dustin said. "Hurt her bad enough, and he might talk."

"And *we're* supposedly the monsters," Tau said. "Gabe, you employ a man who delights in hurting women. You should've seen the way he was kicking her in that alley. Don't claim to have morals and then let a man like him do your work."

Gabe whirled around to Dustin. "I told you to subdue her."

"Let's be honest, you've wanted to hurt her since she betrayed us. I only acted on what we've all wanted."

Adam interjected. "She's our friend! So she left, but we can't hurt her."

"Adam," Gabe said.

Adam didn't back down. "She's still our friend. We knew she was upset about the addiction, and we *are* addicted. She said people would begin to act out. I was pissed about what Brandon did to Dale. You should've been, too. After that I wondered how safe he was. I wondered how I could not have known. She left because so many of us are losing our minds."

"Adam...." The frustration in Gabe's voice was clear. "The benefits far—"

"Outweigh the risks," Adam finished. "But if we have all this honor that we claim to have, we need to rid our team of people who succumb to their addiction. People like Dustin who've hated Raleigh from the beginning. People like Brandon."

"We got rid of Brandon. Dustin, leave."

"What? I'm in this. I found her!"

Gabe nodded. "You'll remain on this team, but you need to leave. You, too, Adam. I need to talk with Raleigh."

Adam studied Tau before returning his attention to Gabe. "Are you sure you want us to go?"

"Yeah," Gabe said. "He's not getting out of these ropes. The inhibitor will last a few more hours at least."

Dustin stomped out, and Adam gave Raleigh a short glance before following. Gabe positioned himself so that he was again sitting eye to eye with Raleigh.

Gabe cleared his throat. "Why are you in Rome? Why aren't you stashed away someplace safe? If Rho was really as great a guy as you say, he would've hidden you so well we'd never find you."

"That's what he wanted. But Rho isn't my boss. We're here trying to take down the synthetic trade."

"Of course you are. But why?"

"It might be Grant and Able's creation, but it's our problem."

Gabe pointed over her head. "No. It's *their* problem. You aren't Designed. You aren't in trouble."

"They nearly killed me. Why are you going after the synthetic?" Raleigh asked. "Why aren't you after the Designed?"

Gabe raised an eyebrow. "You don't know, then."

"Know *what?*"

"Quinn is missing."

"He's *missing.*"

"Yeah, after he went home to visit his sister."

"I'm surprised you let a Modified leave."

Gabe grimaced. "It was a mistake. He didn't come back."

"You didn't have Receps with him?"

"He took a while at the hospital visiting his niece. We didn't have the Receps go in the room."

"Did he run? Maybe he wasn't taken." Nausea tumbled across

Raleigh's stomach. Quinn was a relaxed type of guy, not the kind of person who'd be able to plan a successful escape.

"He liked it with us. Did you take him?"

"No."

"Because you took Dale, I could see you luring him out. Cut off our supply of Lucid."

Raleigh shook her head. "We didn't."

"Did Sigma?"

"I don't think he even knows about the Modified." Raleigh recalled what a shock it'd been to the other Designed. "Surely if Sigma knew, he would've told some of his brothers."

"That was our thought. And if he did, what would be the use of kidnapping? Killing him, sure. But why would he take him?"

The story Rho told her about being imprisoned by the synthetic came to mind. "You think the synthetic may've taken him? You think Ilario took him? We don't think he knows about the Designed."

"Obviously not. We think it's a different one in France. We have guys up there. Coming to Rome was just to be thorough."

"It would be the Normandy one. They took Rho. That's how I met him." Raleigh noticed the odd expression on Gabe's face. "You must've pieced this together by now."

"Sabine."

"Yeah, Sabine. I was there. Everything we said was true. Sabine found me and was treating my blackouts. Then Rho showed up nearly dead with Collin."

Gabe twisted in his seat.

"I saved him," she said. "When I went undercover, it was to save Mu and Tau."

"We aren't like the synthetic dealers. They're trying to turn a product. We're trying to heal the sick." Gabe spoke to her now as he had at Grant and Able, like a teacher.

Raleigh thought of the guy in New York she'd healed. It sounded good, it felt right. For her at least, she wasn't at risk of being addicted.

"At what cost?" she asked. "Not only to you but society? What's the impact that Lucid's going to have?"

"That's a larger question. One we don't agree on or you wouldn't have left." Gabe rubbed his hands together. "What specifically are you doing here?"

"We've partnered with Ilario. Do you know who that is?"

"He's Glen's partner. They started working together. Before, they were rivals."

"Glen's dead."

"I don't think that's right."

"I saw Ilario shoot him in the head over lunch today. Trust me, he's dead."

Gabe whistled through his teeth. "Why would Ilario partner with you over Glen? Do you have a synthetic?"

"We're using mine."

Gabe put his head in his hands. "You're crazy, you know that? Do you have a death wish? Not that I care."

Raleigh continued. "I'm going to find out the location of his warehouses. Then I'm going to give that information to the other synthetic operation in Normandy. That way, they can take Ilario out completely."

"Give it to us."

"No way. You're going to take out the Normandy synthetic once this one falls. We have information that will help you. It will go smoother that way."

"If you have the information to end the Normandy one, give it to me now. We'll take down both."

"No. Once one falls, the other will hide. That's why we need

Ilario to be taken out by the other. That way they're confident and won't see it coming."

Gabe's brow furrowed. "Where is your intelligence coming from? How do you know so much?"

"That isn't the point."

"No. The point is you want me to release you. That isn't going to happen."

"Are you going to stick me in a basement and drain me like you did Tau and Mu? Are you going to justify it by saying I'm in league with the Designed and a traitor and thus deserve it?"

"You do deserve it."

"Fine. Lock us up. But remember Grant and Able has two stains on its hands, the Designed *and* the synthetic. I'm saving your ass by stopping the synthetic."

"We'll bring it down."

"Ilario will never side with you. You might've thought up the same scenario we did and used my Lucid. But it's too late now. It's been done. We're the ones he's working with."

Gabe stood up and kicked the side of the bed. "Screw this. You're coming back with me. You're going to look Agatha in the eye and apologize for what you did. Then you're going to take Mu's place on that boat." With that, Gabe left the room, slamming the door.

C H A P T E R
17

RALEIGH STARED AT at the spot where Gabe had been sitting. She'd made the choice not to coddle him. Tau remained quiet behind her. "I'm sorry," she said. "Maybe I was too firm. Maybe I should've begged."

"No, you did well. He's thinking about it. You mean something to him. I've never seen him show any emotion, and he was raw when he left."

"I was his prized pupil."

"And you and Dustin had a past?"

"Dustin has always hated me. Adam is a friend."

"I got that."

Raleigh moved against the ropes wrapped around her waist and legs. "It's more complicated than you make it seem. Yes, I was friends with them, but I sided with the Designed. It was a hard choice. I admit it. Grant and Able were going to let me become a healer. That's all I wanted. Then I switched sides, and that shocked them."

"I should've trusted that you weren't a spy. I should've gotten Chi's help the moment I saw Gabe."

"Then he'd be tied up with us, and Brent would be alone. No. I don't think there was much you could've done."

There was a pause.

Then Tau said, "Adam had a funny look on his face. I saw how furious he was when Dustin threatened you. Are you sure he considers you just friends?"

"What? Adam? No. There's nothing there. I mean we trained a lot and were close, but he never said or did anything."

"He spoke up against Gabe. Maybe he'll reason with him. There is a chance they might let you go."

"I'm not going without you," said Raleigh.

Tau exhaled. "You might not have a choice, or worse, they might kill me and take you."

There were footsteps outside in the hall. Tau squeezed Raleigh's hand, ready to face their fate.

Adam stepped back in. "I'm going to give you another dose of the inhibitor."

"Adam, I'm sorry," Raleigh said. "I didn't mean to betray you."

"We're not all bad, Raleigh. Not as bad as *they* are. You've seen the video. You've seen what he's capable of," Adam's head flicked towards Tau.

"Not all of them. That's why you have a capture and kill list."

"And you're a capture," Adam told her. "Agatha insisted that we take you captive if given the chance, not kill. We all need to know why you turned."

"I already told Gabe."

"We were friends."

Tau cleared his throat. "Adam, if that's true, you should steal Dustin's gun and shoot us. I know you think being captured is better than being killed. It isn't. They'll hurt her. Think about what Dustin threatened. If you were ever really friends, you'll save her from that."

Adam bit his lip, his brow furrowing. Any concern he had didn't stop him from plunging the needle into Raleigh's neck and walking over to Tau and doing the same. Then he left, trying his best to avoid making eye contact with Raleigh.

"He won't shoot me."

"No, but he might press for them to let you go."

"I think Adam will have little to do with the conversation."

It was Gabe and Agatha who would decide. Gabe would prefer to see her and Tau locked up. It was impossible to know Agatha's mind. At least the woman wanted Raleigh captured instead of dead.

THE PRESSURE OF the ropes on her arms and stressfulness of the situation didn't keep Raleigh from sleep. After the long day, she was exhausted. With no pillow, her head fell back onto Tau's shoulder. In a groggy haze she wondered if it would be all right, but she fell asleep before she could ask him.

It was a restless slumber. Occasionally a noise would rouse her enough to open her eyes before returning to sleep. Then Raleigh felt someone poking her shoulder.

"Raleigh," Adam said, his voice quiet.

She opened her eyes to find him near her. Tau's head rested on hers, his breathing light. He, too, had managed to get some sleep.

"Adam." She moved slowly and painfully.

"Shh. Don't wake Tau."

"Too late." Tau yawned. "Why are you here?"

Adam's mouth was set in a hard determined line. "I'm getting Raleigh out."

"Good," Tau said. "Take her far away. Go to the city, find a cheap hotel. Lie low for two days and then hitchhike. If you can make it to Paris, she has a friend who will help you."

"I'm not going without Tau," Raleigh said.

Tau squeezed her hand. "Yes, you are. Gabe is mad at you, but he's not sure what to do. He doesn't really want to lock you up. If you take me, he'll work harder to hunt us down."

"Adam, I'm not leaving without Tau."

Adam shook his head. "No. Tau will kill me the moment the inhibitor wears off. I'm not strong enough to fight him."

"He won't," Raleigh said.

Adam stared at her. "No. I owe this to you, but if I take him I've betrayed everyone. Come with me. I'll keep you safe. You'll be stronger once the inhibitor goes. We'll find an extraction machine, and you can keep me dosed up so I can fight with you."

Raleigh could imagine Adam's life taking on an eerie similarity to Collin's. "I don't have a port anymore. We took it out so Ilario wouldn't suspect."

Tau cleared the sleep from his throat. "You'll work that out."

"No," Raleigh said.

Adam's eyes turned down sadly.

"Adam, we're not doing this. I'm not leaving Tau. I need to stay. I have to convince Gabe to let me take down the synthetic."

Raleigh could feel Tau shaking his head. "Right now Gabe is trying to decide if he should kill us. He isn't going to let us take down the synthetic."

Adam placed a small knife along the thick fiber rope. "Please, Raleigh. Tau's right. They'll hurt you. This may be our only chance."

"Thank you, but no. I'm sorry. But I can't."

Adam stood up and walked away, peering at her through the dark one last time before leaving.

Tau said, "There goes your chance. I'll remind you of it when we're on that boat."

"And I'll remind you of how you could've been on the boat alone. What time do you think it is?"

"Almost daybreak. I can see lighter sky out the window."

"Lucky you. I get to face this bed that I can't sleep on."

"I wonder what Brent and Chi think happened to us? I told them in the text that I was following you out and mentioned Gabe. Who knows if they understood?"

"I doubt they even got it. None of my texts got through. I bet they think we've killed each other," Raleigh said.

"Yeah, that's the most reasonable assumption." She could hear the smile in his voice.

The door opened. Gabe stood on the other side. Dustin was beside him with Adam a few steps further back.

"You're awake," said Gabe.

"With the comfiness of this sleeping arrangement, it's amazing, I know," replied Tau.

Dustin said, "You're in a good mood. We could ruin that."

Gabe sighed. "We're letting you go."

Dustin inhaled sharply, and Adam let out a sigh of relief.

"What?" Dustin said.

"They're released." Gabe untied them as he spoke. "We'd like to help any way we can with your plan and the synthetic."

She was right. Gabe knew that the synthetic trade was worth more than them.

"Do you think being gone the night will ruin your chances?"

"No," Tau said. "We'll come up with an excuse."

"Good, and you'll pass the information about the synthetic dealers in Normandy. And you'll take Adam. He's loyal to you now, more than he is to me."

Adam stiffened. "What?"

"I know you tried to break them out. I was waiting on the other side to stop you. Raleigh chose not to go, which means she thinks that she has an actual chance of dismantling the synthetic. Yeah, I would love to keep Tau, but Agatha feels that the synthetic is a larger problem than him."

"No! We aren't going to have this chance again, Gabe!" Dustin said. "She fucking *betrayed* us."

"And she stabbed Sigma, and she's working to destroy the synthetic. Trust me, Dustin, I wanted to keep her, too. But we have to look at the bigger picture."

The ropes fell off Raleigh's arms. She took a full breath. "We don't need Adam."

Tau got off his chair. "Yes, we do. Thanks for giving us the help."

"Adam will be our contact when you're ready for our part of the plan. Keep in touch," Gabe said.

"Right." Raleigh straightened her wrinkled, dirtied clubbing dress, imagining that if they had to hitchhike no one would stop. "Are you going to drive us to town?"

"No. I called you a cab. I promise not to follow you."

Dustin stepped in the door. "No. No way."

"Ilario will probably kill them, anyway, if that's what you're worried about," Gabe said. "Either way, Dustin, you need to stand down."

Dustin loomed in the doorframe, scowling, before begrudgingly stepping out of the way.

Raleigh looked at Gabe. "Tell Agatha I'm sorry."

"She's the one who made the call. I'm still not sure it's the right one. Leave. Get back to your mission."

Tau and Raleigh stepped out of the house. Bewildered, Adam went upstairs to grab his things. For the briefest of moments,

Raleigh considered that bringing him might be a trick, but his shock seemed genuine.

"Do you think he's going to be used against us?" Raleigh asked Tau. "We shouldn't be bringing him."

Tau shook his head as the cab pulled up. "He was going to be fired by Gabe. Last night he sided with us. There's a reason Rho won't ever make Collin leave. The withdrawal can be horrible. We'll help coax Adam off Lucid. You owe him. His attempted rescue has cost him."

"It was a stupid thing to offer. Don't forget he was willing to leave you there."

Before she could say anything else Adam was at the cab. "All right. What do you want me to do?"

Tau opened the back door. "Watch my back until the inhibitor wears off."

The three of them slid into the cab, and the car drove off.

18

THEY ARRIVED BACK at the inn before the sun fully rose. Haggard, they walked quickly past reception up to the second floor. Tau marched over to Chi's door and knocked. Raleigh rapped on Brent's. Adam hung back in the hallway.

Raleigh figured she'd be waking Brent up. He couldn't possibly know what this time of day looked like. It surprised her when he immediately opened the door. From the tired look on his face, she could tell he hadn't slept.

"Raleigh." Brent sighed and pulled her into a hug.

She flinched from the pain in her side. Using her Lucid, she calmed its complaints.

"Are you okay? What happened? Where were you?" Brent's eyes darted around, landing on Adam. "Who's that?"

Chi opened his door. His eyes held the same relief and confusion as Brent's.

Tau ushered everyone into Chi's room.

Once inside Raleigh told them the story. "I went to the bar and got some water. Gabe and his crew were at the club checking out Ilario. They spotted me and then took Tau and me hostage."

Brent cursed under his breath. "That's bad. Gabe hurt you?"

"Dustin, a Recep."

"They let you go, and they gave us him?" Chi pointed to Adam. "He's a Recep, isn't he?"

"That's Adam. He's going to help us," Raleigh said. "Look, I told Gabe everything. They're going to leave us alone so we can continue with our plan."

"No way." Brent scowled. "We aren't taking on a Recep. You know how bad Collin is."

Tau put his hand on Adam's shoulder. "He's not the same as Collin. It was my decision to bring him, and I stand by it."

"You accuse Raleigh of being a spy but then readily take one of their men?" Brent marveled.

Tau nodded. "He's proven himself."

Chi crossed his arms. "Good enough for me. Gabe knows we could run, and he let you go knowing that we'd continue to go after Ilario. If we need to, I can call in help."

"We're not there yet," Tau said. "But you should tell your people what happened."

"You should also tell them Quinn's missing," Raleigh added.

Chi grimaced. "We thought that Grant and Able stashed him someplace new. You're sure he's missing?"

"That's what Gabe said." Raleigh tried not to imagine all the awful places Quinn could be.

"I'll tell my boss," Chi said. "If he is gone, Grant and Able have even less Lucid on hand."

Raleigh asked, "How did it go with Ilario? Does he suspect something is wrong, with us leaving like that?"

Chi shook his head. "Brent thought on his feet."

Brent smiled, pleased with himself. "I told him that Tau texted me that he was taking you home. I said that that blonde made you jealous and that you and he got in a big fight. Then Chi said that Tau and you have been flirting for a while and this was the event that made him realize just how interested you were. So yeah, Ilario thinks that you ditched us at the club so you could hook up."

"Not the most professional thing," Chi said. "But I think he found it more entertaining than rude."

Raleigh's mouth went dry. It was one thing to pretend to be a socialite. Over the last few days she and Tau hadn't even pulled off being friends. The hesitation she felt was mirrored in Tau's expression.

"That was the best excuse you could think up? Why couldn't you say that I had a fainting episode and Tau took me home so I could recover?"

Brent considered what she'd said and shrugged. "That would've been good. But I was flustered, and I thought hooking up would be more believable."

"That's not more believable!" Raleigh said.

Chi held up his hands. "It was great that Brent convinced him of anything. We're meeting him tonight. So you'll have to play up the dating angle from here on out."

Being a socialite was hard enough. Raleigh had never had a boyfriend, let alone a fake undercover one. "I can't do that."

"Sure you can," said Brent. "Look at him like he's Rho, and you'll be fine."

"You're with Rho?" Adam asked meekly.

Raleigh rolled her eyes. "No. I'm not. Chi, why don't you fill him in on the plan. Do you think there's some way to incorporate him?"

Brent shrugged. "A dealer? I don't know. It might be best to keep him here and call if we need backup."

"Do any of you have Lucid?" Adam's eyes darted anxiously between Chi and Tau. "I'd love to play backup, but I don't have any."

"No. No using," Chi said. "It's against our ethics. You'll back us up the normal way, with a gun."

Tau told Chi, "He'll go through withdrawals. Ease him off. It's more humane."

Chi didn't look happy. "Have Rho send Lucid. Just enough to wean him off. Adam, can you go a few days?"

Adam said, "Yeah, of course."

Raleigh wondered if that was true. But even if it was a few days, it was better for him than going cold turkey, which was what would've happened if they didn't bring him.

"I'm just glad everyone is safe," Brent said. "You guys scared me. You need to get cleaned up, and we all need to sleep."

"Sleep sounds good," Raleigh said.

Chi asked Raleigh, "You're on the inhibitor?"

"Both Tau and I are. Adam gave us a dose last night."

"A large one," Adam said. "They've got a few more hours."

Chi nodded. "I'll stay up and make sure we're all safe. Adam, come in my room, and I'll bring you up to speed."

Raleigh gave Adam a tiny smile of encouragement. Even if she thought it was a bad idea to have him on-board, it didn't help him knowing it. The mixing of Adam, a part of Grant and Able, with the Designed felt wrong, but there was little choice. Tau was right. It was the least they could do after what Adam tried to do for her. It was odd to have the two worlds muddle together. She imagined Dale would be happy to be friends with Adam once again.

Raleigh ran her hands over her dress, which was still stained with dirt. She turned to the group. "I need to get out of this dress and go to bed."

There was too much to think about, and she needed the rest

if she was going to consider any of it with a clear head. She got
cleaned up and went straight into bed.

A SERENE AND peaceful four hours later, Raleigh awoke feeling
better. Crawling out of bed she was pleasantly surprised that she
could sense Brent sleeping one room over. She headed next door to
Chi's room to let him know she was up. She said an awkward hello
to Adam and then went back to her room to brush her teeth.

Under the harsh florescent light of the bathroom, she observed
how badly her side swelled. The red would eventually give way
to a large bruise. Pressing her finger along her ribs she decided
that nothing was fractured or broken. She'd have to mask the pain
around Ilario and his men.

Tonight would again be busy. It occurred to her that some
people probably lived their lives like this—nights spent partying
and the days in bed. Hopefully, most of them didn't get abducted
and tied up. After freshening up, she returned to Chi's room. She
hated leaving Adam and him together and wondered what the two
talked about. She flopped down on the bed next to Adam.

"How are you doing?" Chi asked.

"Pretty well, considering yesterday. I watched Glen get shot,
got beaten by Dustin, and almost ended up trapped on a boat for
the rest of my life."

"Dustin is such an ass. Gabe needs to let him go. I should tell
Agatha," said Adam.

There was a pause. Raleigh wondered if Adam fully understood
his situation.

Chi didn't mince his words. "You're never going back. If that
story Tau told me is true, and Gabe overheard you offering to

break Raleigh out... this is it. You're with us from here on out. Now that you're up, Raleigh, I'm going to make that phone call to my superiors. Keep your friend company."

Adam asked, "Who are his superiors?"

"I'll let him tell you," Raleigh said. Not that she could tell him much, the Vindex Authority was still a mystery. "You shouldn't have risked coming to me last night."

"I didn't think Gabe was going to let you go. I didn't want you to end up on that boat. I was trying to help."

"It was a bad idea. The world of Lucid is much more dangerous than Grant and Able have you believing. It isn't the Designed that you need to be afraid of... at least not all of them."

"It's hard talking with Chi, pretending that he's a person. I'm worried they'll turn on you."

"Dale used to think so, too. They changed his mind. You can leave if you want. No one is forcing you to stay."

Adam looked at her arm where the port had been. Yes, there was something keeping him there, and it wasn't his friendship to her.

She rubbed her hand over her scar. "What all did you guys talk about?"

Adam rubbed the back of his neck. "Chi thinks that no one should take Lucid. He showed me his arm. His port's been out since he got off the island."

"Yeah," Raleigh said. "He's pretty passionate about no one ever taking any kind of Lucid again."

"But the healers."

Raleigh looked at Adam. "I didn't say that's how I felt."

He worked up a half-hearted smile. "It's good to see you again. Things were different after you left."

"Thanks for warning me in the club, and thanks for offering to get me out.... Even if it was stupid."

"No problem. It's going to be like old times. I always hoped we'd work together in the field. Not quite under these circumstances, but we're trained to adapt, right?"

"Right."

"Brent is Rho's dealer?"

"He's a great guy, but I think he's skeptical about Receps. So don't expect him to warm up to you right away."

"I think that'll be mutual."

There was a knock on the door. A moment later, Tau entered. "Raleigh, you're up. I didn't sense you."

"I'm barricading. At least when we're not around Ilario. But if you can sense that means that your inhibitor has worn off."

"Yeah. And yours?"

"Was gone when I woke up."

"Good," Tau said.

A noticeable shift had occurred between them since he'd given up on his conspiracies. It was clear that he was trying to be nice, but with their history it was still awkward. Adam remained quiet, most of his attention on Raleigh.

Chi came back into the room. "All right, now that both of you are up, I think we need to talk about tonight."

There would be no time for her to recover from yesterday. She couldn't afford to wallow or overanalyze.

Tau was quick to ask, "What did we miss?"

"While you were gone, we spoke with Rubio. Nothing too deep, but it's clear that Ilario trusts him. From the way Rubio spoke, it sounds like most of the time he's trying to tone down Ilario, keep him from making rash decisions. Of the two of them, he's going to be easier to work with. He's level-headed."

"It could all be an act," Raleigh said. Sigma was one of the calmest people she knew and by far the most sinister.

"That's true," Chi said. "But I still think it's the way to go, and Brent agrees."

Tau said, "Great, we'll buddy up to Rubio. I'm not dying to know Ilario. So we're set."

Brent was up and joined them. "Are you meeting without me?"

"I was filling them in on how Rubio is our in," Chi said.

"Great. Raleigh, Tau, can I see you in the other room for a minute?" Brent asked.

Raleigh stood up, and Tau followed her into the other room. Raleigh could guess why Brent didn't want to speak in the other room. She knew he was going to complain about Adam staying with them.

She put a hand on Brent's arm. "I think you need to give Adam a chance."

"Probably, but this isn't about Adam. The two of you have to start to look and act like a couple."

"Yes, obviously," Tau said.

Brent leaned back on his heels. "Well great, because back there I was bowled over by your chemistry. If you act like that tonight, there's no way anyone is going to believe you snuck off last night to be together. Fix it." He motioned for them to get closer.

Mortification danced across her cheeks. "Like now? But it's for show, and Ilario isn't here."

"You practiced being a socialite for a week. I'm guessing, from what I've seen, that you aren't experienced with this sort of thing."

There was no denying that. Raleigh looked at Tau. How experienced with dating was he? They hadn't really gotten that far in any of their conversations, probably because they were yet to have many.

Brent clapped his hands once. "Well, this is nice and awkward. I'm going to go. You work it out."

With that, Brent left them alone.

Tau rubbed the back of his neck, not making eye contact with her. This was going to be difficult all around. Raleigh was used to giving Tau his space. Now it felt invasive to enter it.

She struck up a conversation. "Have you ever had a girlfriend?"

"*Girlfriend* isn't the right word. With the hiding, short-term flings were as serious as it got. Have you ever had a boyfriend?"

Raleigh shook her head. "I was pretty sick before my trip to Belgium. I spent more time in doctor's offices than on dates."

"Besides Rho, who have you kissed? Anyone?"

"A few guys in high school. And Marcel."

His eyes widened.

"I had to prove I made Lucid. It wasn't this trip."

Tau took a step closer to her. This was the most awkward she had ever felt about a potential kiss which was saying something considering the last one had been with Rho. Would their lips taste the same with the Lucid?

"You're thinking about Rho?"

"Yeah."

"Me, too. I'm thinking about how pissed he's going to be at me if I kiss you."

"Rho and I aren't dating, and it's not like this will mean anything, right?"

"No, it won't mean anything."

"Then I guess it doesn't matter." But who was she trying to kid? It felt like the sort of thing that would matter. It was the sort of thing a person couldn't take back. There was also the strong possibility that she was going to be bad at it. The other kisses had been either one-sided or so uncomfortable she'd tried to forget them.

Tau kissed her. It was a chaste, small kiss. His lips were smooth despite the hit they'd taken the night before. When he pulled back, she wondered if he was upset about this new development for their cover.

"This might be more believable if you kiss me back."

"Right."

Raleigh kissed him, making sure she put her hand on the back of his neck. The kisses had a staged quality to them, and she wasn't a good actor. How convinced would Ilario be? Two kisses down and no sparks. Brent was wrong. Picturing Rho wasn't helping. Thinking about the kiss they shared only cemented that this was the last thing she could pull off. They stood awkwardly looking at each other.

Tau finally said, "Right. I'm going to be in charge of this. Okay?"

Wasn't he already? "Okay."

His fingers slid around her neck as he tipped her chin up so he could see her face better. Raleigh's lips tingled in anticipation as he slowly lowered his mouth down to hers. This time the kiss was not chaste. Tongues swirled, and their Lucid mingled. Raleigh's stomach dropped as her legs went weak, her hands reached up to his shoulders to keep from falling. As her fingers gripped him, his hands slid down to her hips so he could better lift her to him. Her skin beneath his fingers was sensitive and alive. They broke momentarily for a breath, and he began kissing her neck. A groan escaped her.

Tau abruptly stopped at the sound, snapping Raleigh's brain back into place. This was for show. Not a real make out session. Tau paused, his lips hovering over the junction where her jawbone touched her neck. Raleigh wanted to lean in, to feel the sensation again but didn't. When he moved away, she stepped back.

Raleigh consciously slowed her heart. What was she doing? Not acting. That was for sure. In the heat of the moment, there'd been nothing false about how much she liked him. The attraction wasn't returned—her mind was quick to remind her body. There was a war inside her, the skin of her lips and jaw eager to go back while her brain put on the brakes.

Finally, Tau said, "I think we'll pull it off fine. I'm going to get something to eat. I'm starving. You should eat, too."

She found her voice. "Yeah. You go. I'll be right out."

Tau walked over to the door, turned the handle, and hesitated. "Don't let me cross any lines that you aren't comfortable with."

"I won't."

Did Tau think that they'd crossed some line? Or perhaps only she had? Maybe he could tell that somewhere in the middle of all that it was what she wanted.

He gave her a long, indiscernible look before leaving. At least Raleigh would have no problem behaving like she was into him. That was one silver lining. Straightening up, she left the room hoping she didn't look flustered.

CHAPTER
19

AFTER EATING LUNCH, they were on their way to meet up with Ilario. They'd given Adam strict instructions that he wasn't to leave the room or contact anyone.

"Do you think we can leave him alone?" Raleigh asked as they walked to the car from the inn.

"Yes," Chi said as he took the front seat along with Brent.

Tau and Raleigh were in the back. She was acutely aware of the mere inches that separated them.

Raleigh stared at the second story of the inn, seeing Adam's shadow behind a lace curtain. "He still thinks you and Tau are evil. There's nothing to keep him from turning on you."

"Yes, there is." Brent started up the car and pulling out of the spot. "It's the same reason that Collin could never leave Rho. The Lucid will keep him here. Now that he's burned his bridges with Grant and Able, he's dependent on us."

Raleigh sighed. "That isn't good."

"No, it's not," Chi agreed. "But that's how Grant and Able keep control of their men. They use the Lucid to bolster loyalty. Adam will need to have his supply and that will come from us... for now."

Raleigh hated what had happened to Adam, what Grant and Able had done to him. The addiction was impossible to ignore. All the Receps at Grant and Able were worse off since she broke out Mu and Tau. She hoped the main reason Adam stayed now was their friendship.

"How long till we get there?" Tau asked Brent.

"A half hour. I'm shocked he told us the location so quickly."

"The warehouse?" Raleigh asked.

Earlier that morning, Ilario had told them to meet up at the lab, taking them by surprise.

"Yeah." Brent nodded. "He's immersing us in his business pretty quickly. I wasn't expecting that."

"Probably because if things go south, he's planning on killing us," Tau added.

Chi strummed his fingers on the car door. "He may need us in the lab since he killed Glen. I get the impression that Ilario did the sales and Glen oversaw the production."

"I hope he needs us," Brent said. "Because the moment he doesn't, we're dead."

Chi turned around to look at Raleigh and Tau in the back. "Remember that you two are a couple now. Can you numb the pain in your side? I don't know if we'll be able to explain those bruises."

Raleigh sat back and dulled her aching ribs. She was lucky that Dustin avoided her face. The shadow of a bruise along Tau's jaw was hidden by a day's worth of stubble.

The directions led them to a two-story warehouse in the country. It was industrial, in an agricultural way. She half-expected to find farm equipment. Weeds ran up the sides of the old brick building, and the parking lot had a few scattered cars.

Ilario leaned up against one of the larger cars, watching them arrive. He smoked a cigarette that he stomped out as they approached. Rubio stood beside him on the phone, ending his conversation when he saw them.

Ilario stepped forward as they arrived. "Good to see you again."

Tau clasped his hand hard as they said their welcomes. "I'm sorry to have cut out last night."

Ilario grinned. "Yes, well, *cut out* anytime you need." His eyes went to Raleigh. He studied her as if she was one of the women from his club, his smile implying that he imagined what might've gone down the night before.

It only made her hate him more. Her cheeks flushed, which prompted his smile to widen.

"These are the labs," Rubio said. "Come, we'll give you a tour."

Ilario's keys clanked together as he walked to the door. "Most of the workers don't speak English, sorry. They're also very upset by Glen's death. Best to keep out of their way."

Raleigh wondered if any of them knew the politics behind Glen's demise or even that he'd been murdered. They were ushered inside, and the pressure of a hand slid down the small of her back, resting inches from her bottom. Turning, she dreaded that perhaps it was Ilario or Rubio. Instead, she found Tau. She slid closer to him and smelled the soap from his shower lingering on his clothes.

"This is the second-half of production," Ilario said. "The first is the mix done in a German lab. Then it's delivered here by truck, and we complete the drug. We forbid any communication between the two plants. The people here don't even know what they're working on. It calms our fears that someone will steal our formula."

Raleigh walked over and looked at the chemistry equipment. "What do they think they're making?"

"An illegal pharmaceutical. As you can see, we have about fifty employees. Weekly, we produce around eight hundred vials. This is what Glen was working on." Ilario held up a sheet of small squares. Tearing one from the sheet, he popped it into his mouth. He took a second and held it out towards Raleigh. "Open your mouth."

Raleigh did, and Tau's hand tightened on her hip as Ilario placed the square in her mouth. The synthetic. Its ragged, unruly behavior slid through her.

She managed a smile. "Could I take one for later?"

"Yes, of course." He pulled off two more squares and handed them to her. "Anyone else?"

Brent stepped forward and took one off the sheet and dissolved it in his mouth. "This is a hell of a lot better than a needle."

Pleased, Ilario said, "Glen was good for something."

Raleigh slid back into Tau. Her heart raced on the Lucid, and her head swam. Her eyes curiously found Rubio was studying her. She tried to act normal but had a hard time with the synthetic jumping around her system.

"Sweetheart, do you need to sit down?" Tau asked.

It took Raleigh a beat to realize he was talking to her.

Ilario looked over. "Is this part of her condition? I thought that the Lucid helped."

Tau nodded. His arm was still looped around her mid-section. "The Lucid lets her control it better. But I think she might be over-correcting."

"I'm fine," Raleigh assured Tau. The words barely came out.

"So what do you think of the lab?" Ilario asked.

Chi nodded. "Very good. Now we just need to see if we can't set up another one in China. How's your Mandarin, Brent?"

"Not good. But we'll figure out something," Brent said.

He walked over near the door where boxes sat. The top box was open, and inside were sheets of the synthetic ready to be rolled out. Raleigh hoped that they ended Ilario and his brand before it ever reached the market. Most people shied away from needles, and the dissolvable form was a dangerous breakthrough.

It was five o'clock, and the workers packed their bags. Raleigh wondered if it seemed like a normal job to them or if they suspected it was something more.

"When can your scientists get here?" Ilario asked.

Chi studied the room. "We could have our lead scientist here in a week."

"A week it is."

Rubio rubbed his hands together. "We're going to gather our dealers. We'll let them try some of the Lucid you have. That way they'll know what they're selling. Then we'll have you speak with your scientists. They should break down the production so that half of it can be done in each of the facilities. We figure it will take a few weeks to get it up and running."

"You think it will be ready that soon?" Raleigh asked.

Ilario lifted his chin and surveyed the plant. "Yes. That's why you partnered with us, isn't it? Speed?"

Raleigh watched the workers put on their jackets. With their aching joints and strained eyes, she knew they put in long days. They moved efficiently and probably worked the same.

Raleigh said, "Yeah, I'm just surprised it's that fast. It's good."

"I'll see you in two days. That's how long it will take to collect my dealers," Ilario said. "If you need anything before then, call Rubio."

Rubio shook their hands, and they got in the car. A few weeks. Raleigh thought the whole deal would take months to arrange. This was going faster than she expected—or liked.

THEY FINALLY HAD some downtime to relax. After the last thirty-six hours Raleigh needed the break. Hopefully, by the time Ilario returned, she'd be more composed.

On the way home they decided to pick up Adam from the inn and get some dinner. Her stomach grumbled, upset with the inconsistent small meals. All of them were in need of a good meal. Brent and Tau stayed in the car while Raleigh and Chi went to fetch Adam.

Raleigh knocked on Chi's door before opening it. Adam was sitting on a chair near the window, looking out. His legs were curled up underneath him like a cat and his eyes were wide—his pupils dilated in the dim light. Sweat clung to his neck, and she could feel heat running along his collar.

"You're sick." Raleigh walked over and pressed the inside of her wrist up to his forehead. The beads of sweat rolled onto her skin. Suddenly, dinner wasn't important. He lacked a temperature, but she could sense his muscles aching. "What's wrong?"

"Withdrawal."

"But you had some yesterday. Didn't you?" Raleigh expected Gabe to keep his men stocked.

Adam shook his head. "We were running low. Only a couple times a week for any of us. The healers need it more than we do. Now we usually get a mix of the Designed stock and synthetic."

"Chi, when will we have the stuff Rho is sending?" Raleigh asked.

"Tomorrow. Or later. Italian's aren't known for their promptness with mail."

Raleigh rubbed her arm. If only she had an extraction machine. Touching her lips, she remembered Tau's Lucid-tinged kiss. It was a considerably smaller amount than a vial, not a good solution, and she didn't want to kiss Adam. She pulled the synthetic squares from her pocket.

"That will stop his body from feeling crummy, but it will only worsen his addiction," Chi warned.

"This is just to hold him until the real stuff gets here." She stared at the square in her hand. "Adam, put this under your tongue."

Adam did it without hesitating. "It's the synthetic," he said a moment later. "An oral dose?"

"Yeah."

Adam sat down on the bed. "This isn't very good."

"No, it isn't." Raleigh hated to be putting Adam on this path. Hopefully, Rho's stuff would make it here soon.

Chi said, "Tau and Brent are in the car. We were thinking of getting dinner. Are you game?"

"Yeah," Adam said, standing. "You aren't meeting up with Ilario tonight, are you?"

"No. He's organizing his dealers," Chi explained. "I saw a pizzeria down the street."

"Sounds good." Adam followed Chi, and the three went down the steps.

Chi frowned as they reached the parking lot. "Didn't we see that blue car earlier?"

Raleigh turned her head. "What car?"

Chi's eyes looked down the road. "I keep seeing the same car. It was here yesterday, too. And this morning."

They got into the vehicle, and Chi voiced his concern about the car to the others.

"Maybe someone who lives nearby?" Tau said.

"Or Ilario's men keeping tabs on us," Brent decided. "Or worse, some of Glen's."

Chi turned toward Brent. "You have your gun, right?"

Brent nodded, studying the street. "Let's not have it come to that, though."

"I don't like the idea any better than you," Chi said. "But better to have it."

Brent put the car in gear. "Let's get dinner."

The pizzeria smelled of garlic and marinara sauce. The large wood ovens heated the building and made her think of camping. They took a large round table in the corner. Pizzas passed by them, the peak of dinnertime had arrived, and acid churned in Raleigh's starving stomach.

Brent stared down at the texts on his phone. He frowned at Raleigh. "Rho's freaking out about the Gabe thing."

Raleigh slapped the table. "You *told* him!"

"Yeah, I told him. Are you kidding? You're lucky that he was already on a flight home when you were kidnapped. Otherwise, he'd be here."

"That's why you shouldn't have told him! The last thing we need is to add more people and complicate this further."

Brent flipped his phone shut. "He's already in the States."

Chi exhaled. "Don't be too sure that he isn't going to come. He called earlier and asked me if he should come out. I told him no, but he didn't seem happy about it."

"Rho and Sigma, those are the two with the biggest bounties," Adam said. "He should stay away from Gabe."

Raleigh drew her attention away from a mushroom pizza wafting by. "Bounty?"

"Grant and Able give more Lucid to the Receps who capture them. It's an incentive."

Raleigh bristled. "And is there a bounty for me?"

Adam shook his head. "No. But we all figured that you'd be with Rho. Everything is going to shit with the Lucid shortage.

They've put a halt to training. All of us were sent out into the field to find you all."

"Have they called in more Modified because Quinn is gone, too?" Chi asked.

"I don't know," Adam said. "After what Brandon did to Dale, we don't have any access or information about them. Dale's fine, right? I hope you're taking care of him."

"Dale's fine." Raleigh looked to Brent, who nodded.

The pizzas Brent ordered came out, and they all munched quietly. Adam stared at Tau and Chi between bites. Raleigh wanted to watch them but repressed her urge. They didn't like standing out, or at least Chi didn't, and ogling them only made them grumpier.

Tau took a sip of water. "Adam, I promise you that we aren't evil. You can quit looking at me like I'm going to jump over this table and strangle you. Any friend of Raleigh's is a friend of mine."

Brent raised an eyebrow and then turned to Raleigh. Yes, her relationship with Tau had changed. Once he learned that she wasn't a double agent, he became much nicer. Or maybe it was when she could've run away with Adam but refused to leave him. Either way, it was new territory. Raleigh could handle suspicious, distant Tau. The new, kind one was a strange Tau who'd kissed her and tossed the world on its side. She watched him as he ate. Casting her eyes down to the pizza, she reminded herself that even if Adam stared, she should not.

"Who's Collin?" Adam asked. "Gabe was freaking out about him still being alive."

Brent spoke up. "He's a jerk...."

"He's a former Recep," Chi interrupted. "He flew us off the island when we escaped. Grant and Able took him for dead, but he's been traveling with Rho, kind of like a bodyguard."

"Gabe and Collin were best friends before the massacre,"

Raleigh told Adam. "I'm sure it was a shock to hear his friend was alive and upsetting to hear what he's up to."

Adam looked down at his port.

Brent said, "Yeah, that's your future. Either you learn to kick Lucid and go off and live a normal life or one of them is going to have to take you on as part of their team."

Adam looked in Raleigh's direction.

Brent snapped his fingers. "Only if we decide you're safe. I know first-hand how unstable Collin can be."

"It isn't your fault," Tau assured Adam. "I'm sure it sucks to be told that you're part of a good cause only to find that they've gotten you hooked on a drug that there isn't much of."

Adam scrunched his nose. "Yeah, I'm not sure how to feel about it. I was pissed about what happened to Dale. Then I was upset that Raleigh left. Then we had the shortage, and now I'm here feeling like crap, addicted. You always said that's what was happening to us. None of us believed you, Raleigh."

Raleigh touched his shoulder gently. "You can stay with us now, and we can work at getting you off Lucid."

Adam looked worried. "I don't think I ever want to be off it."

"We'll help you either way," Tau promised.

Raleigh opened her mouth and then shut it. Tau didn't know what life was like for Collin. He didn't see the way Collin was obsessed with Rho. Would Adam be that fanatical about her? She didn't want that for either herself or him. It wasn't a good situation.

Taking another bite of pizza, she looked at Chi. He was staring at her. His message was clear: No one should ever take Lucid. There was a very good chance he was right. They had too much to do right now with Ilario and the synthetic. Addressing Adam's addiction would have to wait. Raleigh hoped a few more weeks wouldn't do him much damage.

CHAPTER

20

THE PIZZA DINNER served as a refreshing break from the troubled last few days. Adam was in better shape with the synthetic, and morale was noticeably improved. With a full stomach, Raleigh looked forward to bed. The nap earlier had been a poor substitute for missing sleep the night before. Nothing needed to be done tomorrow, and she stopped herself from thinking beyond that.

Climbing the inn's steps behind the guys, she stopped short before the landing. She grasped Brent's arm, halting him.

"There are people up there."

"I sense them, too," Tau said.

"Other guests?" Adam asked.

Chi reached back his hand. "We've booked all the rooms on that floor. Brent, give me your gun."

"Why do you need it?" Brent said. "Can't you do much worse?"

"I've seen the video," Adam added. "There's a reason people are worried about messing with you."

Chi shook his head. "We need to keep our cover. Only influence if it's life or death. Do you understand me? We'll go up and pretend we don't know they're there."

Right, it was unlikely the intruders were common thieves. If they were being robbed, it was probably because of their dealings with the synthetic. They couldn't blow their cover. Her mind wandered back to the night before when the inhibitor robbed her of influencing. It'd been humbling and scary. Those emotions twisted Brent's stomach now. Chi hid the gun. They all walked up the steps. Tau stood near Brent. Adam's shoulders rolled back, preparing to fight. Slowly, they moved onto the landing.

Chi motioned his head to their doors. "I'm going to turn in for the night." His voice was warm, his tone conveying none of the tension they felt.

"Me, too." Brent walked over to his door and took a deep breath. His eyes looked to Raleigh.

She shook her head. The intruders weren't in his room. Frighteningly, they were in hers.

"Good night," Raleigh said.

"Here." Tau put his hand on the small of her back. "I'll keep you company."

"That's one way to put it." She tried to sound flirtatious but knew the joke didn't reach her eyes.

Sensing, she knew the men were on the far side of her room, near the bed. For a moment her stomach flipped at the thought that this might be more sinister than a robbery. As far as she could tell, they didn't have guns, only cold weighted sticks that could be weapons but were more likely flashlights. As she slid her key over the reader, she heard the click of the lock release and felt the two men go still. Opening the door she tried to seem casual, her mind focusing on their hands as they came barreling out. Hurtling past, they shoved her violently out of the way. Tau caught her before she hit the ground.

"Hey!" he hollered after them, but with Raleigh in his arms he was unable to chase them.

Adam and Chi sprang into action, shouting and chasing the duo down the stairs. Tau's hands remained on Raleigh's sides longer than necessary. The danger was gone, but the adrenaline still revved her nerves.

"Why didn't you chase them?" Raleigh asked Tau.

"Because my cover is pretending to be your boyfriend." He released her and stepped into the room.

The suitcase was overturned on the floor and her toiletries toppled haphazardly off the night table. If they weren't undercover, they would've called the police, but they couldn't risk it now.

Brent strode in. "My room's been trashed. Those assholes were looking for something."

"Anything taken?" Tau asked.

Brent shook his head. "Not that I could tell. I bet they were looking for the Lucid formula."

Raleigh looked at her pair of diamond earrings on the bedside table. She lifted them up and let the light bounce off them. "They didn't take these."

Chi and Adam ran in, both breathing heavily from the chase.

"Dammit, they got away," Chi said. "The getaway driver pulled a gun on us."

"Which we could've stopped." Out of breath, Adam kicked the wall.

Chi put his finger to his lips. "We don't know if they left anything here. We'll sweep the rooms."

A bug? Raleigh's eyes darted around the room. If she was going to hide a bug, she'd do it discreetly, and there was nothing discreet about this. Chi was right. It was better to keep their cover, but she didn't think they'd find anything. Raleigh eyed the bed. The sheets were crumpled, revealing a corner of the mattress.

"Do we think they'll be back?" she asked.

"I don't think they were here to hurt you," Tau said.

Raleigh flicked her hair over her shoulder. "I don't think they could have hurt me."

Adam wrung his hands. "Do we think it was the Ilario guy?"

Chi shook his head. "No. He wouldn't compromise the deal. Hardly anyone knows about it. I'd put my money on Glen's people."

"Adam, it's a good thing that you came with us to dinner," Brent said. "Or they would've caught you."

"I bet that's why they chose now," Tau said. "When we were all out."

Chi handed Brent the gun and said to Tau, "The receptionist wasn't at his desk. Make sure he's all right, and then see if he knows when those guys entered. I'm betting they were sly about it but best to ask. I'm going to call Rubio. Adam, help me sweep our rooms for bugs."

Everyone left Raleigh's room with the exception of Brent. The gun sat tight in his hand as he looked down at it.

"If I came back here alone, I would've been ambushed."

"They were in my room," Raleigh told him.

Brent stonily looked at her. "You know what I mean."

"You're worried."

"No shit, I'm worried. We should sweep your room." He put the gun in his back pocket and started to feel around the doorframe.

"You can sleep with me tonight," Raleigh offered.

"What a nice offer. Thanks, but I'm not so shaken that I want to sleep with my best friend's girl." His attempt a joke fell flat.

"You know what I meant. In my room it'll be safer. We'll take

Adam's cot from Chi's room, and you can sleep in here. He'll have your room."

Brent nodded. "Thanks." He still didn't look happy. Their conversation from earlier seemed more pertinent now.

"Brent, if you need to leave...."

"I'm in this because I've lost people I'm close to. They need to be stopped. Anyhow, this whole thing is resting on my shoulders. If I leave, this all falls through. Chi isn't bad, but none of you are very good with people, or I should say you might be, but Ilario is a pig, and it's a good ol' boys club."

"I'm glad you noticed."

"Of course, I noticed."

"At the club you didn't seem to be batting away any of the girls."

Brent squinted at her. "You're not jealous. You felt left out?"

"It's fine. Trust me, I've had enough happen since then that it's completely forgotten."

"Speaking of which, Tau doesn't hate you anymore."

"Apparently not, now that he knows I'm not a spy."

"Then I guess one good thing came out of the abduction."

Adam rapped on the door. "Did you find any bugs? I didn't."

"No. Check my room next," Brent said.

Adam frowned as he left.

"And something bad came out of your kidnapping, too," said Brent, nodding at the door Adam had closed behind him.

"He's not Collin."

"No, but he'll *become* a Collin." Brent helped Raleigh straighten up her things

Adam returned. "No bugs."

"Good. It's your room now. You just got upgraded," Brent tossed Adam his key. "I'm taking the cot in here."

Adam studied Raleigh's face. "Tau's back. The owner didn't see anything. He offered to call the police, but Tau told him no. Chi set up a meeting with Rubio tomorrow."

A day off from Ilario and Rubio was something she'd been happy about. Now it'd been snatched away. She supposed they had to meet and tell him what happened. They got ready for bed. Adam and Chi decided to take turns keeping watch while they slept. Raleigh didn't offer. She was too tired.

That night Brent snored lightly. At least the break-in wasn't keeping him up. It was soothing to have someone nearby, an extra set of ears. Soon, she was slumbering as well. With all that had happened, she had to get her sleep when she could.

BRENT WHISTLED A tune softly under his breath the next morning. She watched as he organized his things. Raleigh had woken up early, the meeting with Rubio causing her to sleep in fits. There was a knock on the door.

Chi entered. "I thought we could prepare for today."

Raleigh shrugged. "As long as we all tell the same story, it should be believable. We were broken into, after all."

"That's what I was thinking," Chi said. "We also need to involve Adam. If someone is keeping tabs on us, they'll wonder why he's here. That, and I think it would be a bad idea to have him stay here alone after what happened last night."

"Do you have a plan for including him?"

"We'll tell Rubio that after the break-in we decided it was best to have a bodyguard."

Raleigh could see the logic in that. Despite his addiction, Adam held himself like a solider. Grant and Able were good at molding their men into appearing composed and calculated.

"I'd believe it," Raleigh said.

Chi nodded and turned to Brent. "Can you give him your gun?"

Brent frowned. "Do we trust Adam? He thinks you and Tau are devils, and he's brainwashed into thinking Grant and Able are great."

Chi scrunched his nose. "We're giving him synthetic Lucid. That's more dangerous than this gun. Even if he can't influence as well as us, he can do it. And a bodyguard would be carrying."

Everything to keep up the cover. Raleigh didn't need Chi to give them the lecture again and was happy when he refrained.

"Does Adam know how to use it?" Raleigh asked. None of her Recep classes included guns.

Chi nodded. "After the last showdown, Gabe insisted they all learn. Adam claims that he's one of the better shots."

Raleigh's stomach flipped. The motivation behind Adam and the others learning was so they could shoot her and the Designed if it came to that. Grant and Able surely couldn't consider their Receps to be anything besides an army.

Brent's furrowed brow meant that he was considering all the ramifications of arming the Receps. "I'm guessing that Adam prefers influencing to a gun. How good a Recep is he?"

"He's in the ninety-seventh percentile." Raleigh knew all the Receps' percentiles. It was still odd to think about what a big deal they made of it during training. "He was able to influence. Not great, but he could. Although it might be harder on the synthetic."

"I'll give him one of your vials to keep on him," Chi said. "He can take it if trouble arises."

"You don't think he'll take it before it's time?" Brent asked.

Chi looked in the direction of the door. Raleigh could feel Adam out in the hall, his nerves raw and his feet itchy.

"He's been starved of it for a while," Chi said. "Let's hope he doesn't succumb to the temptation."

"Is he comfortable being a bodyguard?" Brent asked.

"It's a role he should slip into easily enough." Chi's blue eyes studied Raleigh's face. "I'm going to have him be backup for Brent. He'll stand near both of you, but if things go south I've told him that Brent needs him more."

"Yes, of course." Raleigh planned on protecting Brent, but it didn't hurt to have a backup.

Brent didn't look reassured, but that was because he didn't know Adam as well as she did. Addict or not, he was still a moral guy trained as a fighter, and she had confidence that he would do all he could to protect Brent—if for no other reason than he was friends with her.

Hopefully he wouldn't be tested.

WITH ADAM'S NEW cover agreed upon, they went to Rome. They parked on the street outside the restaurant where they were meeting Rubio. Chi reviewed the rules. Raleigh began to think that he couldn't go on a mission without verbally reiterating the plan. It annoyed her, or maybe it was her frazzled nerves seeking an outlet for their jumpiness.

Chi held open the large doors so they could enter the restaurant. "Adam, don't talk unless a direct question is posed. Blend into the walls."

"I can do that." Adam's expression was severe, with dark patches under his eyes. The decreased supply of Lucid over the last month hadn't been kind to him. He looked harsher than when he and Raleigh first met.

Raleigh marveled at the gaudiness of the hotel. It was a large, ritzy place with a restaurant hosting mostly businessmen. Its best attribute was how busy it was. Raleigh was thankful to be meeting Rubio in such a public place after the rattling event last night.

The hostess escorted them to a large booth that looped around the back corner. Rubio was already there, sipping a cup of espresso.

"Good to see you again," Chi said stiffly as they sat down.

"You've brought a friend." Rubio's eyes studied Adam.

"I've brought protection," Raleigh said. "Last night our rooms at the inn were broken into."

Rubio's face wore an expression of concern and trouble. "That's what Chi told me last night. Were any of you harmed?"

Raleigh let her worries seep into her voice. "No. They fled when we arrived. We think they were trying to steal our Lucid."

Rubio nodded towards Adam. "I'm very sorry to hear that. I can understand your need for defense."

Raleigh guessed that most people who worked with Ilario brought protection. For a fleeting moment, she considered that they should've had someone sooner, for appearances. Ilario probably thought them naïve. But maybe that was part of the reason he took them on as partners.

"It wasn't your men?" Chi asked bluntly.

Rubio held up his hands. "No, I promise you. Why would we? Ilario said that your lab only managed to make around sixty vials. We'd rather have your help in producing more than stealing that paltry amount."

"That's what we thought, too" Brent said. "So, who do we think it was?"

"We have competition up north. In Normandy."

Raleigh glanced at Tau. They didn't think it was the Normandy sellers. They would've kidnapped Chi or Tau before they tried for what was assumed to be a new synthetic. Plus, their style was more violent.

"You think your competition is aware of us?" Brent asked. "So soon?"

Rubio shook his head. "No. You're right. You've been here too short a time. It could very well be Glen's people. The workers don't know what Lucid is for, but a few of the scientists do. They've been furious about his death. Most of them wanted out. But without the synthetic formula, they'd be without jobs."

"So they tried to steal ours?" Brent reasoned.

"You assume they were after the Lucid. But if you're a scientist, you'd be after the formula to make it so you could cut us out. Cut you out."

Rubio was Ilario's right-hand man for a reason. They'd pieced together that it was more than the Lucid.

Raleigh shifted in her seat. "It isn't our fault Glen's dead. I'm still not sure why we didn't include him in this deal."

Rubio gave Brent an amused smile. "You explain to her why."

Brent turned to Raleigh. "Glen's death is how Ilario proved his commitment to us."

"It's like lovers." Rubio's grin widened. "A man might have a wife when a younger, sexier woman catches his eye. He'll leave the wife for the girl. This will create an enemy of the wife's family. They will blame the girl for seducing him away."

"But in that scenario, as it is in ours, the man that left is to blame. It's not the girl's fault. He was the one who was committed," Raleigh told Rubio.

Rubio winked at Tau. "Your woman is progressive and naïve to the nature of people. Raleigh, no one really cares who is at fault. The mistress is blamed. Much like Glen's people will find you at fault for the death of their boss."

"Are we in danger?" Chi asked.

Rubio sat back. "Hiring a bodyguard is a wise idea. The inn

isn't secure. You need cameras and locks. We'll put you up in Ilario's house. It's large. He'll welcome having you as guests after this incident. That way, he'll be able to keep both you and his investment in your Lucid safe."

"That's generous," Chi said.

Raleigh could think of another word. *Creepy.* Visiting Ilario's house made her distressed. She didn't want to spend the night there.

Delicately she shook her head and put up her hand. "I'm not sure we should impose."

"It's no imposition," Rubio assured them. "He'll be overjoyed to have you. He's quite proud of his home and far too many of the rooms sit vacant."

"We'll take you up on the offer. Thank you for your generosity." Chi made the decision without looking to the others. If he had, he might've caught the dread in Raleigh's eyes.

21

THEY LEFT THE breakfast with Rubio. Brent sat behind the wheel with Chi in the front passenger seat beside him. In the back Adam sat behind Brent, Raleigh next to him, and Tau on her other side. With her short legs, it made the most sense to have her in the middle, and, from this vantage point, she could talk with everyone in the car.

"You're insane, Chi!" Raleigh burst out the moment the car got a safe distance away from the restaurant.

Chi's lips bowed downward. "I know. But the inn is no longer safe. If it was Glen's people, we don't know that they won't be violent next time."

"So we're going to stay in the house of a madman!" Raleigh reeled. If an hour-long luncheon had ended so poorly, what would happen with a day long stay?

Brent said, "I see where Chi's coming from with this decision. This shows solidarity with Rubio and Ilario. It also demonstrates their trust in us, by inviting us into their home. But hell. It's going to be awful."

"That's an understatement. My skin is crawling." Raleigh clenched and unclenched her fists.

"I could stay with you if you'd feel safer," Adam offered. "You could play up the vulnerable girl angle."

Raleigh didn't like that anyone would think there was a vulnerable girl angle. She resisted the urge to tell him off.

Tau stepped in. "I'm going to share a room with her. It makes sense. We are an item now, at least in their eyes."

"Raleigh?" Chi asked. "Is that cool with you?"

It was one thing to share a room with Brent who felt like a brother. She and Tau had only recently put the past behind them. Now they were being tossed in together, and she didn't know what to expect. None of these things she was willing to admit.

She turned to Tau trying not think of their kiss. There was nothing romantic about Ilario's. "I'm fine with Tau. But I still think we should get out of staying at Ilario's. You remember that he shot a man in his dining room, right?"

Chi nodded. "To him, it was a demonstration of loyalty. Us going there will be a show of trust. As much as I hate it, it's not like we're safe at the inn. We'll go ahead with the move. Brent, call Rho one last time. We'll have to assume that Ilario is aware of everything we do while we're there."

"We should assume that he's keeping tabs on us everywhere," Brent said. "But yeah, I'll text Rho and tell him that we're going silent for the next week."

The knot in Raleigh's chest loosened. "You really think it'll only be a week?"

Brent nodded. "Ilario's rounding up his dealers. We'll meet them tomorrow. We'll claim to be contacting our scientists, then we'll act."

Chi nodded. "We could take down the labs if we needed, too. The Vindex Authority has been monitoring the lab and followed a van coming from there yesterday. They went to Germany. We have the second location."

"Do we just take them down now?" Raleigh asked. If they took out the labs, then production would end, and the Normandy synthetic could track down Ilario and Rubio.

Chi shook his head. "It would be better to get the high dealers. It's worth the risk. Keep in mind that even if Ilario is dangerous, we have influencing at our disposal."

"Can Ilario influence?" Adam asked.

"Most people don't know what it is. He can definitely sense, and he's addicted. But I don't know his full capabilities."

"On the synthetic, he won't be as strong," Raleigh reminded Adam. "You can't use it as well as the other stuff."

Adam rubbed an anxious hand across his neck. "No, you can't. It's crap."

Chi pulled the vial of Raleigh's Lucid from his pocket. "We decided you should have this in the event of an emergency and only then. It's Raleigh's, not ours. So it will feel a bit different."

Adam put the small clear vial in his pocket, and his eyes met Raleigh's. She could tell by his hesitation that he only wanted to protect her, that he didn't care much for the other guys. At least he wasn't having to guard one of the Designed. But he clearly didn't want to put himself on the line for Brent.

Raleigh touched his arm. "We're all in this together. If things go wrong, get Brent out."

"Sure. If that's what you want," Adam's hand covered hers.

The muscles in his fingers were taut with the withdrawal. Raleigh wondered how much of his loyalty came from the want of Lucid and how much was due to the friendship they forged during training. This wasn't the carefree boy she used to go running with.

"Get packed," Chi said as Brent pulled into the parking lot. "Let's try to be to Ilario's in an hour."

RALEIGH STEPPED INTO Ilario's house with trepidation. The house had touches of its owner everywhere. Ilario may have been gone, but his presence remained.

"We have two rooms here." Rubio said graciously as they walked up the steps. The first room was large with a four poster bed. Rubio held the door open for Raleigh. "This is your room."

"I'll share with her, if you don't mind," Tau said, rolling both her and his suitcases inside.

"No, of course, I don't mind." Rubio smiled at Raleigh and winked at Tau. "Chi will be across the hall. I'll show him to his room while you get settled."

Raleigh stood in the middle of the room fiddling with the zipper on her jacket as she looked around. Nudes hung on the walls, women were put on display. Ilario clearly had no problem objectifying them.

"It's an interesting room." Tau lifted her suitcase onto the trunk at the end of the bed.

Raleigh could guess that Tau, too, had been objectified, probably more often than her. So, she didn't complain about the art.

The bed took up a large chunk of the room. Raleigh ran her hand along the comforter. The fabric was thick beneath her fingers. The last time they were alone they'd tested how feasible they could seem as a couple, a memory that she reflected on more and more often. Tonight they'd be sharing a bed. There was always the chance of hidden cameras. Her eyes looked around the perimeter of the room.

"You think we're being watched?" Tau asked.

Raleigh shrugged. "I don't know."

Tau walked over and whispered in her ear. "It's going to be fine. Ilario is a bit creepy, but who videos a bedroom? Even so, we'll be just believable enough without crossing any lines. I'll make sure I sweep for cameras and bugs before we go to bed. Smile like I've whispered something naughty."

Raleigh tilted the corner of her lip. Tau moved closer to her, brushing her ribs. She pulled back.

He retracted his hand swiftly. "Sorry."

"No. It's the bruises," she explained.

Tau turned her and put his hand on the edge of her shirt. Raleigh expected him to look, but he paused.

"Is this all right?" he asked.

"Yeah."

He lifted the edge of her shirt just high enough to see the blossoming bruises underneath.

He put the shirt back down. "Ouch. Those look bad. Have you tried to fix it?"

"I numb the pain, but it's hard to do all the time."

"Could I try something?"

Raleigh nodded. "Fine, but besides numbing it I'm not sure there's much you can do."

"I'm going to see if I can help with the inflammation. I promise you it won't hurt."

"All right."

Tau concentrated. Whatever he was doing was subtle enough that she couldn't discern it. With each breath her side ached and got worse instead of better. His promise of no pain remained empty.

She started to protest, and then the pain abruptly stopped. A warm joy slipped through her veins. Euphoria. Not the artificial kind drudged up by narcotics. But the natural kind that rose up from too much laughing or a good run. The happiness glided through her, distracting her from her side and anything else.

"I think that will help with the bruising." Tau stepped back.

"What did you do? I feel...." She tried to summon the right word. Content? Secure? Amazing?

"I played with your endorphins. I thought it would take away some of the pain. Better to get rid of it then mask it. Right?"

"Yeah. I've just never thought to do that."

"Moods are just chemical equations. It's hard, but you can learn to influence neurotransmitters if you try."

"It sounds difficult."

"You'll be able."

Raleigh stood agog at his skills. When she thought of influencing, she thought of major changes. This was a small tweak but effective. Tau had stumbled onto something. He understood parts of the body that she hadn't been paying enough attention to.

"You're brilliant," she said. Intelligence was a Designed trait, but he was observant in ways she hadn't considered.

Tau wasn't good at taking compliments and diverted his eyes to the ground. "I'm sorry that I didn't stop Dustin sooner. I should've followed you right away, not taken the time to text Chi. It won't happen again." His eyes flicked up to hers, begging for forgiveness.

It may've been the endorphins, or the butterflies that tickled her stomach, or the weakness that remained in her knees from the day before, but she was at a loss for words.

There was a rough pounding on the door. She jumped a little, remembering where they were. It wasn't safe here. Tau wasn't surprised. He walked over and opened it.

"I'm at the end of the hall." Brent walked in. He casually stood in the room, as if unaware of what he'd interrupted.

Was there anything to interrupt? Subdued, Raleigh reveled in the warmth.

Tau nodded. "Good, this place is big, and I'd rather us all be close together."

Brent stared at the doorway. "I was going to go for a walk. Thought you guys might like to stretch your legs."

"Who all's going?" Tau asked.

"Adam and me. Chi's going to hang out and read a book," Brent said.

Raleigh guessed that Chi's intention would be to keep his attention on Rubio. This was a hypothesis she didn't need to voice.

"Raleigh can go, but I don't want to leave Chi here alone," Tau said. "And I have to sweep the room."

Brent looked at Raleigh. "What do you say?"

Raleigh looked over her shoulder at Tau, the endorphins bathing her in their blissful feeling. She wanted to stay with Tau, but she also didn't want to be in Ilario's house.

"Let me change out of these heels, and I'll join you," she said. While she changed out of the shoes, she tried her best not to think about Tau, endorphins, or the feelings that were threatening to bubble up in her.

They stepped out of the house with the intent of walking through the vineyards. They took off at a brisk pace, enjoying the fresh air. All the foliage was preparing for the winter. The grapevines were planted in narrow rows that rose and dipped with the gently rolling hills. She could imagine how much fun it would've been to play in them when she was younger.

Adam hung back ten paces, his expression blank and his lips pressed in a thin line. With the mud on her feet, Raleigh was reminded of her time at Grant and Able running through the Arizona desert with the red dirt sticking to her legs. Adam was more carefree then. Being a bodyguard was part of his cover, but some of his severity came from his addiction. Thoughts fluttered through her head, her heart light. As her feet bounced down the trail, nothing felt insurmountable. She began skipping through the mud that marred their path.

"Am I missing something?" Brent asked.

"I like walks."

"So do I. But I'm not ecstatic about them. Especially if you consider where we're walking."

"Tau fiddled with my endorphins."

"Is that a euphemism for something? Because I've never heard it called that."

"My side hurt so he helped dull the pain by causing me to release endorphins." Raleigh's stopped skipping, but her arms still swung loosely at her sides.

"I didn't know you could do that. Rho never has."

"I'm not sure I could. Tau is amazing."

Brent stopped, raising an eyebrow. "Tau is *amazing?* Are you sure those are the only things he messed with? Maybe he's affecting your hormones, too."

"He wouldn't need influencing to do *that,*" Raleigh joked.

Brent was more taken aback than entertained.

She laughed. "Really, Brent? You of all people can't take a little joke about attraction?"

Brent started walking again and glanced back at Adam. "I'm just surprised. You and Tau have been awkward as hell to be around. I thought he hated you worse than Collin does. Now you're all touchy-feely."

"That's the cover," Raleigh said.

Brent pursed his lips. "Yeah, but it's really believable. Yesterday at the warehouse I wouldn't have guessed you were acting."

"I thought you couldn't really sense."

"Some things you don't need Lucid to see."

"Well, it strengthens our story. So I'm not going to feel bad about it."

"I'm not sure you have to feel bad about it, even if it wasn't helping with the story."

"Then why do I feel like you're accusing me of something?"

"Rho."

Raleigh could tell that he was going to say something more, but he didn't have to. The name brought forward so many emotions that she knew there were many things he could've followed with.

Raleigh shook her head. "Things aren't romantic with Rho. Things aren't going to be. I know that everyone is teasing me that we're a couple already, but that isn't the case."

"Who's teasing?"

"Teasing isn't as good a word as assuming. Gamma, Dale, Upsilon, and I bet, Collin."

"Collin's been worried about you getting together since you joined us in Paris. You don't like Rho? Is it because he turned you down after the escape?"

Raleigh turned toward him, her mouth flying open. Rho told Brent? It seemed like a nasty thing to do. The rejection on its own was bad enough. It was worse if everyone knew.

"He's a jerk for telling you."

"He told me because I was laying it on thick. You know, prodding him about talking to you and telling him to ask you out. That's when he told me. He said that he messed up his chance. But it didn't seem like it on the train."

A bit of Raleigh's good mood slipped. "Rho wants to make decisions for me."

Brent chuckled. "He makes the calls for everyone. It's going to take him time to realize that if he wants you to be his girlfriend then he has to stop treating you like one of his men and like an equal instead."

It was true and advice that she herself was not particularly following. "We have a lot of things much more pressing to think about than Rho."

"That's the seriousness that I was expecting. I guess the endorphins are wearing off."

Raleigh kicked a rock as they walked between the vines. "I guess they have."

"Tonight's going to be awful."

"You're scared of staying here?" Her eyes flashed back to Adam who was far enough away to miss their conversation. "Rubio doesn't seem that bad."

"No. Rubio's a little too accommodating. This is all going way too smoothly. No hiccups."

"Someone broke into our rooms."

"And didn't hurt us or take anything. All that stunt did was get us to come here. That's the only way we would've come. It feels staged. My gut tells me something's off. Doesn't yours?"

"The whole thing is icky, but no. I guess it's felt more like we've had good luck."

Brent's face was stone. "The sooner this mission is over the better."

Raleigh felt the same. With one last tromp down the path, she prepared herself to go back inside and to wear her cover well enough that Rubio wouldn't suspect anything. At least Ilario wouldn't be there tonight.

CHAPTER
22

BY DINNERTIME, BRENT'S fears had failed to materialize. Rubio was a gracious host. They had a traditional dinner of pasta and salad. Raleigh tried to keep her attention and eyes away from the head of the table, where Glen had been murdered. No one sat in his seat, making it seem like he was still there. Rubio occupied Ilario's chair. The conversation wasn't tense or cumbersome. Only the memory of what'd transpired in the room dampened the meal.

After dinner Rubio insisted that they go swimming. The pool Ilario had installed was impressive. As he put it, it would be a waste not to use it. Raleigh went to her bedroom. The bathing suit Lilia bought for her was conservative enough to be elegant but not modest enough to cover all her bruises.

"There are no bugs or cameras, right?" she asked Tau.

"Not that I could find. Chi checked, too."

After both of them checked one more time, she was comfortable enough to inspect her side in one of the mirrors. A bruise peeked out from the low scooped back of her suit. She tugged on the green nylon hoping to hide it.

Tau walked over to her already wearing his trunks. "Rubio's going to notice that."

"If only your little tricks could help with that." She tugged harder on the suit. No luck.

Tau pressed his fingers on the border of the tender skin. "No. The capillary beds underneath have been messed up, and I'm not skilled enough to fix anything that intricate. Do you have a wrap?"

Raleigh lifted a thin emerald cloth that acted as a skirt in a pinch. "It sits low on my hips. If I edge it up that high it'll look weird."

"You'll just have to get into the water quickly and hope he's not looking at you."

"I'm not going in the water. I'll drown."

"We'll catch you."

Raleigh shook her head. "No. I don't swim, ever."

"Then just go in the Jacuzzi."

"No." Raleigh didn't tell him that back home she used to shower with the bathroom door open so her sister could hear if she fell. Fainting in water, where she could drown, was a nightmare of hers. She put on the wrap. "If he asks, I'll tell him it's because I fainted and hit myself on the way down. That causes plenty of bruising, trust me."

Tau nodded. "Ready to go?"

"Ready."

Despite not wanting to swim, Raleigh couldn't help but admit that the pool was beautiful. Slate stone brought a hit of the rugged outdoors inside, but the room was warm enough to break the illusion. The pool was kidney-shaped with blue lights illuminating the water from below.

Brent, Chi, and Rubio were already in the water. Four girls

Raleigh didn't recognize sat along the side, letting their legs dangle in the water. These weren't the same girls they'd met in the club, but they had the same air about them. They wore risqué suits that Lilia would've scoffed at. It was a relief seeing them. If something serious was meant to go down, she presumed that Rubio wouldn't invite an audience. Adam and one of Ilario's bodyguards stood against the far wall.

Tau got in the water. "Are you sure?" He playfully splashed some water on her toes. A smile lit up his face, and his blue eyes danced. "I'll keep an arm around you just in case."

It was a charming offer. She remembered how nice his hands could feel, and she knew that if he was to plaster himself to her in the pool it would strengthen their cover. With everyone else lounging in the water, she could see the appeal. But her fear of water went deeper than the need to keep her cover. She was overdue for a fainting spell.

"Not right now." Instead of getting in she walked over to the small bar and took a seat.

Tau started to lift himself out of the pool, but Rubio was faster. "I'll get her a drink. You enjoy the water."

Tau lowered himself back in, giving Raleigh a worried look that she didn't return. She didn't need Tau to babysit her. Rubio came over, wrapping a towel around himself. The water dripped off his legs, pooling at his feet as he placed liquor bottles on the counter.

They could hear the chatter from the pool without being part of the fun. Brent and Chi flirted with two girls. A third went over to Tau. He was polite but moved away so that she wasn't indecently close to him.

"She'll be mad that he's taken" Rubio handed Raleigh a drink.

Raleigh tilted the glass in the light. "I'm sure she's not disappointed often."

Rubio smiled. "You're an interesting addition to the group. The others I understand. But this is rough work for a girl."

Raleigh looked up from her glass. "It's a little more violent than we expected. Lucid in the States isn't as harsh. Most of the people who use are athletes and affluent."

"That's because it hasn't dug in its hooks. We haven't dug in our hooks. They have the higher quality product, the one you would've had."

"Yes, yours is really bad," Raleigh said honestly.

Rubio grinned and pulled up a chair. "Which is why Ilario needs you. Is he what you expected?"

"He's rash." She'd spent enough time with the guy to know that he was unhinged.

"He does what he needs to do. Tau and Chi should've left you at home."

"They might've, if they knew."

"Now it's too late, and you're losing your innocence much faster than you should."

"Just as long as I don't lose my life."

Rubio strummed his fingers on the marble counter. "I've never been good at business. I'm not as persuasive as Ilario or Brent. I'm better at being decisive and observant. Do you know what I've seen since you got here?"

The bruises along her side? She shook her head. "What?"

"That your group is the complete package. Tau and Chi are level-headed, you're reassuring, and Brent is a salesman. You were right when you said you needed us for our network and our warehouses. You have everything else."

"We do need the warehouses."

"But Ilario and the warehouses aren't the same thing."

"What do you mean?"

Rubio's brown eyes pierced hers, his words leaving no room for interpretation. "I needed Ilario before. But now, with you, he isn't necessary. I know enough of his business that we could continue without him."

Raleigh gulped down her surprise. "You think he'd leave?"

"No. I want you to kill him."

"What?"

Rubio grinned. "Not you. Your boyfriend. Or Chi. The thing is that Ilario is controlling, and one day he'll kill all of us. The money and power have brought out the worst in him. The dealers are edgy. Glen's death has proved that he will kill anyone. We need a coup."

"Why does it have to be us? Why don't you do it?"

"Like I said, I'm better at the day-to-day operations. I'm not the person who could run this. I'd be toppled. Chi and Tau, they could command Ilario's men."

This was the problem Brent worried they'd step into. Rubio made things so easy so he could have them take out his boss. Raleigh took a long swig of her drink and looked at the guys in the water. Tau gazed at her, a small smile crossing his lips, asking if she was okay. Raleigh didn't return the look. Dread prevented her.

"Tomorrow will be the time," Rubio said. "During the meeting, the higher dealers will pledge loyalty to you, or they will die."

"And what if we choose not to? If we choose to keep Ilario running things?"

"Then you've chosen to keep him as a partner, and you'll be a casualty of his brashness one day."

Tau hopped out of the water, walking over to her. "You look unwell." He put a hand on her shoulder. "Are you going to have an episode?"

Raleigh shook her head.

Rubio said, "We were just talking. Let me know if you agree

tomorrow morning, Raleigh." He swigged down the rest of his drink and headed to the water, diving in from the side.

The girls giggled loudly, their laughs echoing through the long room.

Raleigh looked up at Tau.

"What did he say?" Tau asked.

"We should talk with the others." This wasn't the place. She mulled over Rubio's plan to assassinate Ilario. He was right. Ilario was a wild card. If this wasn't a plot to overthrow the synthetic, they'd be jumping at the chance to kill him. It felt unnecessary to bloody their hands, considering they wanted the Normandy group to do it. But if they wanted to keep their cover, they'd have to kill him.

"I think they're busy." Tau nodded toward the pool.

Brent got out with one of the girls and headed in the direction of the bedrooms.

Raleigh could feel Tau's throat move when he swallowed. In the kitchen there was a lone cook scrubbing the dinner dishes. Raleigh could feel the sore feet of the bodyguard standing next to Adam. The bitter taste of alcohol lingered in Rubio's mouth. She could sense the slick feel of the water up against the girls' feet in the pool. The smell of chlorine conjured up a nostalgia, remembering when she was healthy and used to spend summers in the pool and sun— before she had blackouts like the one she was slipping into now.

———————

LEATHER RUBBED AGAINST her exposed back. Before she opened her eyes, she knew that she was on one of the large sofas in the lounge. Her ears worked before her tongue did, picking up on the hushed angry voices just inches away. Tau and Adam.

"What did you do to her?" accused Adam.

"Nothing," replied Tau. "She does this."

"The last time she did it was when Dustin...."

"Let's not talk about Dustin."

Adam's voice was harsh but low. "She was in trouble. I saw her face before she passed out. What did you do to her?"

"Something Rubio said upset her."

"Shouldn't you have stepped in? Isn't that the reason you two are so touchy-feely? What good are you as a boyfriend if you let her get harassed?"

"I can't monitor her every move, and I don't need to. She's the type of girl who can take care of herself."

"Which is why she should never have sided with you. If anything happens to her..."

"Don't threaten me, Adam. Remember why you're here. I was the one who told her to bring you. Don't make me regret it."

Raleigh dragged her mind into consciousness and lifted her hand to her forehead. "I'm all right. You guys can quit arguing. Adam, I faint. It's awkward, but it's the situation. It had nothing to do with Tau."

"It didn't look that way."

"I caught you this time," Tau told her. "At least you didn't get hurt."

Raleigh sat up. She had to collect herself. "Do you think Rubio could tell I had an overload?"

"No, not while he's on the synthetic. I don't think he has any vials of our stuff. He was surprised when you pitched forward. So I think it's fair to say he doesn't understand how your fainting works."

"What did Rubio say to you?" Adam asked her.

Raleigh sat up and swung her legs over the side of the couch. Her toes pressed into the wooden floors as she mustered the strength to stand. "I need to tell everyone right away. We should go upstairs. Adam, try and discreetly get all the guys to our room."

Adam stood at attention, clearly comfortable accepting orders from Raleigh. He threw her one last concerned glance before going back to the pool.

"Do you need me to carry you?" Tau asked.

"No, of course not. I'm fine now."

"Last time you lay down for a while afterwards."

Being trapped in the trunk didn't really count as a leisurely rest after passing out, an observation she didn't voice. She found her balance and headed toward the stairs. Tau's hand was on her back, guiding her. Even though it wasn't necessary, she didn't stop him. If Rubio caught sight, it would be more believable. They went up to their room. After shutting the door, Tau began to remove his trunks.

Raleigh rapidly diverted her eyes.

Tau paused. "Sorry. I figured that I shouldn't stay in these because they're wet. I can go to the bathroom to change if it makes you uncomfortable."

"No, it's fine," Raleigh said. "I'll look this way, and you can keep facing the direction you're facing." Quickly, Raleigh slid out of her suit. Since it was dry it came off easily, and she hopped into her nightgown. By the time she was dressed, Tau was, too and still facing the other way. "Done."

Before Tau could turn around or say anything, there was a knock on the door. Raleigh could sense Chi on the other side. Tau went to open it.

"Are you all right?" Chi asked Raleigh as he entered.

"Was it hard to get away?"

"No. Adam said you were embarrassed, and I told Rubio I needed to check on you. What's up?"

"We should wait for Brent," Raleigh said.

Chi looked toward the door. "He's busy."

"Adam will have to interrupt."

Brent came through the door. "Adam did interrupt me. I finally get to have a bit of fun on this trip... and Raleigh faints, and we all have to be rounded up."

"It isn't that." Raleigh looked to Adam who was nearest the entrance. "Shut the door."

"What's going on?" Brent asked.

"Rubio wants us to kill Ilario tomorrow." The words sounded as surreal as when she heard them.

"What?" Chi exclaimed.

The others muttered similar outraged expressions.

"That's what you were talking about?" Tau asked.

Raleigh braced her hand on the bed. "Yeah, he says that Ilario's unstable."

"No shit," Brent said. "He's just figuring that out now?"

Raleigh rolled her eyes at him. "No. He figured it out a while ago and said that Ilario has to be brought down, but he's not in the position to do it. Something about not being a good leader."

"Bull. He doesn't want to take the risk," Brent said.

Chi put up his hand. "No. He's supposed to be Ilario's right-hand man. If he does it, the dealers may not recognize him as the boss, but someone who took advantage of an opportunity may have a chance. If we do it, as outsiders, it will simply be us taking over his territory. Not that it's that different. The dealers might not follow us any more than him."

"He thought they would. They're scared of Ilario." Raleigh couldn't blame them, Ilario scared the crap out of her, too.

"Or that's what Rubio wants you to think." Brent slid his fingers through his hair, his gesture full of frustration. "I knew this was too easy. Now we know why. Rubio has probably been whispering in Ilario's ear what a good idea this is just so we can do his dirty work."

Raleigh didn't like how flustered Brent was getting. "We don't have to kill Ilario. We can tell Rubio no."

Chi exhaled. "No. We can't tell him no. If we don't kill Ilario, Rubio will turn him against us. Rubio won't want us around because we know he wants his boss dead."

"We could tell Ilario." Tau's voice lacked conviction.

Chi shook his head. "Rubio is right. Ilario is impossible to work with. We have to agree to this."

"I've never killed someone," Adam said quietly.

Raleigh wished that she could make the same claim. Images of the man she took the life of still haunted her. She pushed them aside. "It won't be you. Rubio wants Chi or Tau to do it."

Brent didn't seem surprised. "Because they need to inherit the power. I'm their dealer, you're their financier, and they'll run the operation with Ilario gone. Adam, you killing him isn't enough of a statement."

Adam let out the breath he was holding while Tau and Chi exchanged a worried moment. Neither one wanted to do it, but both had killed before. Leaving the island, everyone had gotten blood on their hands. The difference was that it had been in self-defense, to some extent. This killing was unprovoked.

Chi decided. "I'll do it."

Tau stared into his brother's eyes. "Are you sure?"

"This is *my* mission. You're here to take care of Raleigh and Brent."

"When will you do it?" Tau asked.

"During the meeting," Raleigh said. "That's when Rubio wants."

"You'll do it then because the dealers will see it as a show of power." Brent's tone barely contained his anger.

Chi said, "Fine, we'll do it then. I don't want you in there, Brent. This could escalate quickly, and we might all be relying on our barricades and influencing."

Brent didn't argue. "I'll take a call. I'll leave the room and run."

"Go with him, Adam," Chi ordered. "He'll need you more than we do, and who knows how strong those dealers will be with influencing. Hopefully, not at all. But we can't assume that."

Adam turned to Raleigh. "You might need me."

"I'll be there to watch her back," Tau said. "Stick with Brent."

Adam squinted at Tau. "Let Raleigh decide who she wants to have her back."

"I want Tau. Adam, Chi's right. Guard Brent and get as far as you can from here." Raleigh noticed a pang of sadness in his eyes.

Adam was her friend, and it was clear he only cared about her safety. "If that's what you want."

"It's decided then," Tau said. "Everyone get some sleep. Tomorrow's going to be a tough day."

Everyone but Raleigh and Tau left the room. Alone once again, they walked to opposite sides of the bed. She watched as he threw back the covers and climbed in. Raleigh slid into her side, leaving the middle of the bed a border between them.

She broke the heavy silence. "Do you think it will work? A lot could go wrong. The dealers could attack us."

"Rubio's going to want us to live." Tau propped his head up with one arm. "Likely he didn't act sooner because he's not as good at dealing as Ilario. I can't see him sending us to our deaths."

"I don't like trusting Rubio."

"Neither do I."

"Why not just take down the whole thing tomorrow?" Raleigh asked. "If the higher-level dealers are there, why not?"

"We need to get the warehouses. That, and if we take them down the Normandy bunch will be cautious. Chi said that with Ilario's synthetic gone they'll be less guarded. No. It needs to be them, not us. Get some rest. We have to be alert tomorrow."

Raleigh turned over and attempted to fall asleep. It was hard. Tau's warmth drifted over the patch of bed between them, reminding her that he was there. She could hear his short, normal breaths give way to the slower, longer ones of slumber. After replaying all the things that could go wrong in her head, she eventually nodded off.

CHAPTER
23

RALEIGH AWOKE TO sunbeams peeking around the corner of the curtains. The blankets were bunched around Tau as he slept with one leg exposed. She wasn't sure what she'd say to him when he woke up. So she got up, choosing to face the day.

The downstairs of the house smelled like France... like crêpes. The savory aroma of chives and onions drifted past her nose, making her stomach grumble. Down to the kitchen she went, catching sight of Ilario before she sensed him. He saw her, too. It'd be rude to go back upstairs. It looked like the two of them were going to have breakfast. A cook stood over the griddle. With a smile, Raleigh walked in.

"You're up. Hopefully your stay here last night was restful." Ilario motioned toward one of the empty wooden chairs at the table.

Unlike the one in the dining room, this table's worn wood wasn't pretentious. The age made her think it was an antique. It didn't look like the type of furniture he would own, and she guessed it had come with the house.

Raleigh tucked her hair behind her ears and sat. "This smells good. How did it go with your dealers?"

"They'll all be here tonight to try your wonderful Lucid." He smiled wider at her.

The cook brought over one of the crêpes. Vegetables edged out from the thin white pancake, and the smell of cheese mixed with the smell of egg.

"Espresso?" Ilario asked.

"Please."

Ilario said something to the chef who then delivered a small cup of the rich caffeinated drink. It was dark and bitter, the perfect start to a day that she could only see ending badly. Sipping it, she tried not to squirm under Ilario's scrutiny.

The thick silence was the type her mother never let stand. Instinctually, Raleigh wanted to break it. The thought of her family gave her a pang of sadness. Her mother would be losing her mind if she knew what Raleigh was up to—not only hanging out with drug dealers but plotting assassinations.

"What are you thinking about?" Ilario asked.

"My mother." She chose honestly, too many lies had been told already. "I was thinking about how she'd love this crêpe. She was always trying new things in the kitchen."

"She's dead?"

Raleigh realized that she spoke of her in past tense. That life was now gone. It was safer for her parents if Ilario thought them dead. "Yes."

"I'm sorry to hear that. I assume that she didn't intend for you to be a drug dealer?"

Raleigh trained her eyes on Ilario. "It would break her heart. But her main goal was for me to get well, and the Lucid helps. So, hopefully she'd understand, even if she didn't support me."

Ilario sipped his espresso, drumming his fingers on the wood. "It can be dangerous. Rubio said your rooms were broken into. I should've offered to put you up from the start."

"Rubio thinks it was Glen's people looking for the formula."

"Did they find it?"

Raleigh shook her head. "No. We didn't bring it. None of us are biochemists. We leave that to our scientists, like you do. Do you think it's worth looking into who broke in? Or is that a lost cause?"

"It's worth figuring out. If it was Glen's men, I need to end that threat." Ilario's voice was casual. "One thing you're going to learn working with me is that I eliminate all my enemies."

"I hope you consider us friends."

Ilario laughed. "Of course."

Chi walked into the room. "Good morning." He leaned over and patted Raleigh's back. "How did you sleep?"

The sleeping was fine. It was the waking hours that she was worried about. "Good. You should try these crêpes. They're delicious."

"My favorite. Part of why I have a French cook," Ilario said.

A befitting last meal, Raleigh realized. It was unsettling knowing what they planned. Chi smiled a grin that belied nothing about what he was charged to do tonight. She let the two of them converse as she finished eating. Her bites were measured. She didn't want to look like she was too eager to get away. When Rubio entered, she regretted not scarfing her food down.

Rubio greeted them and took a seat next to Chi, foregoing breakfast but politely accepting an espresso. They spoke as though nothing were amiss. Ilario eventually turned his attention to Chi, and when he did, Rubio's eyes met Raleigh;s and in them was a question. With Ilario facing away, she gave one short nod. Rubio gave her one firm nod in response.

The plan was set.

TOO QUICKLY, THE morning slipped into afternoon. Then supper. Before long it was evening. The blue sky was inked out by black clouds, and by the time of the meeting, a steady rain pelted the ground. They were to gather in the front sitting room. It was an ideal room because Raleigh could sense the whole house from there—and a clear path existed to the front door. Brent and Adam would have a place to step out for their phone call. Along the back wall, a large window overlooked the vineyard, bringing a bit of serenity to a room that was bound to be filled with tension.

Raleigh and the crew waited in the dining room. Ilario wanted everyone to meet at the same time, which meant they were isolated until everyone arrived. Brent seemed calmest, wearing his charm like armor. They all had their defenses. Adam was dosed with Raleigh's Lucid, and, for once, was at peace. Finally it was time.

"And these are the new partners," Ilario said as they walked in.

They went around the group shaking hands and trading names. All five dealers laid claim to a region of Europe or America. Raleigh tried to remember as much as possible. Some of them didn't say where they sold, but their accents gave hints. They needed to remember all they could in order to pass on enough information to Chi's people and his mole with the Normandy operation.

The dealers were serious men. None of them had the manic joviality of Ilario. Bodyguards lined the walls, Adam's just one face in the crowd. These men didn't look comfortable. Their eyes darted around the room, guns under vests and tucked inside waistbands. Muscles twitched, and stomachs knotted. Rubio appeared to be right. The dealers didn't trust Ilario.

"Where is this new product that we had to come all this way for?" a gruff man from Madrid asked in a heavy Spanish accent.

Ilario went over to the case Brent brought. He pulled out enough for each of them, himself, and Rubio. As Ilario presented the Lucid, their pupils dilated. It was hard to tease out how much tension was due to the situation and what portion should be attributed to addiction. These men likely fell on the spectrum for sensing abilities. As they injected Raleigh's Lucid, she tried not to look any of them in the eye. She wasn't supposed to be skilled enough to feel the way it altered them, and she tried not to let that show on her face.

"It's phenomenal," a British one said, looking at their team. "And you want us to sell it?"

"I'm sure it won't be hard." Brent smiled, diffusing some tension. "Yes, we want you to sell it. By myself, it would take a long time to build up a base. I'll be looking to you to distribute."

"That we can," an American said. "What regions are you looking at?"

Brent pulled out a map of Europe. "I have some dealings in France." He started marking territories.

The guys explained who they sold to and the breakdown of the trade in Europe. Raleigh was excited that they were so forthcoming, but it could easily change in a moment.

Brent's phone buzzed. He looked down. "It's an emergency in the States."

Ilario's attention perked up.

Chi asked, "What's wrong?"

"One of my athletes had a heart attack and is in the hospital."

The dealers all nodded. "That can happen," one said. "Some people can use it too well."

"Could you excuse me?" Brent rose from his seat.

Ilario's face faltered for a moment before returning to normal. "Yes, of course. Take your call."

Brent headed toward the front door, and Adam peeled himself from the wall, following him. Ilario watched Raleigh. She acted as though nothing was wrong. Not once did she look to the door.

She pointed to the map. "You're not as widespread in America as I thought."

"With this new version of Lucid, we'll get there," the American dealer said. "The American market is dominated by a costly high quality recipe. Our Lucid couldn't compete, but this will."

Dealers all over knew of the Designeds' Lucid, but people didn't know where it came from. Chi was right. They were a part of this. People in America had the real thing, and that's why the synthetics weren't gaining traction.

"The Americans also pack their prisons with dealers. Lucid isn't the only thing I sell," said a man who looked Greek. "If I never go there, I will be happy."

His lack of interest wasn't a common sentiment. Overall, most of the dealers seemed eager to capture whatever part of the market they could, probably because they were at the top end of sales and could have people in the US and never need to travel there themselves.

Five minutes after Brent left, Raleigh caught Chi's eye. It was time. She readied herself, sensing the men in the room and preparing her barricade. Tau prepared, too. It was now or never.

Ilario hunched over the map. Chi removed his gun in one fluid motion and fired. The noise cracked through the room, shocking the dealers. A man like Ilario was bound to be killed at some point, but none of them expected that time to be now. Their hearts raced, and their eyes appealed to their bodyguards as they dived down around the coffee table. Ilario's bodyguard drew his weapon but was shot in the chest by Rubio before he could take aim at Chi.

The room erupted in chaos. Tau pulled Raleigh off the couch and positioned her behind his back.

"What have you done?" one of the dealers shouted, pulling out his gun and aiming it at Chi.

Rubio shot him in the chest. Unlike Ilario and the guard, this man didn't die right away. He fell across the table and map, bleeding a red wave across the paper.

Raleigh couldn't pull her attention from the dying man, the fear of her own mortality making her sweat. It was just supposed to be Ilario. She could sense the bodyguards converging on them. If they were lucky, the deaths would stop now.

"Right, this is over!" Rubio said to the dealers. "Ilario was a crazy man. He killed Glen, and he'd kill any of you if you crossed him in any way. Chi has done you a favor."

They put up their hands and sat back down on the sofa. Raleigh wondered if Tau would sit. She was happy when he remained standing. There was no way she could stand next to two bodies and pretend nothing was wrong. They needed to be frozen.

Tau's hand tightened on her arm. "Not yet," he whispered.

"We want you to side with us," Chi boomed. "Our product is better than what you had. This is the same arrangement, just not with Ilario."

"Yes," Greek dealer said, his face blotchy and red with sweat. "Yes. I will not act against you, neither shall my guard."

"Yes," said the Spaniard.

Rubio looked at Chi, a slow smile spreading across his lips. "Well, look at that. Your plan worked."

"Our plan," Chi said.

Rubio fired his gun, hitting the Spaniard. After the Spaniard fell, he aimed at Chi's leg. As Rubio's finger compressed, Tau froze him in place. Rubio's guard jumped forward, and Raleigh froze him. And then, for good measure, she stopped everyone. They were now standing in a room of live mannequins.

"What was his plan?" Raleigh asked. "Why did he shoot that guy? Why was he going to shoot you?"

"To take full control," Chi said.

Tau pulled Raleigh to the door. "We need to leave. It's over."

Raleigh agreed. But they'd missed something. She paused, staring at Rubio. "That makes no sense. He still doesn't have the formula."

The large window that showcased the vineyard broke, glass shattering into the room. It sliced the immobilized dealers, leaving them bleeding.

Tau pressed Raleigh down to the ground. She waited for the sound of bullets, but there were none. There was a whizzing, and then the room was engulfed in mustard-colored smoke.

"Cover your mouth." Tau pulled his shirt up over his own mouth.

Too late. Raleigh could already feel the sedative effect of whatever chemical was suspended in the plumes. Tau yanked her across the floor. As they moved in the direction of the door, she could feel the people she held immobile go black. No point in influencing them now, not when they were sedated, and she was well on her way.

The room swirled, and her head drooped. Shots began to ring out behind them. She saw masked men enter and kill the dealers. Rubio was on the ground, unharmed. She tried to lift herself, but her body felt tethered to the ground. Tau also struggled. Blinking, she tried to stay awake, knowing that unconsciousness was a death sentence. With that thought she slipped away, her fingers laced through Tau's.

C H A P T E R
24

RALEIGH LIFTED HER head off the ground. The biting damp cold had roused her from sleep—not that it had been a natural, comforting slumber. Her eyes slowly focused on the world wobbling into view. She steadied herself against the concrete and pushed herself up to sitting while grasping her queasy stomach.

Tau was on the ground not far from her and Chi a few feet beyond him. They, like her, were wearing scrubs. Neither were dead or hurt. Their bodies were just heavy with sleep, as hers had been.

Where were they? It couldn't be good. The nausea welled up, and Raleigh dry-heaved in the corner. She wondered how long she'd been out. Between heaves, Chi began to stir.

Lying back on the ground—to help deal with the spins—Raleigh tried to make sense of everything. Rubio had some other plan in mind. It wasn't simply taking over Ilario's empire.

"Where are we?" Chi asked.

"I don't know," Raleigh replied. "I just woke up."

"You've been sick?"

"I'm dizzy."

"My port is back." He turned his arm toward her.

So was hers. It felt more natural to have it there than not. Rubbing her hand over the tubes, a shiver went down her spine. Someone had installed ports in their arms, changed their clothes, and put them in this chamber. Cell was a better description. It was a fifteen by fifteen cement box with no windows or furniture. The high ceiling echoed their voices. Twin steel doors lined one wall. On the walls on either side of the massive doors were small single doors. The free wall had a box that resembled a book return at the library.

Chi lifted himself up and glanced at his brother before walking around the room. He grabbed the metal handles on the twin doors. Raleigh could see the muscles in his arms work to no avail. Frustrated, he went over to the library return box and opened it. It was empty and small, too tight to fit Raleigh's torso. Chi let the door clang shut. Then he was back over to the first of the two doors.

From her vantage point, Raleigh could see a toilet, sink, and tub. She peeled herself from the ground and walked the short distance to the wall. She braced herself. "Is it just a washroom?"

"Yes. No window." Chi strode across the room to another door.

Raleigh wasn't as fast. But she saw what was in it—four cots with blankets and an extraction machine.

Craning her neck, she asked, "How did we get in here? Is that a camera by the vent?"

"Yeah, and we should assume that they can hear us as well." Chi was turning in circles, as if he expected to find a crack in the room.

"I don't sense anyone outside. Where do you think we are?"

"I don't know."

Tau groaned, sat up, and clasped his head. He rose, his hands pressed to his temples. "What happened?"

Chi filled him in with the meager amount they knew. "It had to be Rubio. That's why he shot those dealers. He's working for someone else."

Raleigh had caught the expression on his face when she'd influenced. "He wasn't surprised when we froze him."

She ran her hands over her scrubs. Her mind traced back to the first time she met Rho. There'd been a lot going on with him being on the cusp of death. His clothes weren't her focus, but now that she saw the scrubs on her, Tau, and Chi, she remembered.

Raleigh studied her legs. "The pants. This is the same kind of thing Rho wore when we found him. We've been taken by the Normandy synthetic."

Applause emanated through the room. *"And Raleigh guesses it."* Rubio's voice echoed from the speaker above. *"Nice to have you all with us. That was an ingenious thing you tried to do, topple Ilario by using your own Lucid. Gutsy."*

Raleigh looked up at the speaker. "So I take it you're with the Normandy people?"

"Yes," Rubio said. *"I've been undercover with Ilario. I was the one who prompted him to side with Glen. By combining our enemies, it made it easier to take them out. Then he shot Glen, helping me. All while you fell into our lap."*

Raleigh turned to Chi. How could things have gone so wrong?

She glanced back up at the speaker. "Now you're the only one in the synthetic market?"

"Bingo. And we just ate up a big chunk of yours, too. Ilario was so stupid. He never considering just why exactly your Lucid was so much better than his. The moment it hit my bloodstream, I knew it was the real stuff. From there, it wasn't hard to guess that it might be you. After we installed the port, we extracted some. Amazing stuff, Raleigh, really."

Panic edged out the remaining sedative in her system. "Where are we?"

"*Underground,*" Rubio said. "*Holding Rho was too hard. Too much upkeep having him sedated all the time. It didn't work out in the end. Thus we built this underground bunker. People will put food on a conveyer belt, and it will be transported to you that way. They'll never be close enough for you to harm them.*"

"So you're giving us food?" That was one good piece of news. The claustrophobia of the space was stifling, and her instincts were kicking in. They would need food, and hopefully the sink had water.

Rubio cleared his throat. "*Here's how this is going to work. You'll be fed twice a day, once in the morning and once in the evening. In exchange for food, I expect you to extract and fill four vials per person per day.*"

Four vials in one day was a lot. It would keep them pretty drained, not that they needed much energy while locked up.

"I'm not giving you anything," Chi said, his hand reaching for his port.

"Don't pull it out," Raleigh said.

"I'm not some animal they can use."

"We don't want you bleeding to death," Tau said. "There's nothing here to patch you up."

Chi's fingers hovered over his port and then lowered.

Rubio spoke again. "*If you don't fill the vials, you'll starve. All of you have to participate.*"

"We'd rather die!" Chi hollered.

Raleigh didn't agree. If it was between starving to death and handing over four vials a day, the choice to her was obvious. "Chi, we should give it."

"No way. I vowed that no one would ever take my Lucid again, and that's a promise I plan to keep."

Raleigh looked at Tau, who studied his brother.

"We can't go long without food or water," Tau said.

"There's water in the bathroom. We can go a while without food."

"It won't be pleasant," Tau said.

Chi scoffed. "Of course, it won't."

"We could die," Raleigh said.

Chi gave a sinister laugh. "You've never read studies on people kept in isolated, small spaces, have you?"

Raleigh shook her head. "Why?"

"We'll go crazy before we starve."

"With that kind of attitude, we sure will," Tau said. "I say we give over the Lucid."

"It's not up for debate." Chi walked into the bedroom.

Rubio's voice came on overhead. *It won't be just food. It will be books, blankets, anything you need. Think about it.*

The buzzing of the intercom died.

Raleigh's stomach tightened. She asked Tau, "What do we do?"

"Not much, for now."

———

AN HOUR PASSED. Raleigh's bottom hurt from sitting on the cold concrete floor of the main room. Tau sat across from her, one leg extended out in a relaxed way. Chi was still in the bedroom with the door shut. The air was chilly and stale. Eventually the door to the bedroom opened and Chi returned, calmer than when he left. Tau and Raleigh didn't say anything as he walked into the main room.

Chi cleared his throat. "I know that you both would give over your Lucid. I'm sorry that we disagree on this. But I'm not going to apologize for having values... that you should share."

"No, but you should feel like shit because we shouldn't have to die for your values," countered Tau.

Chi pointed at the box near the vent. "It's Rubio's fault, not mine. Blame him."

"I'll blame both of you," Tau said angrily.

Chi huffed. "I knew I should've only brought Raleigh. The rest of you don't know how bad Lucid is. You're too invested in your own survival to understand how vital it is to end the trades."

Tau stood up, his eyes falling level with his triplet. "You've been brainwashed by your bosses. You're just as fanatical as Sigma, just about different things."

"Sometimes I can't believe that we share the same genetics. How did you end up so spineless?" Chi took a step closer.

They were mirror images of frustration. Both of them had their hands clenched and their legs braced to fight. Raleigh imagined that it would be balanced. The two were identical in every way, meaning they could do a lot of damage before either one was a clear winner.

She jumped up and squeezed into the small space between them. "Hey, not here. Let's say you do beat the crap out of one another, then what? The only medical supplies in here are toothpaste and brushes. Nothing to stitch either of you up."

Chi moved her back. "Don't play moderator, Raleigh. Let Tau try if we wants to."

Raleigh was behind Chi, but she could see Tau's troubled and angry eyes. She wondered what emotion he saw in hers. Whatever it was softened his response.

"Raleigh's right," said Tau. "What would it accomplish? Even if I kick your ass you're way too stubborn to give in. Fuck this." He kicked the metal door. "How did we not see this coming?"

Chi took deep breaths, stepping back from the confrontation. "We knew something was off. Too bad we couldn't figure out what."

"Yeah, but shouldn't you have known?" Tau's eyes were on the vent.

"Second-guess me all you want, but I did the best I could. At least Ilario is done for."

Tau put out his hands. "Ilario is gone, but the Normandy group will be stronger."

"Ilario was so wicked that Rubio didn't stand out," Raleigh said quietly.

Tau kicked the wall again and sat. Raleigh lowered herself down next to him.

Chi watched them for a moment before taking a seat. "Thank you both for your sacrifice. It will not be in vain, even if we didn't bring down the Normandy group."

It was in vain. If what Rubio said was true, then Ilario and Glen would've been taken out regardless of their involvement. All that work, and they'd only succeeded in getting captured. It was a pointless sacrifice.

Chi eventually said, "At least we're not alone. It's easy to go nuts in these types of situations. We're lucky to have each other."

Raleigh wrapped her arms tighter around herself, the thin blue scrubs not very warm. "I can't imagine being alone. Why are there four beds?"

"They got Rho. It's reasonable to think that they're after all of us," Tau said.

That made Raleigh think, "Then at some point they'll open the doors if they add a fourth," she whispered as quietly as she could.

"Already dreaming of Rho being added to our group?" Chi asked.

Tau tensed.

"Maybe that's the opposite of what you two want. Either way, I'd think Rubio would incapacitate us before he opened those doors."

Raleigh tried to ignore Tau's glance. "Do you think Brent made it out?"

Chi dropped his head. "Your guess is as good as mine. Hopefully, Adam helped him. I know people will be looking for us. We could be anywhere."

Raleigh considered the chip in her shoulder. She didn't know if the signal would be strong enough to get through the concrete. Even if it was, Trevor said they had to be within a few miles. Yes, they'd found Rho, but they knew the region. She didn't dare bring it up now. The last thing she needed was for Rubio to know.

"People will be looking for us." Raleigh felt the muscles in her shoulder spasm.

She was being influenced.

Tau stared her squarely in the eyes. He, too, remembered her chip.

"If we're going to survive this we're going to have to keep our heads and think logically," Chi said.

"The few weeks until we starve?" Tau asked.

Chi gave his brother a level glance. "A lot can happen in a few weeks. We need to keep our wits."

Tau let go of his anger enough to drop it. "The first thing we need to do is establish the time. I'm dead tired. It might be from that drug they used, or it might be that it's nighttime. There's a clock on the extraction machine."

"It's a timer so we know when to extract next," Chi said, correcting him. "But yes, we could set it and measure time that way."

Tau stared at the extraction machine in the room. "I say we start it now. We'll consider it midnight right now. I think it's night."

"How would you know?" Raleigh asked. She didn't venture to guess the time.

"My circadian rhythm. I worked the night shift one summer stocking shelves at a grocery store. Anyhow, when I was bored I used to pay attention to the subtle hormone differences in people. Glucose regulation, thyroid, all of that. Mine got thrown off, too."

"You must've been really bored." Raleigh couldn't help but be impressed. Tau was knowledgeable about things she hadn't even thought to consider.

Tau shrugged. "Endocrinology fascinates me. I became more sensitive to my own natural rhythm. The Lucid helped. After a while, I could tweak it. That's not the point. The point is, I think that it's nighttime."

Raleigh looked around. Without the sun there was no way to prove that it was night. And statistically, it was virtually impossible that he just happened to guess the right time. "What does it matter? Let's just sleep when we're tired."

Chi pointed at his brother. "Tau's right. Our circadian rhythms will get messy. When people are deprived of light or sensory input, they end up with wacky notions of a day."

"How do you know all this?" Raleigh asked.

"It's a form of torture," Chi said. "Never hurts to be well-read."

Raleigh put her hand against the cement wall. "Will it be warmer during the day?"

"Not underground, it won't be," Tau said. "Ground temperature is pretty stable throughout the year. That's why basements are cool in the summer."

"You read that?" Raleigh wondered what other kinds of books the Designed guys read in their spare time.

Tau shook his head. "No. My room was in the basement growing up."

"Midnight, right?" Chi said, staring the clock. "All right, let's get to sleep."

They all walked into the bedroom.

Raleigh lay down and wrapped her arms around herself. It was spooky in the small room. Fear had been niggling at her all day. Logically, it was the small space, being caged or the potential starvation that was frightening her. Illogically, it was the fear of the dark. "With the lights off?"

"What are you worried about?" Chi asked. "Nothing's going to come for you down here. We can't get out which means nothing is getting in."

"I'll leave the bathroom light on," Tau offered.

With the thin bit of light, they went to bed. Raleigh's aching stomach and troubled mind put up a good fight against her efforts. It didn't help that the futon mattress was hard, and the blanket was itchy and thin. She, eventually, succumbed to restless dozing.

It was cold, and she hugged herself, trying unsuccessfully to get warm. She was half-awake and foggy with sleep when she saw Tau get out of bed. He took the blanket from the fourth bed and laid it across his brother. Raleigh hadn't taken it, despite being cold. It didn't feel fair when they were all chilled. Now she wondered why Tau gave the extra one to Chi who was sleeping pretty deeply—and was the reason they were all hungry.

Tau lifted his blanket onto Raleigh.

She sat up. "You'll freeze."

"I thought we'd share. No sense in us all being cold."

Raleigh scooted over, and Tau climbed in bed beside her. His fingers glided over the spot her chip was in before he influenced her muscles in that area to contract. If there were night vision cameras, the move wouldn't reveal anything. Raleigh wanted to tell him that she didn't know how good the signal would be, but her confession wouldn't change things, and it would alert Rubio. She kept quiet.

It didn't take long for her to warm up with two blankets and Tau next to her. There was no point in overanalyzing it, not at this hour, not when she was finally comfortable enough to really rest.

"GODDAMMIT, CHI!"

Tau's voice woke Raleigh up. The two had indistinguishable voices, so it helped that Chi's name was included in the curse.

"Don't pin this on me!"

"And who should I pin it on? You're going to get us all killed. You know that going insane thing, it's going to get worse."

Raleigh heard them, but she couldn't sense them. Their barricades were up. Getting out of bed, she took small steps in the direction of their voices in the main room. The sliver of light from the bathroom no longer made it through the door, and there was no light to aid her. Inching toward the doorway, she kept her hands up so she wouldn't hit the wall as she skimmed her feet along the floor. There wasn't much in the room to run into, but she was careful regardless. Eventually, her fingers found the doorframe, and she entered the other room.

"Why did you turn off the lights?" Raleigh asked. In the dark it seemed like the rooms could go on forever. When she spoke now, her voice echoed back, reminding her of the small size.

"We didn't," one of them said.

"I can't tell your voices apart in the dark," Raleigh admitted.

"We need to extract." That had to be Tau's voice. "I'm starving. I don't care about your damn morals. Right now there's Designed Lucid on the market, like it or not. We might as well add to it if it means saving our asses."

Raleigh moved in Tau's direction.

"If we do, our asses aren't worth saving," Chi said. "We can have this conversation all you want, but it's going to get old."

Raleigh could tell who was who now. Her fingers found Tau's, and she slid up beside him, feeling comforted by him if little else.

She said, "Tau's right. This is an awful way to die. Plus, our Lucid is better to have on the market than the synthetic, right? Less addictive, less deadly and that whole thing?"

Silence. They chewed on her words.

Chi spoke. "Yes, it is better, but they'll make more money with ours than the synthetic. Most likely they'll stretch it by mixing the two. Even with only a bit of real Lucid it will go for more."

"They have a lot of money," Tau said, "and the market just became theirs. Ours is a drop in the bucket. We need to stay alive. People are looking for us."

He didn't say their brothers, and Raleigh knew that the Vindex Authority was their best bet.

Chi exhaled. "Rubio! Turn on the lights!"

No answer.

A lump formed in her throat. The darkness was unbearable. "Please, Chi. Please do it for me. When you asked for my help, I gave it. Now I'm asking for yours. You both know that I won't make it as long as you without food. I'm not built as strong. No one is. I know it's giving your Lucid, and I know you don't want to do it. But sometimes you have to do things you disagree with. Keep your morals, but look at the bigger picture."

Tau spoke. "It's going to be a really awful, drawn-out death in the dark with no food."

The hairs on the back of Raleigh's neck to stood on end. She'd never been fond of the dark, but she hadn't known she was so scared of it. The thought of her last week of life being in pitch-black was too much.

"Please!" she shouted. "I can't do this! I can't! Starving is one thing, but this feels like being buried alive!"

Tau's hands cradled her head to his chest. "It's all right. You're all right." His arms slid down around her, holding her tight.

There was no response from Chi. Raleigh doubted that he was going to change his mind. It was frustrating, but even with Tau's help there was no way they were going to force him to extract. The darkness made her skin clammy, and even though she knew that there was nothing lurking in the corners, her instincts were on high alert.

Raleigh could no longer hear Chi's light breaths. "Did he leave the room?"

"Let him." Tau snorted. "He's such an ass. There's a reason none of us call him brother."

A beep sounded from the bedroom, making her jump. The small red lights of the extraction machine broke the dark. Chi had given in. She didn't know if it was the arguments they'd made or her begging that convinced him. But she didn't question it. None of them spoke as the machine preformed its job.

It took them three quarters of their "day" to collect four vials each. They put them in the small box and waited. The darkness messed with Raleigh's mind, and she was filled with bitterness toward Chi for holding onto his pride.

Five minutes after they deposited the vials the lights flicked back on. The brightness was blinding. Raleigh's hands covered her eyes, as joy filled her.

Half an hour later they had their first meal—eggs, toast, broccoli, and milk. Nothing to hint at where they were. Raleigh scarfed it down.

That night, Tau skipped getting into his bed and got right into Raleigh's. Between the warmth and the food, she found sleep easier.

CHAPTER
25

TWO WEEKS PASSED in a lazy way that stretched out each moment like taffy tugged through a machine. Over the days the small space had been filled with books, board games, and even jump ropes. But none of the items relieved the suffocating claustrophobia for more than a few minutes.

"You should do some more push-ups," Chi said to Raleigh, not losing count on his way to a hundred.

He and Tau had been working out for hours each day to relieve the boredom. All the exercise burned up the small number of calories they were eating. Now they were gaunt, their muscles strapping across their slender frames.

"It isn't going to change that we're here." Raleigh pressed her head against the cement wall.

Exercise proved a poor distraction, and she hated breathing in the stale, cold air. A run in the mountains was the only kind of workout that sounded appealing. Closing her eyes, she could picture the well-worn path near home with all its twists and dips. Her mother and father usually set one day of the weekend aside for family hiking—even with Raleigh's condition. The thought of her mother's face drew her from the memory of the mountains.

"What's wrong?" Tau had just finished his push-ups and was sitting next to her on the floor. It was a loaded question, as everything seemed to be wrong these days.

"I was thinking about my mom." They'd swapped stories about their pasts but never anything too specific. Rubio didn't need to go after their families, but none of them wanted to risk it by revealing too much. "She never wanted me to come."

"You told her about synthetic?" Chi asked, shocked. No doubt he was worried that more people might find out about his Vindex Authority, the organization that had failed to find them.

"No. I never told her about the synthetic. She never wanted me to go to Belgium in the first place."

"She wanted you to go to college and live a simpler life."

"No. She wanted me to stay at home. Imagine, she thought that my passing out at college would be the worst thing that could happen."

"If you'd listened to her, you'd never have met Rho, or Grant and Able, or us," said Tau. "Do you regret not listening to her?"

"No." Raleigh was certain about that. It was worth it to have made her own decisions, even if they led her here. There was no guarantee that her life would've been good if she'd listened. A million scenarios could've played out. She could've gone to college and then been discovered by Grant and Able. Gabe may've been a true mentor, and she might've hunted the guys she had come to know as family.

Chi went from pushups to crunches. "Really, you should do some pushups. It will take your mind off your family."

Raleigh told them what they already knew. "I don't feel good."

"You might hold up better," Chi insisted.

Of the three of them, Raleigh was faring the worst. Like them, she'd gotten thinner. The exhaustion of the extractions painted the delicate skin under her eyes lavender and blue.

Chi stood up, stretching his arms above his head and yawning loudly. "I'm taking a bath. See you in a bit."

Raleigh and Tau found themselves alone, or at least as alone as they were going to get with the camera overhead always on. Tau eyed the Monopoly game at their feet.

He sat ridiculously close to her. At all times she knew the exact distance between them. Right now it was two inches, between their shoulders.

"I don't care about Rho." Tau looked at her. "Or my brothers."

"Chi's a bit grumpy. But I don't think you have to discount them all on his behalf."

"No. I mean I don't care if Rho likes you. We're the ones trapped underground. We're right for each other, and I hate that these stupid politics are keeping us apart."

"Me, too."

Tau closed the two inches, wrapping his arms around her and sliding her across the cold ground toward him. When his lips touched hers, sparks ran across her skin and a tug, deep down in her stomach loosened. She'd wanted this so badly for so long and now that it was happening, she almost burst with joy. Grabbing his shoulders, she didn't want to let go, the kiss making her lightheaded and breathless. Her next breath made the stale air manageable for the first time.

This was how one lost track of time. Tau kissed her neck, the mint taste of his mouth and his calm Lucid still tingling on her tongue. For a moment she was free. The cold dry bunker no longer had its terrifying grip over her. The joy and giddiness of Tau's kisses brushed away the impending doom.

They no longer spent every moment considering the time, losing track of it, or at least ten minutes until they heard a throat clear. Tau drew back, his eyes staring into hers. Raleigh couldn't bring herself to look away, her heart thudding in her chest as the Lucid from his kiss sat on her lips. She wondered if the wild look he gave her was partly due to her Lucid.

"I'm glad that you guys finally decided to do something other than look dopily at one another like emotional teenagers. But remember, there are three of us down here, and there *is* a bedroom."

Raleigh blushed as she turned to Chi. His hair was wet from the bath, a towel slung over his shoulders to catch the drips.

Tau spoke. "It sort of just happened. We'll do our best to not make this weird."

"Of course, it's going to be weird. Besides the three of us being locked up, don't forget the cameras or that she's dating our brother."

"I'm *not* dating Rho," Raleigh said.

"Rho doesn't seem to know that," replied Chi.

Raleigh fiddled with the bottom of her shirt and Tau grabbed the Monopoly game.

"Rho rejected me."

"I don't want to get in the middle of your love life," Chi said.

Tau opened the game and looked at his brother. "Then don't. We're waiting on you to start the game."

Chi sat down and removed his metal game piece—the racing car—from the box. Tau picked up the top hat and dropped the iron into Raleigh's hand. Her brain didn't want to focus on the game. She focused on the lines of Tau's forearms as he shook the dice. One look at Chi and she knew that if this was going to work they couldn't ignore that he was there, and right now that meant including him in the game. Watching Tau move across the squares she trained her attention on winning, rather than him.

─────────────

THE NEXT MORNING Raleigh took a bath. Chi and Tau bathed every other day, shaving their faces as if they were going to work. She didn't bother with a routine, taking baths sparingly. The water was warm, but the dampness on her skin when she got out scarcely made it worth it. There was also the ever-vigilant camera in the corner unflinchingly pointed her way.

With her and Tau now together, she was self-conscious that she might smell, and the best solution was a bath. The hair on her legs grew slowly, but it was starting to drive her nuts. With one leg propped up, she ran the razor over her calf, leaving smooth skin in its wake. A small nick caused a few drops of blood to fall into the water. She watched it dilute before dragging the razor again. Cleaning it off, she started on the other leg.

"Rubio! You're not keeping your end of the deal!" Chi yelled, his voice echoing in the small space.

Raleigh hastily finished and got out of the tub. Tau and Chi spoke heatedly on the other side of the bathroom door. Dabbing herself dry with a thin towel, she slipped into her scrubs, regretting the damp patches that formed where the cloth met her skin. After sopping up the water in her hair, she dashed out.

"What happened?" she asked.

"There's no dinner," Tau said.

They all looked into the box.

"Just our vials from before," said Tau.

"Did the conveyer belt break?" Raleigh asked.

They often heard the belt when it was delivering their food and goods. Then the box would open in the back while locking in the front. It wouldn't unlock until the back was sealed. But the vials hadn't been removed this time.

Chi shook his head. "No. I didn't hear it even try. Rubio! You know the deal."

"If he's listening, shouting won't get your point across any better," said Tau. "You're hurting my ears."

Panic skipped across her shoulders, the heat warming her in a malicious way. If the water hadn't already been on her skin from the shower, she would've broken out in a sweat. "Why wouldn't he take our vials?"

The boys looked at her. Chi's concern manifested as anger.

Tau reached out and touched her shoulder. "I don't know."

"Maybe he can't," Chi reasoned. "That Lucid is the most valuable thing to them. He wouldn't leave it."

"Do you think someone is stopping them? Do you think it's... Rho?" Raleigh knew that Rho would dig up half of Europe to find her. It was the only hope she clung to. People were looking. Brent and Adam, hopefully, had gotten out and told the others what happened.

Tau shook his head. "Rho would get you out first, before harming them."

"What about your people?" Raleigh asked Chi. Would the Vindex Authority care so much about ending the synthetic that they'd abandoned them? "Would they take down Rubio before getting us out?"

Chi's face became stone. "Ending the synthetic is the most important thing. We all knew that it might cost us our lives. Yes. If they had the shot they would do it, even if it meant not finding us."

Raleigh's stomach dropped. He was serious. The Vindex Authority didn't give a care about them. The most important thing was the mission, not the people in it. Their mission must be accomplished at all costs.

"No," Tau said. "No way. That's cruel."

Chi didn't apologize. "They do what needs to be done. They will look for us. They'd rather us not be dead. But if they have the shot, they'll have to take it."

"They're never going to find us," Raleigh said, her breathing becoming shallow and her head fuzzy.

Chi snapped his fingers stunning her from the terror that'd swept her up. "We can't think like that. We need to hold on as long as possible. The longer we make it, the better our chances. With water we can last weeks."

Raleigh did not miss the quick glance he gave Tau. Tau's brow knit in the middle, and he looked down at his hands rather than at her. She realized that they would make it a few weeks. She wasn't Designed. She wouldn't make it as long. They had many things in common, but she wouldn't weather this as well.

"I'm going to die first," Raleigh said.

Tau influenced a muscle contraction over her chip, like he'd done their first night in the bunker. This time the message was clear—*don't lose hope.*

"We aren't going to talk like that," Chi said. "We keep saying attitude is key. We hold on as long as we can."

Tau stepped closer to her. "Raleigh, you don't have to starve to death. With the Lucid we can influence you into an easier end."

Chi put up his hand before Raleigh could respond—not that she had the words. "We aren't talking like that. We carry on as if nothing has changed. A least we won't have to extract anymore."

"I'll black out," Raleigh reminded him.

Chi shook his head. "They're draining you. You need to stop. Blackouts or not."

"Your blackouts...." Tau stared at her arm. "When Gabe and Dustin were taking us hostage, you lost consciousness."

"So?"

"Before you did you sensed everything, far more than I've ever been able to sense. The same thing happened at that dance we went to with Lilia. But we haven't been able to sense anyone above us. They've built this deep and far away enough from people that we can't sense. But they based that off what we can do. Not what you're capable of."

"Good. A plan. It's been too long since we had one of those," Chi said.

"I've extracted twice today. It'll be a day or two before I black out," Raleigh said. "But even if I sense someone before the blackout it will only be for a moment. That's not long enough to really influence. And I'd be working blind. I have no idea how to get us out."

"One thing at a time," Tau said. "First, let's see if you can actually sense someone."

Chi's palm opened, three vials resting in his hand. "We don't have to wait days. Tau and I will extract and then you can take five."

"Five vials?" Raleigh wondered if she'd wake up from the mental outage that would cause, an end that would be better than starving to death.

"That's too much," said Tau.

"If we're going to do this, we should do this," Chi said.

"What if that much is toxic?"

"That's the thing. For us, it can't be. We make so much that it can collect and do no damage. With her it builds up, but then she shorts out and shuts down. I don't think it will hurt her."

There was a difference between guessing and knowing. Raleigh hated the rush that came before a blackout and the loss of control. She'd never before imagined a scenario where she'd purposely cause it. Raleigh didn't want to take the vials unless it was her only option.

She stared at the camera. Was Rubio really dead? Her eyes moved over to the large duct beside it. "What about the vent. We didn't try it before because of the camera, but who cares now?"

"That ceiling is high," Chi said.

Raleigh knew the beds were bolted to the floor. "You could lift me up."

"Let's try it," said Tau.

They headed to the main room. Tau got down on one knee and lifted his hands. "Have you ever seen the way cheerleaders do this? Put your knees on my shoulders. I'll stand. Then you stand up."

Raleigh wobbled on Tau's shoulders, but he managed her weight well. As she stood he transferred his hands to her ankles, holding her in place as her fingers reached for the vent. It was out of reach. Down she climbed, and she didn't even have to suggest what they were all thinking—Chi was going to have to be part of the tower.

Chi lifted Tau onto his shoulders, like a four-year-old getting a ride. Raleigh climbed up, Tau lifting her the last part of the way as she fumbled for footholds while trying not to kick Chi in the face. By the time she stood on his shoulders, their tower of bodies swayed.

Chi didn't complain about the weight, but Raleigh acted quickly. Her fingers reached the vent and she yanked before seeing that it was screwed in. Turning the small metal bolts with her fingers, she was happy when they gave. The grate came loose and she tossed it to the floor with a clang. Her fingers gripped the edge of the vent, and, with all the strength she could muster, she hoisted herself up.

She climbed into the vent. It was barely big enough for her to fit. Chi let Tau down, and the two of them stared up at her.

Chi asked, "Can you get out?"

"I don't know," Raleigh said.

The connecting vent was smaller than the opening that she was perched in. It took all her effort to fit her torso. Her hips got caught. They were too wide to fit. She was trapped. The claustrophobia of the bunker was nothing compared to being half-squished into the vent. Frantically she swung her legs, using the momentum and gravity to dislodge her top half. The rough lip of the vent scraped against her skin, cutting it and her scrubs, as she shimmied back out.

"I'm going to fall!" she said as she tumbled down.

Tau stood under her, arms out. His angle and timing made the catch anything but graceful. She landed mostly on him, sending him backwards onto the hard ground. His body cushioned her fall, taking the impact as he let out a deep grunt.

"Sorry." She levered herself off him, trying to ignore the scrapes on her stomach from the vent.

Tau got up. "It was worth a shot." He rubbed the small of his back and eyed the cuts on her lower ribs.

"Should we try again?" Chi asked.

"No," Raleigh said. "There's no way I can fit, and if I can't, then you can't either."

"Then it's the vials," said Chi.

Raleigh nodded. It seemed like that was the only option left. If they didn't do something, they'd die anyway. A Lucid overdose was preferable to starving. She walked into the bedroom and lay on one of the beds. Chi and Tau took turns extracting, adding the two new vials to the three they already had.

Chi placed the vials beside her head. Then he extended her arm, exposing her port. Tau positioned himself on the other side of her, his fingers wrapped around hers.

Raleigh focused on Tau's blue eyes instead of her nerves. What if the Lucid overload pushed her into a blackout and she never got out?

"If you get out, tell my mom that I'm sorry."

Chi plunged in the first vial. "This isn't going to kill you."

Tau's fingers squeezed hers, and she tried to keep her attention on his face. Chi injected the second vial. The Lucid sprinted through her, their calmer version warring with her erratic one for receptors. It felt like her body was gearing up for a race. Anticipation tap-danced through her heart and around her veins.

"That's all five," Chi said.

Raleigh wasn't listening. Up, up, up. Her mind drifted out of the bunker and past the familiar sensations of Chi and Tau, expanding like the beam of a lighthouse. It searched for the people around them, reaching out. Miles, that's how far it soared. There wasn't a person to intercept her mind's message. Then all the light that consumed her, all the sensation, snuffed out as the dark took hold, plunging her into the familiar foreboding of a blackout....

"Raleigh?"

Tau's voice came through. The heaviness crushed her. The cuts on her stomach beginning to crust over. She didn't need him to tell her that she'd been out a while. She tasted the time on her breath and in her muscles.

"Chi, she's back," Tau said.

Chi was on her other side. "Did you find anyone?"

"There's no one for miles. We're trapped. There's no way out." Raleigh gulped down the fear. It may've been better if she never came out of the dark. This was their tomb, and it was waiting for them to die.

CHAPTER
26

THEY WAITED FOR starvation to end them. The first two days Raleigh listened to her stomach grumble. By day six she was too dizzy to get out of bed. After the experiment with the five vials, she'd given up extracting. She'd had one blackout since, and it was the only moment she'd been liberated from the coffin they called home.

Tau lay beside her on the bed. She rested her head on his chest, listening to his heart beat in perfect time. Sixty beats per minute. If there wasn't a clock on the extraction machine, they could've used him. His fingers slid through her hair, twisting the ends before letting them go to unravel. It was intimate and comfortable. Raleigh was falling in love.

The unfairness—that she connected with him so shortly before her end—broke her heart. And it was her end. She guessed that she'd only hear his heart beat about a thousand more times before her own gave out.

"If you stayed with Grant and Able, you'd be a doctor. Gabe would never have let them bury you in here," Tau's voice echoed in his chest to her ear.

Raleigh imagined Brent's guy in New York and how right saving him had felt. The missed dream haunting her equally as much as the man she killed and the fraying of her family ties.

"You'd be on the boat and better off," Raleigh countered.

"I'd rather be down here, anyway. On the boat I didn't have you. I'm sorry I was such a jerk to you. I should've trusted you sooner. Maybe if I wasn't so focused on you, I would've seen Rubio for who he was."

"None of us could've guessed. Quit beating yourself up about it. While we're saying our regrets, I'm sorry I tortured you."

"You don't need to apologize for that again," Tau said. "This is depressing. We should think about something else. If we get out of here I want to spend the day with you in Rome, walking the streets and meeting people, like we should've had a chance to do. This is my first international trip, really, and I didn't get to be a tourist at all."

"If we get out, I want to bring you to Colorado to breathe in the mountain air." Raleigh took a deep breath of the stale bunker air. "You can meet my family, and I can patch things up."

"Do you think your family would've liked me?"

"Uncle Patrick would've insisted you tell him all about your endorphin tricks. Thalia is shallow, so she'd like you just because you're hot."

"So I'd win over the sister and the uncle. Not too bad. What about your parents?"

"I never brought a boy home. It's hard to say. You're probably too exciting for my mom. She'd want me to date someone boring."

"And your dad?"

"Always wanted me to be happy. So he'd like you."

"Do I make you happy?"

Raleigh lifted her head. It rushed with the small movement. He sensed her and lifted his hand to cradle her chin. "You make me as happy as a person trapped in a bunker could be."

Despite the sadness, her body was too tired to cry.

"Yes. You've been the only bearable part of this."

"Then I'm sorry to go. At least you'll make it a week longer than me."

Tau shook his head. "I'm not going to starve to death. They aren't going to find us. Chi's frustrated. I'm sure he'd be willing to do me in if I asked."

"No, you have to try," said Raleigh. "Please, and if you make it, go to Colorado and say goodbye for me."

"You aren't serious."

"I wrote notes to my parents." She pointed at a notebook on the ground, "And there's one for Dale, and one for Rho. Please deliver them. Will you promise me?"

Tau lowered her head to his chest. "I will. But don't get your hopes up about me getting out. They haven't found us by now, and I can't see another week making a difference."

Dizziness narrowed her vision. "I'm going to faint."

"You're going to black out?"

"No. Faint." The words barely came out as the world narrowed to nothing....

"She might never wake up," Chi said from the main room.

Proving him wrong, she opened her eyes.

All those years doctors compared her blackouts to normal fainting, but the two were very different. If anything, fainting was worse. She didn't feel like herself when she came back—her brain was muddled, and she remained light-headed.

Tau shouted, "This is so messed up. Your stupid company should've found us."

"Blame me all you want," Chi said, "but I'm as dead as you'll be, and I'm sad to see her go, too. Just because I'm not making out with her doesn't mean that I don't care about her."

"I'm falling for her."

"That's a stupid idea. How did you see this ending?"

"I didn't plan it. It took me by surprise. A month ago I couldn't think of a person I disliked more."

Chi's voice was soft when he spoke, comforting. "You're meant for each other. I know our brothers assume she'll end up with Rho. But they'd be miserable together. She's more of a risk-taker. Not that it's done her good this time."

"I'm not as brave as her."

"Neither am I. But I know that a person like her needs to make their own choices. That's why I knew she'd help with the synthetic. She's moral, and she's driven. You work well because you support her."

"Too bad that we'll never see where it would've gone. I'm sick of daydreaming my hours away," Tau said.

"Daydreams are far better than the nightmare we're living."

"Do we help her along?"

Chi didn't answer right away. "The longer she can go the better. Not to be morbid, but a body is going to stink."

Then smell she would, because this was the end. A blackout was imminent. She didn't know if these were her last conscious moments or not.

The Lucid washed through her, bathing her mind in its depths. She used it to sense all of herself, from her angry stomach that she'd been trying to ignore, to her tired muscles that were wasting from no food, to her heart which—despite everything—

kept beating. The Lucid coursed through her slowly at first and then more aggressively.

She could sense Chi and Tau in the other room. They were pained in their hearts, not just their stomachs. Chi told the truth when he said he would regret her death. Out of the bunker her mind stretched, gaining the freedom her body would never have again. What was above she didn't know, but she kept reaching. Then she found a person with an ache in his knee and a restless fidget in his muscles.

"Collin!" Raleigh shouted at the top of her lungs. Then the blackout took hold.

RALEIGH WAS BEING carried. With each step, she shifted and came back to consciousness. Looking up, she saw Kappa's smiling face. Behind him, the sun winked at her through a thick mess of trees. A forest. The bunker was gone.

She was free.

"Hey, hey! Look who's awake." Kappa pulled her in closer as he walked.

"Is she?" Tau walked over. "Raleigh, are you all right?"

"I'm doing better now." A smile tugged on Raleigh's lips. Teary-eyed, she'd never felt such relief.

"Rho wanted to be here," Kappa said. "But we didn't think it was best, with Gabe. We've sided with him for now. Unbelievable, I know, that's how badly we all wanted you found."

Raleigh tilted her head back. There Gabe was, hiking in stride with Collin down the makeshift path. Two men who were very similar in nature but separated by their ideals.

"Adam and Brent, they made it to you?" Raleigh asked.

"Yeah. They're fine. Chi's people at the Vindex Authority contacted Rho. They gave the information to take down the Normandy group to Grant and Able. We knew you were in a bunker, and we planned on breaking you out that night."

"You took them down a week ago, didn't you?"

"Yes. The feeds from the bunker went to a facility. We knew that you were somewhere, but the location we had was bad. The bunker we found was empty. They had more than one. Four. We've been looking all week. This one wasn't even marked that well in the notes we found."

"I'm amazed you found us," she said.

"Your chip's signal didn't get past the metal and concrete. But then we could all feel you sensing all of us. We were ten miles away, Raleigh."

Tau spoke. "Just think, your blackouts saved us."

Raleigh returned her attention to Kappa. "How long does this alliance with Grant and Able last?"

Kappa's face darkened. "The Normandy synthetic didn't have Quinn. We think Sigma has him."

Raleigh's mind swirled. Sigma had Quinn. Why would Sigma need a Modified? "That's weird. Isn't it?"

"Not only weird but likely bad," Gabe said. "We're sided until we get Quinn out. Rho's admitted that Sigma's more of a threat than us."

However strong the alliance was it didn't hold up to having Rho be here now. She was hesitant about putting much faith in their agreement. Faith. Hope. Optimism. These all had new and deeper meanings for Raleigh, and she'd never underestimate the terms again.

"I want to go home."

"Dale wants to see you, too," Kappa said.

"No. I want to go to Colorado. If the synthetic is gone, and Grant and Able aren't trying to capture me, there's nothing in my way. I want to go home. Not forever. But I need to see my family."

"All right. I'll tell Rho," Kappa said. "Just hang in there."

Right. Getting out of the bunker didn't undo the weeks of havoc and damage to her body. Closing her eyes, she knew she only had to make it a bit longer. The fresh air reminded her how close she was. Soon she would be in the mountains back home.

When they reached the road, she discovered that they were in Germany. It was a surprise. It made sense that the Normandy synthetic wouldn't be foolish enough to dig their bunker near the last place they held a Designed, but she'd guessed they were somewhere in France. Once they made it out of the woods they piled into a van and drove to a small airport. America was only a plane ride away.

Grant and Able let them use their jet—a clear indication of differences being set aside. Raleigh was starving, but the doctor on board insisted that she introduce food to her system slowly.

They gave her ice chips to chew on and a bag of fluids and nutrients through her port. Raleigh had millions of questions bombarding her brain, but her body was too tired to entertain any of them. The recliner chair she was in was comfortable. Tau sat in the one beside her, and across the aisle was Chi. Empty chairs faced hers. The others were in the back getting things ready for takeoff.

With the plane in the air, she drifted off. When she awoke she found Tau's hand in hers. He was sleeping, his long lashes making his face angelic. Raleigh reveled in the warmth of his touch. She was used to sensing people and too often she forgot the joys of her own sensations. With his fingers clasping hers, she was reminded. The sleep, nutrients, and freedom were intoxicating. They were going home. She was never going to see a bunker again, and she'd be hard-pressed to go into anything as deep as a basement. Out the window playful white clouds gave way to blue sky—as if the world was welcoming her back.

"You're up." Gabe said, sliding into the seat across from her. He leaned forward, his elbows on his knees.

Raleigh knew it was time to deal. She withdrew her hand from Tau's, wondering if Gabe noticed. Everything was political these days, and, somehow, holding Tau's hand felt like a stand against Rho—not that Gabe was the sort of guy to mention such things.

"Your plan to end the synthetic didn't go smoothly," he said.

"And you teamed up with the Designed. We're both surprising each other now."

"The Vindex Authority needed us to take out the Normandy synthetic. They're an odd business. Secretive. Do you think we're on their destroy list?"

"That's a good question. But I think that they expect us to destroy each other, leaving the other so weak there's nothing they can do. Why were you on the rescue today?"

"You're using our jet," said Gabe.

"But you're not flying it. Why not just send Kappa and Collin?"

"I wanted to talk with you, and I didn't think I'd get the opportunity otherwise."

"What's so important?"

"Collin's convinced that not all the Designed are bad."

"You may've noticed that I feel the same," said Raleigh.

Gabe looked down at his hands.

She wondered where he was going with this conversation. "Don't tell me that you're going to change your tune and say that you like some of them?"

"No. Nothing like that. I'm simply going to say that some of them pose an immediate risk and others hardly any." His eyes flicked to Tau. "Sigma has Quinn, and our healers and Receps have been rationed as a result."

"None of us are going to give you our Lucid."

"If they could see the good that we're trying to do, the good that I know you saw in us...."

"I don't know. Maybe trapping them on an island wasn't the best way to ask. That, and I'm not so sure about the good anymore. Adam isn't the same. He used to be a really sweet guy. It makes me wonder what you were like before you took Lucid."

"Chi's gotten to you," said Gabe.

"No. I'm just not prepared to accept Lucid as a miracle drug. That was part of why I left. I'm not sure how I feel about it."

"You think it's more bad than good?"

"I just tried to stop a nasty synthetic operation and ended up shoved in a bunker by another organization that forced me to do an exhausting amount of extractions. This might not exactly be the time to ask."

The corner of Gabe's mouth lifted. "Fair enough."

"You didn't honestly come along because you wanted me to convince the Designed to give you Lucid?"

"No. I came along because we now have a common enemy. Sigma. I saw you stab him, and I know that their brotherhood has splintered as a result. You have Rho's ear and a voice among them. We put our differences aside, and we took out the Normandy synthetic. What if we teamed up and took out Sigma? We could have Quinn back safely. Better yet, with the synthetic market gone, we could send him home and pay him for his Lucid."

That all sounded good to her. "What about after?"

"We leave the Designed that went against Sigma alone."

"But you need the Lucid."

"We have a few other Modified. I'm not going to get into it."

His hands went up. "All of them can work safely from home like Quinn, if this pans out."

"I don't know."

"What's not to know? This works in your favor, Raleigh. Rho will be safe. All the non-threatening ones will be. You can go to college and become a doctor, and then we'll hire you. This is the best of everything."

Her venture to take down Ilario taught her an important lesson. Things never went to plan. "This isn't the type of decision I can make on my own. I need to involve Rho and the others."

"Great," Gabe said, standing. "That's all I'm asking. Have the conversation. I'm glad you're alive. We'll be landing in an hour. All of you are getting off in New York. Rho didn't want me to know where you're hiding Dale. Do me a favor? Make sure Sigma doesn't get him."

"That is something I can agree to," Raleigh said.

Gabe walked to the far side of the plane and rejoined Collin and Kappa. Chi was still sleeping across the aisle. She looked over to find Tau awake.

"How much of that did you hear?"

"It's a good deal, but I don't trust him. I don't think he trusts us, either. The only reason this works is because of you."

"We'll see what Rho says."

"Raleigh, a lot happened between us in the bunker. Gabe is right. You have Rho's ear. You have standing in the group. Nothing can jeopardize that." The tips of his fingers traced the ridge of her knuckles. "If Rho was worried about how everyone would see you and him, I've got to believe that things will go over worse for us."

"You think the others would care if I dated you instead of Rho? Your brothers aren't that shallow."

"I think the focus needs to be on getting Quinn back. Then

we can figure out what to do about Grant and Able and Sigma. If nothing else *this,* would only distract us. I care about you. But the time isn't right."

Raleigh gulped down her frustration. "I see."

"No, you don't. This isn't like Rho turning you down. I'm not doing that. I'm simply saying that dating me is doing you no favors. We'll bide our time. Eventually, it will be right."

"And if it isn't?"

"Our relationship can't detract from what's important."

Raleigh agreed. "Do you think Chi will tell?"

"I think Chi doesn't talk to them all that much, and it's a little too gossipy for him to mention."

Raleigh withdrew her hand and let the subject drop. Kappa navigated his way to a spot across from her. Maybe not pursuing Tau was for the best. Raleigh didn't want to give up Tau, but she also didn't want to lose her authority in the group—two things that at least Tau was convinced could not co-exist. It was the logical course, but her heart splintered at the thought. Tau had become as necessary as air. She didn't voice it, forcing her eyes from his to Kappa.

Kappa raised his eyebrows. "I assume Gabe made you some kind of deal."

"Yeah. We'll discuss it when we see Rho."

"I think you could sell him on just about anything. He texted me every hour we were searching. He's on European time. Now would be the time to push your agenda."

An agenda that would only be pushed if she and Tau weren't dating. She didn't need to face Tau to know that he was thinking the same thing. In the next few hours, Rho would have to agree. If she was ending things with Tau, it was going to be for a good reason.

CHAPTER

27

THEY LEFT CHI in New York. It was strange to see him go. When they were in the bunker Raleigh assumed that they'd be together for the long haul. Now he was gone, and Tau remained. They took a flight to Chicago with Kappa and Collin.

If it was odd leaving Chi in New York, it was even weirder to be in the Windy City again. Raleigh had changed since leaving. She now knew what she was capable of, good and bad.

When they entered the small house Dale bounded up to her. "You're back!" He wrapped his arms around her, but not too tight—like he was concerned that she'd break. Pulling back he said, "You don't look so good."

"I'll be fine."

Upsilon and Gamma said their hellos, and Rho hung back, waiting for the others to say their greeting before sweeping her up in a tight embrace. He didn't release her right away. Instead, he kissed her forehead. It was the kind of thing that would've delighted her a few months ago. Now she had to fight from looking at Tau's response.

"You're alive and back, and I'm never letting you out of my sight again." Rho's voice was light and happy as he took a step back. "How was your flight?"

"Interesting. We have a lot we need to talk about. Gabe offered me a deal."

"I bet he did," Rho said. "But we won't discuss it now. You're weak and need to get your strength. It's safe here. You should rest, and then we'll figure out what to do."

Raleigh couldn't argue. Her legs were barely keeping her up. The extractions and lack of food had taken their toll. "A rest sounds good."

Rho turned to Tau. "Do you want to go back to working with Mu now?"

Raleigh froze. She couldn't imagine Tau leaving. She turned to him and caught the same emotion in his eyes. It was a good thing that they barricaded because his eyes hardly contained their connection.

"I'd like to stay here a while if you don't mind," Tau said.

"Of course not. Thanks for having Raleigh's back. I owe you."

"No, you don't. I'd gladly have her back anytime."

"I'm glad to see that you two are on the same side," Rho said. "It's been a productive month."

"I thought you'd be mad about how things turned out," Raleigh said.

"I'd be mad if you were dead, and I know I haven't been very pleasant to be around all week." He looked at Dale and the others. "But right now, I'm relieved."

Raleigh swayed a bit on her feet, and he wrapped an arm around her shoulder. They headed up the steps. Even though her feelings for Rho had shifted, she was glad to be back. She didn't step away as he walked her up the stairs. As they passed out of view, she let her barricade down. It wasn't needed now.

Rho spoke about the steps they'd taken to find her and the sadness of finding an empty bunker instead of her.

Raleigh's attention remained one floor down, thinking of Tau. There was a lot they had to discuss concerning Lucid and Sigma over the next few days. It was going to be a difficult road. As she stepped onto the landing, she felt Tau's squeeze on her shoulder, right over her chip.

I'M KATE TAILOR. My first job was building planes, my second working with worms, my third, snug behind the pharmacy counter. Now I spend my time at a messy writing desk with two sleeping cats and dozens of stories scrawled across scrap paper.

I've been writing stories in my head—and sometimes murmuring them under my breath—since I was five. Over the last few years I've committed them to paper. I write stories that I wanted to read but never found. If you're looking for something interesting, I hope you've found it here.

Besides writing, I love my husband, kids, and cats—less so on writing days. I also love the mountains, rain, cappuccino, worms, board games—not Monopoly, not EVER—and friends.

To learn more about me—and my writing, because let's face it, you probably don't care about the worms—visit my website at www.katetailor.com.